Island o

WITH

Island of the Naked Women

INGER FRIMANSSON

Translated by
Laura A. Wideburg

Pleasure Boat Studio: A Literary Press
New York
2009

Island of the Naked Women
by Inger Frimansson

Translation from Swedish by Laura Wideburg

ISBN 978-1-929355-56-3
Library of Congress Control Number: 2009920808
First U.S. Printing

Design by Susan Ramundo
Cover by Laura Tolkow

Pleasure Boat Studio is a proud subscriber to the Green Press Initiative.
This program encourages the use of 100% post-consumer recycled paper
with environmentally friendly inks for all printing projects in an effort
to reduce the book industry's economic and social impact. With the
cooperation of our printing company, we are pleased to offer this book
as a Green Press book.

A Caravel Mystery
Caravel Mystery Books is an imprint of Pleasure Boat Studio:
A Literary Press
Our books are available through the following:
SPD (Small Press Distribution) Tel. 800-869-7553, Fax 510-524-0852
Partners/West Tel. 425-227-8486, Fax 425-204-2448
Baker & Taylor Tel. 800-775-1100, Fax 800-775-7480
Ingram Tel. 615-793-5000, Fax 615-287-5429
Amazon.com and **bn.com**

and through
PLEASURE BOAT STUDIO: A LITERARY PRESS
www.pleasureboatstudio.com
201 West 89th Street
New York, NY 10024

Contact **Jack Estes**
Fax: 888-810-5308
Email: *pleasboat@nyc.rr.com*

Screwdriver in his hand
screwdriver in his
jabbing
hand.

How it sinks in, like butter, how things gurgle, things break
things silence.
Silencing, silence, all silent.
Red heat, in eyes, on hands, all the small hairs
of the hands.
A geyser, upwards, gushing.
A man fighting back with no strength,
no strength left.
Falling into a desk edge,
a sharp edge to the temple.
The smallest child knows to protect the temple.
Behind it is the brain and everything
a living person thinks and does.

Still the screwdriver
sinks into the naked throat
gurgling, gushing, all gone.

Acknowledgments

I would like to emphasize that none of the individuals in this book are real and any resemblance to persons living or dead is a coincidence. I would also like to thank those people who helped me in my research for this book, especially the farming family Göran and Yvonne Nilsson as well as Arne and Elsie Nilsson. I also would like to thank Professor Ole Matsson, retired Police Commisioner Hans-Eric Sergander, Gunnar and Åsa Fritz-Crone, Bror Sköld, Lorenz Berglund along with the employees of Södertälje City Library.

Thanks also go to my husband, Jan, for his usual support and constructive advice as well as to my two daughters Helena and Hanna, who also read this book and shared their opinions with me.

Stockholm, Spring 2002
Inger Frimansson

The translator would like to thank her mother, Joy R. Wideburg, for her insightful comments and editing throughout the translation of this novel.

Seattle, February 2009
Laura A. Wideburg, Ph.D.

The End of September

1

SHE WOKE HIM right before dawn. Her voice was thick and husky from sleep.

"Tobias . . . time to wake up. The wind's died down."

He was lying in bed, his arm raised at an unnatural angle, his hand in a fist. When her voice reached him, he punched as if he had to defend himself, and his fist hit the wall. Still half-asleep, he swore out loud.

"Damn it, I'm coming already."

She'd turned the light on in the hallway, and stood backlit. Through her nightgown, he could make out the strong, well-developed contours of her body. He stood up, and a fringe of his hair fell into his eyes. Animal stench still seemed to permeate every strand of hair on his head. He'd made sure to wear a cap out in the barn, but it hadn't helped.

She carried the stink of the animals, too. He'd noticed it the minute he arrived on Thursday. She probably wasn't even aware of it.

"I'm going to go get dressed," she said, and her voice was not yet her natural Sabina-voice; it was thick and forced. The stairway groaned as she walked away. He heard her breathe.

"All right, I'm coming," he whispered, and his voice hung in the room.

Tobias rolled up the blinds and pushed away the curtains. There was frost covering the grass, and the chill was sharp and direct. A low hum came from the boiler, which sent out warmth as if it were the house's very own blood circulation. He'd been sleeping pressed against the wall, warmed from its life-giving heat. His own body odor—strong, familiar—now mixed with the animals' scent; the air all around him was filled with it, their manure and their sweat.

His smell was no longer his own.

He experienced a brief moment of dread.

He stood in the middle of the floor, standing straight but tired, and adjusted the clothes he'd been sleeping in. The wallpaper in the room was the same—wide, silver-white ribbons with ornamentation. That heavy, old-fashioned furniture and the tapestry on the ancient chair's upholstery. No one could bear to sit on the lumpy seat for long; the back support was an anatomical joke. When he was a child, he'd lost himself in its pattern of fairy-tale trees; the tips of his fingers had traced the embossed velvet surface.

The sofa could be pulled out and made into a bed. When he and Görel were newlyweds, they'd often slept there, quiet and breathless during the marriage act. Görel had never felt comfortable in this house. Not even when they were alone. Strange noises and knockings made her tense. She would jump up from her chair and pace between the windows.

"I know someone is out there, Tobi. Someone wants to break in!"

It took a great deal of his patience to calm her down again.

Outside, the dogs had already sensed that people were up and about. Their deep, calm barking showed they knew he was there; nothing escaped their acute hearing. They would stretch their necks, point their noses to the sky, and howl that ancient wolf cry: *There's a human being at the edge of the forest! And a deer!*

They were kept mostly in the dog yard. Not pets. They were meant to guard, hunt, and herd animals.

Sabina was already in the kitchen, completely dressed, wearing her green sweatpants and her sweater with sleeves that were much too long. She'd rolled them up over her wrists, but they kept sliding back down. She was massaging her hands with hand lotion, kneading them.

"I've started some coffee."

Tobias nodded, sat down on the chair closest to the window, heard the soft sound of her heels on the rug. On the table was the container of butter, a sticky butter knife straight up in it, and a plate with sliced liverwurst, rather dry around the edges. She was slicing tomatoes, and the seeds were sliding all over in the juice.

"I can make some hot cereal for you if you'd like; it'll warm you up."

"Hot cereal?"

"Oatmeal."

"Hell, no. My mom stuffed that into me when I was a kid. I had enough to last the rest of my life."

Her back was to him as she stood in front of the counter, her hair in a strong, twisted braid, intertwined and shining warm.

"Were you able to sleep at all?" she asked.

"A bit."

"Is the bed soft enough for someone like you?"

"Someone like me? Cut it out."

Her eyes were like blades in the whiteness of her face.

"Of course, you're used to much better accommodations, what with being on TV and all."

He didn't bother answering. She had dragged the cot out of the attic and added an extra mattress. Honestly, he'd had much more comfortable beds, but since she'd made the extra effort, he was touched. He slowly buttered a bit of dark, sweet rye bread, and pulled apart a few slices of the liverwurst. A scratching noise at the door made him look up. Sabina's face turned soft and open; she looked at him and smiled.

"He's learned to behave, and he's clean, now," she said contentedly.

It was a golden retriever pup. Not a very useful creature. The old man had bought it for her because she'd been longing for something soft. Sabina went to open the door and ice-cold morning air was drawn in along the floor. The puppy scooted through the door-way, his nails tapping. Sabina squatted down to the puppy; her hand was big and flat on its head.

"What do you call him?" he asked.

"I already told you. Frett."

"Fred?"

"No, you heard me, Frett."

"Frett? But that's a kind of polecat."

"What?"

"It's another name for a polecat."

"I just thought of it out of the blue. It's short enough, he hears me when I call him, and he comes right away."

She sat down in front of him, legs apart, the puppy in her lap, his tan paws hanging over her arm. An odd shyness came over To-bias. It seemed she expected him to say something, something awk-ward and unnatural for him.

"Frett," he said, thoughtfully. The puppy's ears pricked up.

"These little ones are just so cute, aren't they?" she kept prat-tling away.

"Sure."

She was sitting there, rubbing the puppy's warm earflaps.

"Lion cubs are also cute," flew out of his mouth. "And tiny baby tigers, too."

Stomping sounds came from the staircase. Adam had woken up. He was unshaven, and his greasy hair hung straight to his neck. He went right for the table and thumped down next to his mother. The puppy let out some whining noises. Adam gave it a confused look.

"You're scaring him," Sabina said. "You have to be calm and gentle around animals. You know that already. You can't just come barging in like that."

"I'm hungry."

"Then you'll have to move so I can get through."

Adam got up, leaning away, and Sabina slid her way past him, letting the puppy loose onto the floor. The puppy immediately began to play with an empty toilet paper roll.

"So it'll be you and me and Adam," she said to Tobias from the stove. "And Hardy is coming, too, Hardy Lindström, if you remember him." Her voice dropped. "He often helps out. It's hard to find people who are available and have the skill to help these days. And he's good with Adam. He even has a few ideas. . . ." She turned and cast a glance toward Adam. "Some kind of singing tour."

Tobias had a memory flash: a tall, sinewy man with a haircut that made him resemble Jesus. He'd arrived on a Vespa the last time that Tobias had been at home. He'd shaken hands as if they were friends, but he didn't want to speak.

"Hardy's my manager," said Adam in a voice that even sounded somewhat normal. Adam broke apart a piece of hard tack and dunked it into the butter container, then licked it clean with the tip of his tongue.

"Stop that, for Chrissake," Tobias said.

"What's he doing?" Sabina came to the table with the coffee pot. "Do you want a warm-up, Tobias?"

Tobias nodded. "What kind of tours? Is he still doing that Elvis crap?"

Adam laid his arm on the table. It was wide and grayish in the light.

"You wanna arm wrestle?"

"Not in the middle of breakfast, you moron."

Tobias instantly berated himself. He really ought to watch what he said; he really ought to have more patience. Something was wrong with Adam; Adam couldn't help it. He was developmentally disabled, or something like that. Adam had gone to a special school in the city, but Tobias doubted that he'd learned much. Adam could barely even write his name. But oddly, he had an almost sick interest in Elvis Presley and loved wearing glittery training suits with belt and scarf, and, surprisingly, he had a melodic and beautiful voice. He'd learned all of Elvis's songs, and he sang them well, there was no doubt about that.

"So he's got time, does he?" Tobias said toward Sabina's back. "Doesn't Hardy have a job?"

"He was working at the sawmill, you know, but they've cut back and laid off fifteen people."

"Is he coming the whole way here?"

"No, we'll meet at the bridge. Finish up, and I'll go take a peek at Carl Sigvard."

"How's he doing today?" Tobias pointed toward the ceiling. Sabina shook her head.

"He's awake a great deal of time now. He has a lot of pain, but he refuses to take any medicine for it. You know how he is. He's always been against that kind of thing."

"I don't see why he has to be so damn stubborn. I thought that most people get wiser with age, but not him. How old is he now? Seventy-five?"

"You ought to be ashamed of yourself, not knowing how old your own dad is. Don't you remember he turned seventy-one on August third? Hardly two months ago!"

Tobias finished his coffee. It was hot and bitter.

"Well, he's too old to keep working. People usually retire at seventy-five, and some folks even retire earlier than that, if they have a chance."

Sabina squatted down next to the puppy. Quietly, she said, "Your father is the kind who will never grow old."

Tobias found himself standing on the bridge. The air sweeping into his nostrils was below freezing, and it stung. Everything appeared to stand still. Some of the bushes had broken down during the night, and the currant berries had withered and shrunk. Tobias lit a cigarette and looked out over the field of stubble. The sun was about to break through as if leaking some warmth with a few rays. But it was too late. At the very end of September, the leaves of the birches had already turned golden and were beginning to fall. Frost coated the fence. Below them, on the road, the Räcklinge bus thundered past, followed by three cars. The cars seemed to be hoping to pass the bus; he watched their shadows. In the pen, the dogs were howling their thick howls; they sounded slow and tired even though it was morning.

Suddenly, something thumped him between his shoulder blades and he whirled around. Adam stood there, wearing his plaid jacket, collar turned up, happy.

"Love me tender," he moaned. Tobias saw remains of food on Adam's teeth.

"Calm the hell down. Where's your mom?"

The rough giant of a man danced a few surprisingly skillful steps and wriggled his backside in rhythmic jerks.

"In the gh . . e . . e . . to!"

Sabina was already walking toward them with Billy, the border collie, who would help them drive the steers. There were about twenty cattle, all young, at pasture out on Shame Island, and now they had to be brought in. They would have been fine if it were only cold, but the eternal winter rain would give them pneumonia. Actually, they should have been brought in a week ago, but it had been too windy. Now the weather had turned and the wind was still.

And of course, there was that accident with his old man, the accident which had thrown off all the farm routines.

They took their seats in the car. Tobias was in the back seat with one of the herd dogs, and Adam was in the front passenger seat. Tobias didn't have much room for his knees. Sabina was driving, and the car smelled of gasoline.

"Do you have a leak somewhere?" Tobias asked, leaning forward toward Sabina. He would have been able to rest his chin on her collar bone if he had wanted. "It stinks like hell in here."

"No, that was the reserve can. Before I thought to tie it down, it fell over and dripped a bit back there."

She turned onto the road. The asphalt glittered. The entire field of stubble was filled with sunshine, golden and warm, but Tobias' fingers were still freezing. Tobias had borrowed his old man's work clothes to pull over his own once they got to the water. He held on to the dog's paws, warming his hands from those hairy toes. The dog looked at him in a friendly way.

"How are we going to get them onto the raft?" Tobias asked.

"You mean the steers?"

"Yeah."

"You have to be careful not to scare them because then they become hyper. You can't control them once that happens, and their fear is contagious. Scare one and you've scared them all. Then they'll spread out over the whole island and we'll never catch them."

"But won't they get scared the minute they see us land?"

"Nah, they're actually a curious bunch. We usually go out and check on them once a week or so because you never know, something could happen. They could get caught or go down. We had one with his head stuck in some branches; he'd tried to fight his way out and was completely exhausted. Carl Sigvard had to crawl up to him and try to free him. Afterwards, he was totally docile."

"Which one, Dad or the steer?"

Sabina laughed softly.

A lumber truck with logs from Viks Kvarnlunda Sawmill was in front of them. Adam grabbed Sabina's right arm.

"Pass him! Pass him!"

She slapped his face.

"I've told you not to touch me when I'm driving! Listen to me, I've told you a hundred times! It's dangerous, Adam. We could drive into the ditch!"

The overgrown man began to sob. Sabina softened.

"Don't worry. We're going to be there soon. So there's no point in trying to pass him now. What do you think, you think Hardy's there yet?"

Adam hiccoughed and stopped crying. "Love me tender, love me true," rumbled out of his throat.

How does she manage, Tobias thought. *Adam is nothing but a full-grown child. It's grotesque. He's never going to be normal. Sabina will never be able to stop caring for him, like other parents once their children are grown. Her responsibility will never end until one or the other of them dies.*

Tobias thought back to when Adam and Sabina had moved in. When was that now? Ten years ago? Adam was seventeen, and Tobias' old man had agreed to let him move into the house with

Sabina. Adam could help out with some of the chores. He was certainly strong enough and many hands were always needed on a farm, especially since Tobias had no intention of taking over.

Tobias' father had met Sabina at an outing in the village. The village community would organize dance evenings in those days, and word spread to other areas, even to some of the bigger towns, so people came from all over.

It's not like the old man didn't have other women at times, but he hadn't found one that he wanted to have in his own house, at least not until he met Sabina.

And he had to take Adam as a package deal.

They were nearing the lake, called Fagerlången, with its many islands and coves. When he'd been a boy, Tobias had kept his own little boat there and he'd liked to row about aimlessly. In those days, there weren't life vests or any of that other safety stuff, but he'd been just fine. Of course, he'd fallen in a few times, but he knew how to swim and so all he had to do was heave himself back up over the edge of the boat and let the sun dry his clothes.

Things were different now. He would never dare let his daughter Klara even go down to the edge of the water by herself. *You change so much after you have your own children. It's ridiculous, really*, he thought.

Finally they arrived. The water was like a mirror, totally still. The air was so cold it brought tears to their eyes. Tobias went behind one of the boat houses and took a leak before he put on his father's work clothes. They felt stiff and uncomfortable. He rubbed his hands together, making a dry crackling sound. He then blew his nose.

The raft was tied up at the dock. It was made from waste lumber and oil barrels which hadn't been detoxified, which was probably why the old man got them on the cheap. The raft was used two times a year, first, when the young animals were brought to the island and then in the fall, when they had to be brought back again. The pasture out there was excellent. The old man leased part of it. He'd offered to buy all of Shame Island, but he wasn't successful.

Tobias walked toward the raft. Sabina was bending over it, filling the motor with fuel. Adam had also climbed on board and was holding the rail.

"I'm freezing," Adam said sullenly. "I forgot my mittens on the stairs."

Sabina was just about to reply, but at that moment a man appeared from behind the boathouses. They hadn't heard him. He must have just been silently waiting, perhaps spying on Tobias while he changed. Not saying a word. Tobias did not find that thought pleasant. Hardy was somewhere between twenty-five and thirty. He strode toward them, stamping on the ground, his hands deep in the pockets of his leather jacket. He had a green military backpack slung over one shoulder. Hardy Lindström, live and in person. Now Tobias recognized him — Hardy's blonde, curly hair under his hat; Hardy's short, off-yellow beard which looked dyed.

"I'm so glad you're here, Hardy," Sabina called out, and there was a pleading note in her voice. She'd finally gotten the motor started; it sputtered and coughed. Hardy nodded, and lifted one long leg over the rail, and there he was, standing on the raft with the rest of them. The dog slinked over and sniffed him. He didn't howl, hadn't howled. Hardy pushed him aside with his foot. Hardy's laced black boots reached up around his lower legs, and his pants were stuffed into them.

"Hi there, Adam," Hardy said. "How're things going?"

A tiny nerve started twitching in Adam's left cheek, right under his eye. Adam grinned, spit flying from the corners of his mouth.

"How're things going?" Adam echoed.

"Great, kid, just great. Never better."

Only then did Hardy appear to notice Tobias. Sabina was busy steering the raft, maneuvering between the piers.

"Thanks for coming to help us," she called as her hands slipped on the rudder.

"I see you already got reinforcements. A professional from Stockholm, huh? You think he knows how to do the job?"

"You've got eyes. You know that's Tobias. And I know you've met before," Sabina replied.

Hardy turned to the side, cupped his hand as a shield and lit a cigarette. He didn't offer one to anyone else. His spent match bobbed on the surface of the water for a while before it disappeared. Hardy took a few greedy drags. Then he walked over to Adam and gave him the same kind of thump on the back that Adam had given Tobias. Adam shook himself; his glance slid to one side.

"How are you doing these days?" Sabina asked Hardy.

"What do you mean?"

"Well, how is everything?"

"Everything's all right."

"What about your mom?"

"Nothing wrong with her far as I know."

Tobias tried to catch Sabina's eye, but she was busy steering the boat, setting its course toward Shame Island. It was the largest island in the lake, but no one lived there. No one had even built a summer cabin there.

"Shame Island, what a hell of a name," he burst out, mostly to change the subject and make things easier for Sabina. His own voice disgusted him at once. He heard the sound of his old man's voice in his own, a tone he wanted nothing to do with.

A glimmer of light came into Hardy's eye.

"Do you have any idea why they call it Shame Island?" Hardy asked.

Tobias didn't answer.

"They used to leave the women there, the ones that were married and did the deed with other men. They rowed them out there like we bring the animals. And they left the women there as naked as the day God made them. They probably wished then that they really were animals with pelts on, those old whores."

"Those old whores," repeated Adam. The nerve under his eye twitched more strongly.

"Cut it out," said Sabina.

"Well, it's true. They starved to death out there, that is, if they didn't drown themselves or freeze to death instead. No food, no clothes."

"I'm sure that's nothing but a legend," said Tobias. "Do you really believe that old tale?"

Hardy stuck out his chin and his yellow beard bobbed.

"Let me tell you, people found stuff out there, in the crevices. I've found some stuff, too. You can come to my place and take a look."

"Oh, come on, that's just an old wives' tale!"

The sound of the motor sputtered away as they neared Shame Island. Some grebes, untouched and secure, were settled in the clumps of reeds. Tobias could see their shiny amber eyes. Their mating season was over, they had nothing to protect any longer. Soon they would lose their characteristic chin-beard and have their winter feathers.

Thinking about the coming of winter made his stomach hurt. He would have to get started on his new book to make some money. His two-year grant from the Swedish Authors Union would end when the year was up. Now he would have to prove that they were right to give him the money. He'd have to accomplish something.

"Hang on tight now!" Sabina said. "We're about to land."

With a great bump, the raft's momentum carried them right onto the sand. Sabina sucked in her lower lip. Her face was flaming red, her braid stuck out of her kerchief.

"Now you know what to do," she whispered. "Quietly, nicely, and then everything will go smoothly."

2

IF HIS GOD-DAMNED LEG HADN'T BROKEN . . .

Carl Sigvard had been in the loft with his pitchfork. He'd been climbing around like a mountain goat, sometimes standing up, sometimes on all fours, his old limbs as flexible as they'd ever been.

And then when he least expected it, he fell.

It had been a rainy day, but not at all chilly. Late in August, yes, but not one of those Augusts with so much cold and rain that the entire harvest ran the risk of going straight to hell. Still, there had been rain for four weeks in a row, and maybe he was worrying all his hard work would go for nothing: the seed would rot in the fields, too heavy with mud to be saved. Perhaps those were the thoughts which distracted him that morning, because all at once there was nothing under his feet, nothing holding him up, and he fell. The last thing he heard was the cracking sound his own skull made when it hit the cement.

Sabina's face had not been in focus. She'd been leaning over him, her swollen lips open. Through the pain, he noticed how she was shaking. Behind her was the boy, Adam. He noticed Adam's stiff, straight neck and heard the boy repeating *mamma*, dull sounds calling for his mother. Sabina was not listening. For once, she was not entirely focused on the boy. She was on her knees in the manure, her fingertips hovering over him, but it seemed as if she didn't dare touch him, fearing he would break if she laid a finger on him. His mind drifted off again, but he must not have been completely unconscious because later certain details came back: how he floated above the stalls as if he were resting on a waterbed. He was floating a bit above Sabina, saw her rounded shoulders, her hunched back, her hair hidden under the kerchief she always wore when she went out to the animals. And he remembered other things too: how she'd stood in the hallway in front of the mirror, how she twisted and tied up her hair, the kerchief's pattern of flowers. Her glancing at herself in the mirror, the way she did when she thought no one was watching. Her glance of fulfillment and desire.

He could still do the deed.

It would be many more years before he no longer could do the deed.

This was what he usually thought.

From far away, the harsh sound of sirens. Carl Sigvard had opened his eyes, and Sabina still sat there. The boy, Adam, had gone down on his knees in the manure, too, his bloated cheeks sagging.

He wanted to ask Sabina something, or else blame her: "You haven't gone and done anything unnecessary, have you? Called the ambulance when you didn't have to? And here they're coming with sirens on and everything."

Something like that. But not one sound came from his lips. That was when he felt the first touch of confusion.

Two girls came in, wearing red overalls. Two girls whom he thought had to be from town, their feet so small and neat that they risked slipping in the animal dung. There was the clinical smell of lotion, that sweet clinical smell of city.

They had a little trouble getting him up on the stretcher. For the most part he'd been worrying about his head, but now he realized that other parts of his body had been broken. One of his legs, the left one, seemed loose and strange underneath the blanket.

"What is your name? Can you tell me your name?"

That little girl had a blonde pony tail. And she was acting like he didn't even know his own name!

"His name is Carl Sigvard Elmkvist," Sabina rushed to answer and as she saw him lying there in the stretcher in all his brittleness, she no longer could keep her tears from flowing.

The girl raised an eyebrow.

"I want to hear it from him, please. Carl Sigvard, do you know what day it is?"

So stupid! So goddamn stupid. And then there was the boy like a lump in the doorway. He was making howling hoarse sounds. Sabina ought to comfort him right away, or he would break out into a fit of rage she would not be able to stop.

He no longer remembered the trip to the hospital, just waiting on a narrow, unsteady cot. Out in the hallway, there were folks sitting on chairs, and there was a ray of sunshine on the bright but somewhat dusty floor.

Finally a doctor appeared. Good Lord, was he ever young. There he stood in a white coat and he had pink cheeks.

"You can thank your strong physique that you're still alive."

He remembered he felt obstinate as if everything were someone else's fault, not because of his own clumsiness up in the loft.

He had stayed in the hospital for more than a week, and he had various operations on his back and his one leg. There were cracks and breaks throughout his skeleton. He'd never before been the kind who hurt himself, and he'd only been in the hospital once before, the day that Tobias was born.

3

THEY STEPPED ONTO SHAME ISLAND'S SHORE.

The whole time Sabina had watched Adam, her finger pressed to her lips: "S*shhh!*" The herd dog stayed near them. He'd done this before; he was just waiting for his command.

"Let's stay here awhile and let them take the initiative," Sabina whispered.

She sat down on a driftwood log which had floated ashore and landed a bit up on the grass. The dog sat next to her, impatient, his gaze fastened on her mouth. A few minutes later, there was rustling in the leaves. The cattle were coming, cautious but curious, their breath rising like puffs of steam from their nostrils.

Tobias stood with one foot on a stone. He was wearing his own rubber boots he'd brought from Stockholm. He rarely used them there, and he'd had to go to the basement and dig them out. Tobias wiggled his toes, freezing, standing, watching the animals become braver, their brownish white hides, their breathing which made his thoughts drift to the sound of balloons, picturing balloons up in the air until the whole sky filled with them, and that other sound, pregnant panting, that sound which came from women in labor, controlled, exactly measured breathing. From the corner of his eye, Tobias saw Adam's heavy, hanging face. Adam was tense because he knew there was something that he had to keep remembering. Adam watched his mother's finger: *quiet now Adam, shhh.*

The first steer had come to the sand, a little bit away from Sabina. He'd set his hooves firmly and reached out his neck, his wet, gray muzzle coming close to Sabina's skin. Sabina wrinkled her forehead and sneezed. Was the steer attracted by the happy pattern of Sabina's kerchief, did he think it was edible? Sabina was sitting up straight on the log, her hands, red from the freezing weather, resting on her knees. Her work gloves had slid to the ground. Another muzzle was approaching her hands. Sabina moved her foot and the steer scooted away. Sabina smiled.

"Golden noses, you are all so curious," she said in a low voice.

Hardy was counting them. "I only count nineteen."

"There has to be twenty. The other one will come soon; he'll notice that these are missing."

The raft was ready, and they'd placed planks to make a solid gangway. Hardy went back to it and opened the fence on each side. He drove sticks into the ground and they heard him swear dully as he forced them into the frozen mud.

"I believe they want to go home," Sabina explained to Tobias. "They'd never come here so quickly otherwise. I think they're longing for their warm stalls."

"They wouldn't if they knew what was coming," Tobias said drily.

"No, but that's just the way it is."

"Turned into entrecote and roast beef."

"Don't think like that. It doesn't help."

Adam grunted and suddenly pointed toward the forest. "There he is, there he is!"

The sand puffed up around their hooves as the steers hopped away in little leaps to pause, their sides heaving, their ears straining for every sound.

Sabina sighed.

"It's good of you to let us know," she said. "But please keep your hands to your sides, hold them in place, Adam, because you're scaring all the animals away. Now let's spread out. It's time to get them on board."

The dog was standing with his tail raised, every muscle in his black-and-white body ready to work. As soon as Sabina gave him the sign, he sprang into action, like a streak of lightning into the bushes. Twigs snapped and broke. There was a moo, high, but without panic. The steers were three years old and had spent two summers on the island. Maybe they were remembering the warmth of their stalls and the comforting sound and smell of their companions chewing their cuds around them.

We don't want to harm you, Tobias thought. *At least not now. Come on boys, climb onboard now!*

With the dog's help, they guided the animals through the temporary pen and up onto the gangway, keeping them calm. Tobias feared that the clomping of the hooves on the wooden planks might scare the animals coming up behind the first, but that didn't happen. The sound disappeared in the noises of the herd, their steaming bodies, and he followed them up, guiding them to the raft's stern. They huddled together and stared at him. He saw their big mild eyes, and he wanted to pat one of their warm, bulging stomachs, but that would be stupid. It would make them nervous.

Sabina stepped on board; her boots were wet to the tops.

"There really is one missing, Tobias. We have to search for him. Do you think you and Hardy can go look together? I'll stay here and keep watch on these."

"Where's Hardy now?"

"He was right behind me, coming from that direction. Take the dog with you. We'll wait here and hold down the fort."

That silence. Tobias was not used to it. He stopped behind the rise of the hill and held his breath. The dog had run away somewhere; maybe he'd gone with Hardy. That type of dog was bred to herd animals, his total instinct and focus.

A drumming noise over his head made him jump. It was a woodpecker. He peered up and caught a glimpse of dark red feathers. A black woodpecker, he remembered. His third grade teacher had once made the class memorize ten different kinds of woodpeckers, but she'd never taken them out to the island. There were young animals out to pasture even then, and his teacher had been afraid of cows. Afraid of cows! How could she have taken a job out in the country? What was her name again? He couldn't remember. But she'd taken up with their local Lutheran priest. The whole thing had been quite a scandal since he was married and had four children.

Where had she gone?

The priest was forgiven for his sins and remained in the pulpit to preach on Sundays and instruct the children coming up for confirmation. But what had happened to the young teacher? Tobias thought about what Hardy had said about Shame Island. Without being able to help it, he felt vaguely aroused. He stood there, shoulders tense and shivering in the raw cold rising from the ground. The air seemed to surround his body, forcing its way even into his rubber boots to slide up his calves.

I have to move, he thought. *I have to find this steer so we can go home.*

He made his way up the slippery slope, going to his knees to peer down inside a crevice, and he heard a strange noise, a short and cut-off bellow. There it was, the lost steer. It was brown and white, and was lying wedged in down between the rocks. When it saw Tobias, it began to thrash its head about and bellow more loudly.

"Now, now, there, there," Tobias said as he slid down on the moss and sand, using his elbows to stop. The animal must have been badly hurt, perhaps broken a leg. Otherwise, it would have gotten up and fled. Tobias could go right up to it now and touch it, laying his hand on its hard flat forehead. It had a white star in the middle of all the brown.

"How are you doing, buddy?" he said helplessly. "Did you break your ankle?"

No, it was even worse than that, he understood, and he took the animal by the horn. The horn was warm and smooth. "There, there," he said again, and the great head swayed, nostrils flaring, the stink of fear.

"How the heck do you think we're going to get you home when you go around doing stuff like this?"

There was a movement to one side and the steer threw his head up so quickly Tobias had to let go. The dog had come; it had tracked them down. Tobias grabbed the dog's collar and told it to sit. The dog breathed heavily and gave a weak whimper.

"What do *you* think we should do? Any ideas? You've done this kind of thing before."

The dog put its head to one side and seemed to think. Its jaws were half-open; its tongue rolled around inside its mouth, pink and wet. Then it lifted its muzzle and began to bark.

Hardy was on his way down the slope. His hat was pushed back, a twig caught in the cord around the hat's crown. He must have fallen down, too; his pants were wet and muddy at the knees.

Hardy went right up to the animal on the ground and kicked it in the side. A thumping sound, a dull, hollow noise.

"Get up!" Hardy yelled.

Tobias let go of the dog. His stomach was burning.

"What the hell are you doing? Don't you see it's hurt?"

Hardy's ice-blue eyes fixed on Tobias.

"How do you know? Are you a vet or what?"

"Anybody can see that this animal is hurt."

"Sometimes they're just lazy; they just refuse to move." Hardy lifted his boot, ready for another kick. Tobias leaped forward.

"Why are you so fucking brutal? Just calm down, okay?"

To his surprise, Hardy stepped away, pulling out a crooked cigarette from his chest pocket with two fingers. He lit it, blew out some smoke.

"We have to think about how we're going to go about this. Calmly, using our heads." Tobias pointed at the animal lying on the ground. "We have to find a solution."

"You'll certainly think of something," Hardy said, sneering.

"I just don't get you. Have I ever done anything to you?"

Hardy smiled, his lips creeping from behind his bushy beard. He took off his hat, saw the twig, and brushed it off with one jerk.

They stood glaring at each other for a moment. Hardy breathed smoke from his nose. There was something wrong with that nose. It appeared to have been broken, as if someone had given him a good punch and it never had healed properly. He rolled the cigarette on his lower lip.

"So, Mr. Vet," Hardy spit out. "What're you going to do?"

"Dammit, cut that out. Sabina is waiting for us. We have to go back."

Before Tobias could do anything, Hardy walked back to the heifer and kicked it in the tail.

"Get up, goddamn you. Can't stand up, can you? We're in a hurry, don't you see, Mr. Big Shot Veterinarian is in a big hurry."

Tobias' eyes felt suddenly red and hot and he leapt forward, but slipped on the damp grass and almost fell over. Hardy stood there, rocking on his heels.

"It was just a test," Hardy said calmly. "Just to see if it's playing around."

"What the fuck is wrong with your head?"

"So you're a shrink, too. A vet and a shrink!"

Tobias whirled around and began to climb up the slope, half-crawling, his whole body shaking. He felt warm, and sweat broke out on his back, under his arms, down around his stomach. He realized that the dog was following him, but when he turned to check, the dog had turned around and was heading back toward Hardy. Tobias wanted to call the dog, entice it over to his side, but his lips were as stiff as bark. His heartbeats thudded up through his throat all the way to his temples, a hard, moaning hiss. He scrambled over the edge and turned his head. Hardy was watching him. He'd put aside his backpack and was taking a last deep drag on the cigarette, which he then threw aside.

Tobias walked away. As soon as he was out of sight, he began to run. His rage burned within him and he wanted to scream out loud. When he was getting near the beach, he slowed, knowing that he shouldn't cause any panic. Sabina was standing on the beach, looking the other way, with the animals behind her like a tight, brown-and-white wall. Some of them were mooing, and he thought he heard her answer them from his place on the slope above. Then Sabina turned around and caught sight of him, and he saw a flash of worry in her eyes. He stroked his hair in order to calm himself down as well as to straighten it out. Then he scratched his neck.

"What's up, Tobias?"

Her face appeared pale and overwrought.

"What happened?"

Before he could answer, they heard a bang from the direction of the forest, the sound of a shot being fired, and at the same time, the dog began to howl.

4

THE TELEPHONE RANG.

Carl Sigvard was dozing, probably due to those pills that Sabina insisted on forcing down his throat. They made his mouth dry, befuddled him.

He searched for the receiver. Sabina had gotten a long line so that he could have the telephone next to his bedside table.

"Because I cannot remain at your side constantly, as I must see to the animals." Sometimes she had an old-fashioned way of speaking, using words which other people had stopped using a long time ago.

The plastic was cool against his palm. Did he have a fever, too? Goddamn it!

"Elmqvist," he said, noticing his tongue was swollen from lying down so much, blocking his normal tone.

There was a tiny girl's voice on the other end.

"Hi. It's me, Klara."

"Klara, how are you? This is Grandpa."

"I recognize your voice, you know."

"Hmmm. So, you recognize my voice."

She giggled in an affected manner.

"Are you feeling any better now, Grandpa?"

"Much better, much better indeed."

"Is Pappa there?"

"No, he's not."

"He isn't?"

"He's out on Shame Island, bringing in the steers. They all left early this morning. What time is it now?"

"Ten forty-nine."

This young folk's way of telling time was something he had trouble getting used to. Ten forty-nine, he'd have to figure that out.

"Aren't you supposed to be in school?"

"I am in school, but we have recess now, I'm calling from my cell phone."

"I see."

"I tried Pappa's cell already, but he never turns it on."

"No, that may be." Carl Sigvard cleared his throat. "How are you doing, Klara? Everything fine?"

"Yeah, everything's fine."

"Shall I tell your father to give you a call when he returns?"

"Nah, it wasn't anything important. I can call back later."

There was a moment of silence. Carl Sigvard thought it must cost a great deal of money to just call on the cell phone for no reason. Tobias would have to pay for it. Or maybe Görel, her mother. But Görel didn't seem to have a great deal of money. Nor his boy, for that matter.

"What are you doing now, Grandpa?" he heard her say, and at the same time a rising swell of noise came from behind her, her recess was probably coming to an end.

"I'm just lying here in bed. But maybe I'll try getting up in a bit."

"Okay. Keep on getting better. I have to go now."

"Bye-bye, my little Klara." He thought, my little Sweetie-girl. Of course, he wouldn't say that. She would be embarrassed. She was much too old for childish pet names. How old was she again? Fourteen? Fifteen? She really wasn't a kid any more, though she had a high voice which resembled Görel's.

Carl Sigvard rolled onto his side and replaced the receiver with great effort. His back had started to complain again; it hurt to be lying in bed all the time. He wasn't made for this kind of thing.

He'd been active and on the go his whole life. His muscles were going to atrophy if he had to keep lying in this damned bed. They were already thinning down so that his legs looked like seed potatoes and had a bluish tinge. The first twenty-four hours they'd put on support stockings so that he wouldn't get blood clots, and already underneath those stockings, his legs had started to atrophy, flesh and sinews shrinking, everything getting weaker and weaker.

When Sabine unrolled the stocking layer, something else sloughed off which was not a part of him. Sabina, sitting there with her hair loose, had grimaced and turned her little cute nose away.

"What the hell was that stuff?"

"I guess I'll have to wash your little toes, since it'll be a while before you'll be able to take a shower," Sabina said.

Carl Sigvard closed his eyes, all at once feeling as if he could no longer look at this all-too-familiar room with its boring old furniture. He wasn't used to seeing it in the light of day, and everything was worn out and dirty. Like himself! That wallpaper, with marks from the leak last winter. That chair underneath Sabina's yellow robe. That picture over the chest of drawers, it hung crooked; he saw that now. And its scene, that certainly wouldn't cheer him up, that huddled little hovel with its grass roof and the melting snow and the fields beginning to show their barrenness. Lean and demanding, as in real life.

Svava had brought the picture with her when she moved in. Svava, who'd been Tobias' mother. Why had he left it up there? That picture was of some Icelandic hell-hole, a family farm probably. He'd heard she'd gone back to Iceland and married some knotty Icelander. They were probably singing Icelandic folk songs every evening, *ridum, ridum,* whatever the hell it was called. No matter what was going on those crazy Icelanders would start singing. Once when Svava's brothers had come to visit, they did nothing but strum their guitars and sing the whole damn day, and no food was put on the table because Svava was too busy to bother, stamping to the rhythm and swinging her hips and not at all acting like her usual self.

Jaou, she used to say instead of a good Swedish *ja,* and he would imitate her way of answering him. *Are you there, Svava? Jaou.* But now she wasn't there anymore, which was all the same to him, and now here he was lying in bed like a sack of rotting turnips, when he should be outside. And his lungs were really aching for some fresh air.

As he lay there, he tried to call up a picture of Sabina in his mind, of her body when she would just get out of bed, how she stretched her arms straight up to the ceiling and how her hair fell like a tangle of cotton all the way down her back. He saw her thin, white nightgown, thinking of her breasts with their large brown nipples, larger than any he'd ever seen on any other woman, and remembered how he nursed them, sucking them, lying with his chin on her stomach, yes, nursing just like a calf.

Sabina was still beautiful. Not like when they'd first met, but in another way, a more inner beauty. They'd met more than ten years ago by now, but before then, he'd lived alone in this house since November, Nineteen-and-Seventy, the time when Svava took their boy and disappeared.

He'd been doubtful about letting Sabina into the house, a person who did not know his habits and who wanted to come right in with all that new stuff. He'd gotten offers from other women before, that's for sure, but it was only Sabina he dared take in, and that in spite of that malformed offspring she'd had to drag along, who'd have to live on the farm with them. The kid would not have managed without her, with his child's mind in a body big and strong as a grown man's.

That first month, she stayed in the same room with her boy.

"We'll have to take things step by step, and you're going to have to be patient, Carl Sigvard," she said. She always used his entire name, no nicknames like Kalle or Sigge. Svava'd done that, but not Sabina. His name sounded pretty whenever Sabina said it.

Adam slept in the room farthest away, the one which had been Svava's sewing room. Every evening, Sabina put the beds in order, pulling out the trundle bed and smoothing out sheets and blankets.

She even slept with that half-man in her arms. He sucked his great big thumb, his beard stubbly, his eyes shining underneath his brows.

"He has to start feeling safe and at home here," she explained. "If we give him some time now, I promise, things will be better later."

And she was right. She knew all about that boy, that man, whatever the hell he was. She was the one who had carried him and birthed him and let him nurse at those big nipples, just as Carl Sigvard did now. Surprisingly, the thought did not affect him, the boy's flabby lips sucking at the same breasts he now sucked.

With time, he saw that the boy was strong and could do some of the chores necessary on the farm. That is, if you made the request the right way, if you asked him and explained things to him and if you were gentle and thankful afterwards. Then he'd even do the chore again. Carrying in the wood, for example, or, like now, helping round up the steers.

And then there was the whole thing with Hardy. They'd been forced to take him on, although there was something slippery and unpleasant about that man. Nowadays, it was practically impossible to find someone who was able to help out. Hardy was a cheater, that's what he was. He'd been away in prison, too, and everybody knew it even though his mother Ann-Mari tried to convince people that he'd attended school in Gothenburg. Carl Sigvard was surprised that Sabina let Adam hang around Hardy so much, though he said nothing about it, since it was good to not have the boy following at his heels all day long. But that Hardy was not proper company, that was clear, and he felt an instinctive repugnance at having to ask Hardy for help.

Carl Sigvard knew exactly what Tobias was thinking: *Time to stop farming now, Dad. Don't you see?* But Tobias would never say that out loud, at least not in Carl Sigvard's hearing. His son had some sense of respect, after all. And that's why he showed up now, when he was needed, breaking off that important book writing of his.

Tobias had come up to the room to talk only on the first two days. He was probably afraid of taunts and jeers, of course. Tobias had stood at the threshold of the room and greeted him by nodding without a sound as if he would rather have turned around and gone back downstairs.

"Come here and let me take a look at you!"

Tobias had a thin face and black hair with strands hanging in his eyes, as if he wanted to hide something, hide himself from other people and their staring. He resembled his mother. He had that redness which could suddenly blossom on his neck whenever he felt cornered, that gap between his front teeth, those cheekbones.

He had looked like a little nomad as he lay in Svava's arms while she loosened some of his swaddling clothes.

"He looks like that picture of your father, the one hanging in the living room," she said.

Carl Sigvard didn't see anything of the kind. Tense, leaning forward, he sat with his newborn son on his lap, his son's head in his cupped hands.

The thought came to him, *Is he really mine? Why does she keep pointing out a likeness?* There was no doubt that the boy looked like her. *He* certainly didn't have those colors or features.

As the boy grew up, his doubts faded.

But then she took him with her when she moved out, before the boy had even turned ten years old.

5

A WHIRL OF AIR BLEW over the surface of the water, changing its color from clear as glass to rippling gray. Tobias twisted around and saw Sabina's eyes, flickering, the same gray as the water.

"What was that?" Sabina whispered, and pulled at the knot in her scarf as if she were having trouble breathing.

Then they saw the herd dog coming back, black and slinking, not in a straight line toward them but aimlessly, zigzagging.

"Billy!" Sabina hunched down and called the dog to her in a raw, commanding voice. "Come here right now!"

The steers were getting nervous behind them. They stomped their feet and pushed each other, and the raft began to sway. The dog sat down, its head at an angle. Then it got up and dug about in the sand.

"Billy, come here!" shouted Adam in his hoarse, animal voice.

"He fired," said Tobias. "When we heard the shot. That was him."

Sabina nodded absent-mindedly. "The steer, wasn't it?"

Tobias nodded.

"It had been hurt, right?"

"It couldn't stand up. It had broken something, but it was alive."

"We could have called the vet."

"It probably wouldn't have helped."

Sabina's forehead wrinkled with irritation.

"This is just going to be a lot of hassle. Now we've got to figure out what to do with the meat, and that means someone will have to come back here and take care of that. Not to mention that the freezer is already pretty full. So we'll have to try and sell it as fast as we can."

"Isn't Hardy a bit egotistical? Shouldn't he have come here and asked us, I mean, asked *you,* how you wanted to handle it? Before he shot the steer?"

"Maybe so," she said in a brusque voice. "But he probably wanted to end its suffering."

"End its suffering? Nonsense! You should have seen the way he was treating it! Sabina, I don't like the guy. There's something wrong . . . up here." Tobias tapped the side of his head.

"You think that I have many choices?" she spat out. "You think it's all that easy to find people out here?"

"What about all those other folks who lost their jobs at the sawmill? Maybe one of them is a pleasant, normal human being?"

"Well, we don't have any of them; we have Hardy. He has his drawbacks, but at the same time, he is a hard worker. And he's really good with Adam. He's the only one who can make Adam feel good about himself, like he is a real person."

"Hardy's a sadist. I don't see how you can trust him!"

She wasn't listening to him; she kept on talking. "Sure, it's different for you. You can work with any person you choose. If you don't like one publisher, you can change to another one. That's not the way it is out here with us. But you don't understand how it is here."

The hair on the back of Tobias' neck rose and he shuddered. Hardy was coming, his backpack hanging from one shoulder, his cigarette lit. As he came, the dog had lain flat on the ground and then tried to crawl underneath the raft. The sight was unreal.

Hardy jumped on board, snapping his fingers. The dog followed, whining, and lay down as close as possible to one of the oil canisters.

"What's wrong with him?" Sabina asked.

"Don't ask me," said Hardy. "Not my dog. Can't read his mind."

Sabina bent over and petted the dog's fur. It licked her hand.

"We heard a shot," Sabina said.

"Yeah."

"So, was it you?"

"Yeah, it was me."

"So it was absolutely necessary?"

"What do you think? That I just fire away whenever I feel like it?"

"That's not what I meant."

"What did you mean?"

"Well, nothing, really. But I guess this means that we have to come back here."

"That'd make sense."

"But you know I don't have time for this. Today is all booked. We've got to get these animals into the pens, shave them and clean them up. We can't sell them looking like this." She gestured at the muddy, matted flanks. "Unless they're squeaky clean, we won't get what they're worth."

Hardy chuckled. "You got this expert from Stockholm to help you. So everything will work out just fine."

Tobias was standing with his hands in his pockets, and he felt his hands clench into fists. Again, this rage, this rising fury. He thought he'd learned years ago to control his feelings, make himself impervious. He'd covered himself with layer after layer so that he wouldn't be provoked, wouldn't hit back, wouldn't lash out. He'd taken to writing instead, turning his feelings into words, using them well, earning money with them. In fact, his latest book had been a crime novel, his breakthrough to the reading public, finally, after four poorly selling books. The last book had even come out in paperback. He'd found himself looking at it in the rack at the train station while waiting to catch his train, and it had given him a fluttering sense of contentment. Big fat letters: *THE NIGHT*, and then his name underneath, his own name, somewhat smaller and in a more cursive style: Tobias Elmkvist. Round, thick letters. His name. He stood there incognito and enjoyed looking at the cover of his book picturing a few foggy light posts by a taxicab. *I wrote that book you have for sale*, he thought, as he bought his cigarettes. *Bet you little bimbos have no idea it was me.*

And what if they had known? As if they would even care!

Sabina managed to get the raft's motor started after a few tries and they all helped push it off the beach. The animals stomped around and let loose dung which began to cover all the boards, but they showed no signs of panic.

Hardy leaned over the railing, taking one drag after another. His hat was drawn down over his eyes. His profile looked as if it were chiseled into wood, his cheeks edged in golden stubble so each coarse hair was distinguishable.

"So what did you use?" Tobias found he had to ask.

Hardy nodded toward his backpack.

"You hardly have room for a moose rifle in that."

"Hardly."

"So you run around carrying a handgun?"

"Now, Tobias," Sabina began, but interrupted herself because another boat was on its way over the lake, a little motorboat.

"Keep an eye on the animals," she commanded in her stern voice. "There might be a wake."

It was easier than Tobias had expected to bring the animals into the barn. The dog was a great help, and now all nineteen of them were under one roof, calm and uninjured. The next step was to corral them one by one and shave off their shaggy coats. Food animals, about to be transformed into organic, locally raised beef, could not be shaggy and dirty. The slaughterhouse would refuse them.

Tobias was still wearing his father's blue overalls, his cap jammed down, flattening his hair.

It was too tight across his forehead, but it wasn't adjustable. He knew that he'd have a headache later; one was already pushing its way out from inside his head, ready to burst into full bloom. A flowering headache? Perhaps not a good metaphor.

He was alone with Sabina now. Hardy had gone back out to the island, this time taking the small boat, and he'd taken Adam with him. Together they would take care of the meat from the dead steer.

Tobias felt a wave of relief. A time out from Hardy, if he could call it that.

He had a tuft of hay in his fist, to entice the young animals, one by one, until they followed. Then he'd give one push so that the gate of the pen would fall and hold them tight. He found out these animals were clever, too, and you couldn't trick them too many times, no matter how much they wanted to get the dry, good-smelling hay. If they managed to duck aside, if their horns didn't go through right away and they figured out what was ahead, well, then it would take a long time for them to forget.

Sabina was standing at the ready with the electric clippers. A shimmer of chaff covered her skin like powder. Her overalls' zipper had slid down slightly and he discovered she was wearing a necklace underneath, glittering between her breasts, two golden hands entwined. He hadn't seen that piece of jewelry before. That she even had a piece of jewelry surprised him; she didn't seem to be the kind to like fripperies. She'd also put on head protection to keep her hair clean from dirty, swishing tails. He'd gotten a smack in the face from a tail right after he'd momentarily taken off his cap. It hurt like hell so that his eyes filled with tears, and, even worse, his hair was covered in shit.

"Pay attention," said Sabina. "This little sweetie is really hungry."

The animal's large head was almost through the gate, but then one of its horns got stuck. The steer stuck out an impossibly long tongue. Tobias lifted his hay-filled hand. He clucked his tongue and coaxed until, finally, both horns moved through. Quickly Sabina pushed the gate down and locked it. The animal lowed with surprise, but calmed down and began happily to chew the hay. Those blunt, grinding jaws. Tobias stuck out his fingers and scratched the steer between its horns.

"The clipper plug fell out. Can you put it back?" Sabina yelled, and he bent down and pushed the plug back into place. Sweat was dripping off Sabina's face; she was streaked with dust and rubbed-off skin.

Now that the steer was in position, she was able to shave its legs and hindquarters, its tail and stomach. The large tufts of hair fell like lightweight potato peels and strewed over the slotted floor, trampled down by cloven hooves. Shaving did not seem to bother the animals; it seemed to cause no pain or even a tickle. Tobias watched Sabina's hands, tanned, lumpy, unbelievably strong.

A picture floated into his mind.

She and his father.

No.

He brushed the picture away, blinking hard.

The steer was finished, completely shaven now. Tobias sprayed red paint on its forehead, the same kind they used on sows which had been mated. At that, the steer finally started, suddenly afraid, now that the procedure was over.

"You dumb beast," Tobias said. Sabina laughed.

Sabina had borrowed a boar a few months ago. The boar had mated with more than half of the sows by the time Tobias arrived. He looked over to the latest pair, now sleeping side-by-side, the boar and his now well-inseminated mate. The enormous pink and black male had one of his cloven hooves against her side, up over her back, as if embracing.

"You've got to take a look at this," he called to Sabina. She stood on her tiptoes and looked down into the pen.

"Yep, they're really cute, aren't they? Our boar had to be slaughtered. He was unable to perform. Simply put, he was burned out."

"Nice way to go, though. I mean, before."

"You could say that."

Tobias took a few steps down the walkway, looking into the pens with the piglets scampering about. When they were six weeks old, they were separated from their mothers. They were just like active small children, never totally quiet, curious but easily scared. They jumped up with their front hooves on the side of the pen, looking at him with their unusually human eyes. Of course they didn't recognize him. Not his movements, nor his voice. Although he was raised on this farm, it was long before their time.

And by now, he'd turned into another human being altogether.

"Want to start the next one?"

"All right." The smell of ammonia in the air stung his nose. He thought about how he would take a shower later this evening, stand under the streaming water and scrub his skin so clean that his skin would seem to be falling off his body. But it would not be enough to get rid of the stench.

One day, before he and his wife had divorced, his father had come to visit him in Södertälje. His dad and Sabina. That was in the middle of the nineties, when some agricultural event was taking place at Älvsjö Event Center. His old man had found a new suit somewhere, as well as a dark blue overcoat. In spite of the new clothes, he still carried the barnyard smell. Sabina was new then; she'd just moved into the house. She'd been wearing a red dress and Tobias couldn't help noticing her breasts, though he felt ashamed the minute he did. The two of them stayed the night, and he and his wife stayed in Klara's room. Görel was in a relatively good period in those days, and she'd made a wonderful fish stew and baked caraway bread; he could still remember that.

Where'd they put Adam that day?

He knew a neighbor, Erik Malmfeldt, had taken care of the animals. His father trusted Malmfeldt. The neighbor was out of the picture now. He'd had a stroke and was put in an old folks' home.

But what had they done with Adam that day?

Tobias turned toward Sabina and watched her hand with the clippers, how it moved back and forth like a plow, while the hair fell in clumps. She turned off the machine.

"How does it look? Good enough? Think I'm done with this one?"

"I see a spot near his tail, but then he's done, I think."

Sabina shaved the last bit of hair.

"You can spray him, now."

Tobias carefully sprayed a red mark on the hay-chewing steer's forehead. This one had stood still during the entire shaving, just chewing away. When Tobias lifted the gate, the steer jumped into life, backed wildly out, and almost slipped in the mess on the floor. The steer made a few nervous leaps back into the herd.

"How many do we have left?" Tobias asked.

"Don't know. I think we've done five, maybe six of them."

He stared into the herd, trying to count the number of paint marks.

"Ready for a coffee break?" she asked.

"A bit."

"Let's go to the house. I should look in on your father."

Your father. Not Carl Sigvard, but *your father*, as if she were making a point. A point of what? He took an awkwardly large step into the hallway and barely missed tramping on one of the barn cats. It hissed at him and slinked away between two milk canisters.

They walked over the yard together. The frost had melted away; water ran and dripped next to the house's walls. They walked past the dog yard and Sabina let out the little puppy, Frett. One of the gray bitches had adopted Frett as if he were her own. Frett ran toward them with his unsteady bounds, but then sat down to pee. Tobias laughed.

"Look, he's peeing like an old lady! Hey Frett, lift your leg. You're a guy. Don't you get that yet?"

"He's still so small," said Sabina as she picked up the puppy. "You're a good boy, Frett, a really good boy!"

Tobias brewed the coffee while Sabina went upstairs. Her mumbling voice came from up there, with the old man's short, sharp replies. Lying in bed had made him all whiny. He wasn't used to being cooped up inside as helpless and ungainly as a seal on dry land.

"Come closer and let me take a look at you!"

Tobias had not wanted to go upstairs; he didn't want to face all those unasked questions. It was enough that he'd promised to help out for a few days, since things had obviously reached a crisis. He had no desire to confront his father's bad temper.

"Come closer and let me take a look at you!"

Not an invitation, not a request. A command.

The old man had nothing to say about Tobias' books. Tobias had sent the latest one, just as he'd sent all his previous ones, with his hand-written dedication: *To Pappa with best wishes from the author.*

The first few times, his father had thanked him, at least, but he had also made it clear to Tobias that a farmer has no time for reading.

"Once evening comes, you get so damned tired. Up at the crack of dawn, you know, then non-stop all day long. *You* don't live this kind of life."

He almost said, *"You* chose *your* life."

But don't provoke him, don't get drawn into a fight!

Sabina was coming back downstairs now. Tobias heard her feet thumping down the stairs.

"The worst thing of all is his using that bed pan we got from the hospital," she said quietly. "The thing makes him stopped up."

Tobias felt mean. "You'll have to give him an enema."

"Why would you say such a thing?" She was sucking on her middle finger as if she'd gotten it stuck somewhere.

"Oh, forget it. The coffee's ready now. What did you plan to do with these frozen *bullar,* put them in the microwave?"

She nodded. "I'll have to bring him coffee, too."

They sat across the table from each other after she'd returned from bringing the old man his coffee. There was a pinched look in the corners of her mouth. Tobias bit into his *bulle*, the cinnamon taste so hot from the microwave that he almost burned his tongue.

"It's been a while since I've had a home-baked *bulle*," he said, trying to be contrite.

Sabina looked up at him from where she sat.

"I can imagine."

"Tastes wonderful."

"Thanks. How are you eating these days?"

"Oh, I manage with a little of this and a little of that. You know how things get when you live alone."

"But what about Klara? Doesn't she live with you sometimes?"

"Not so often these days. But when she does, I pull everything together for decent meals."

"How are you and Görel working things out?"

"Not so well."

"But she's managing all right, raising a teen-age girl on her own? I know how tough that can be."

"Görel has her happy pills. That's how she does it. I don't think she'd manage otherwise. But she and Klara seem to get along. I've suggested that Klara spend more time with me, but Klara doesn't want that. She often goes to stay with Klara's parents. They have a large home in Pershagen, the rich folks' neighborhood in Södertälje."

"I see." Sabina drank more coffee. Tobias noticed the light hair above her upper lip.

"What's that you got there?" The question suddenly flew out of him.

"Huh? What do you mean?"

"That necklace you're wearing."

"Oh that. It's nice isn't it? Your father gave it to me as a birthday present. I think it's wonderful."

"Huh. I had no idea that the old man could be so generous. I certainly never saw that side of him."

She kept quiet and stared at the table, drawing her thumb along the woven threads of the tablecloth. He grabbed her hand suddenly and turned it over. One of the nails was twisted and darkened.

"There's nothing wrong. I just got it stuck in something earlier."

"*Sabina!*"

There were loud thuds coming from above their heads. She carefully drew her hand away.

"I've got to look in on him. He's in a great deal of pain."

6

HE HEARD THEM IN THE HOUSE NOW. Why weren't they coming up to see him? Why wasn't she bringing up his tray with his coffee bread? So they could eat together alone? Instead she'd just brought up a mug of coffee in a cup with a damned advertisement on it. Gullvik's Plant Protection. He was half-sitting in his bed, slurping his coffee so hard that drops ran down the cup. She'd put that goddamned steel bed pan somewhere; who would ever imagine a normal person could really take a dump in that?

What the hell, Sabina! Come up here!

The district nurse had left a pair of crutches nearby, brand new and awkward. She ought to have known that he'd never be able to use them! He couldn't balance on his damned leg and his back wouldn't hold, so that the crutches fell with a bang which echoed throughout the entire room. His underarms were all sweaty and he felt as if he'd throw up.

Sabina was there, wearing her soft sweats.

"Oh, sweetheart, sweetheart!" Her small affectionate words fell over the bed, fell over the pillow where he was lying, bouncing like rubber balls.

"You've got to get the shit out! I just can't!"

Her hands under the blanket, burning in his asshole, his naked, tired skin. He had hemorrhoids, big red welts; she seemed to twist and pull.

"What are we going to do, Carl Sigvard? What are we going to do with you?"

"The hell if I know."

"But you've got to get this out! You're getting more and more constipated!"

"If I could get to the outhouse, there wouldn't be any problem."

He was used to the outhouse, that old-fashioned secret house. He needed to be left completely alone with these kinds of private doings. Certainly when Adam was yowling his awful music at the highest volume in the main house. Even his mother couldn't get him to stop the noise.

"Why don't we ask the district nurse?" Sabina was saying now. "Shall we ask her to stop by? She probably has some kind of medicine. There's all kinds of useful preparations these days. You're certainly not the first one to have this problem."

She tried to laugh. He threw his newspaper so hard that it flew apart.

"What the hell are you two doing in the kitchen?"

"What do you mean?"

"What are you two doing?"

"We've just gotten back from the island."

"Yes, I know you went to the island."

He shut his mouth, stared out the window, at the weak sun and washed-out colors.

"And we got all of them in," she continued carefully. "All but one. It's still out on Shame Island."

"It's still out there?"

"Unfortunately, yes."

"Did it drown?"

Sabina drew in her lower lip, held it between her teeth, sucked in some air.

"No."

"What happened to it, then?"

"Hardy had to shoot it. Hardy and Adam are out there right now, taking care of the meat. We'll try to sell it, and I'll check with the neighbors."

"Why did he have to shoot it? Was it injured?"

"Yes, it was."

"So six thousand crowns went straight to hell."

"No, no. I'm going to check with the restaurant, too. They sometimes buy meat under the table. They've done that before."

He lay there silently awhile, staring at the ceiling and the shiny copula of the lamp. He noticed that it had cracked; he'd never seen that before.

"So Hardy's out there now," he said after a while.

She nodded.

"With Adam. Tobias is here at home. He's helping me with the clipping."

"Huh."

"We just came in for a moment. We needed a coffee break."

"Listen here . . . ." These abrupt shifts in light; things weren't like this before. All the edges were washing out. Sabina sitting on the bed looked blurred. "Can't you come up later? You and the boy, I mean Tobias. Can't you two just come up here and sit for a while? It's so damned lonely. Can't you come up?"

She stroked him around his chin, and the tears couldn't stop themselves from running down his face.

"Of course, Carl Sigvard. You know we'll do that. But not right now, because we have to get so much done. You understand, don't you, sweetheart? You know how much we have to do right now. But we'll come on up this evening, all right?"

He swallowed. He couldn't speak due to a lump in his throat.

7

"I HAVE TO MAKE A FEW PHONE CALLS," Sabina said. "I have to
deal with this meat, you know. We'll have to try and sell it."

"All right."

"Do you think you could take out the sow, the one with the
boar, you know, and let a new one in? And just spray a little red
paint on her side. Don't forget that. We don't want to let her in twice
and have the boar use up all his resources."

"Sure, sure, of course. How many does he manage in one day?
Just one?"

"Well, no, he can do three in a day. He's in his best years."

"And so am I!" Tobias joked, but regretted saying it immediately.
Sabina chuckled.

"Well, if you're anything like your father . . . !"

Tobias pulled on his boots and started getting ready to go out
again, but then thought about his cell phone. He'd had it off the
whole morning; maybe that wasn't so smart. What if the publisher
called? Both Görel and Klara knew he was here at the farm, and
even Marit knew, so if there was something important, they could
always call the land-line to the farmhouse. But what if the publisher wanted to share some good news? Like maybe the latest
book had reached the best-seller list? Or maybe television had
asked to make a movie of it? Maybe he'd been nominated by the
Swedish Academy of Crime Writers for Best Mystery Novel? You
never know.

His cell phone was in his jacket pocket, and he took it out on the veranda and turned it on. It started to vibrate the minute he turned it on. He'd gotten a message. Better listen right away.

Frett had sneaked out the door with him and began to chase a leaf blowing by. The reception here in Kvarnberga wasn't the best. Tobias had to walk around for a while until the bars showed a high enough level to receive. He tapped in 2-2-2 and pressed his hand to his other ear so that he wouldn't miss anything. There were three messages. The first one was just a scraping noise before it was turned off again. The second one was from Klara.

"Yes, uh, hi, it's me. Why don't you ever turn this thing on when I call? Love ya."

Nothing else. He'd have to remember to call her this evening. She was probably in school right now.

The third message was received "Today, at nine forty-five." He immediately recognized Marit's nasal, quick voice. She often sounded stressed, even when she wasn't.

"Hi, Tobias. How's everything out in cow country? You haven't forgotten me, have you? I miss you."

He'd been going out with Marit for two years now. Two years to the day. Marit was a library assistant at Södertälje City Library. They'd met after she'd contacted him about giving a reading at the library from his short story collection which had just come out. *Fountains of Near and Dear.* It was a stupid title, he realized after a while. Maybe poetic and unusual, but completely crazy. In spite of good reviews, the book hadn't sold more than 200 copies. No one could make a living from that. As luck would have it, even the Swedish Writer's Union realized this and gave him a two-year grant.

His publisher, Titus Bruhn, had steered him toward this mystery novel thing. "You have something going in your short stories," Titus said, "which can be developed into something more. You have fantastic descriptions of people, tension, relationships." Titus had even offered him an advance, which Tobias declined, although it felt good for his self-esteem. It certainly did.

Tobias lit a cigarette and punched in the number to Marit's workplace. She answered immediately.

"Södertäje City Library. Marit Stenhägg."

"Hi there, Stenhägg woman."

"Oh, it's you. Hi there."

"Hi."

"Did you get my message? Why don't you have your cell phone on?"

"You've got to realize that I'm not in the city. I'm out in the bush, which has damned awful reception."

"Well, that seems odd. It can't be that far from civilization."

"You wouldn't think so, but that's the way it is."

"How are you doing, Tobias? How's everything going out there?"

Tobias felt strangely wordless.

"Well, everything's under control," he finally said.

"Yes, and . . . ?"

"What do you mean, 'and'?"

"I mean, when are you coming home?"

"I don't really know. I'll be here for a few more days at least."

She lowered her voice and sounded childish. "I miss you and I want you to come home now."

"I miss you, too," he said automatically, and, at the same time, he began walking again, and as he walked, her voice was cut off. He turned off his cell phone and drew a last drag before he stamped out his cigarette in the mud.

The second he entered the barn, he knew instinctively someone had been there. He put on his cap and looked around. The piglets were playing as usual.

He saw no one, but just as he was thinking he was mistaken and was about to go into the pen with the boar, a shadow fell over the floor and he jumped.

"Hi, Tobias," a woman's voice said. "God, I frightened you, didn't I? Sorry about that."

The woman looked about his age. She had hair dyed an awful red cut in some kind of punk style. Her eyes were heavily made up, and so was her mouth. It looked totally out of place in here—the word *discrepancy* flew through his brain. Her face was round and friendly. A thin, white scar ran down her left temple. She held out her hand, and he took it, surprised at the strength in her grip.

"No, it's just I thought I was alone here," he said as an excuse.

"I heard that you were home helping out, and I thought I'd drop by."

Who is she, who the hell is she? Probably someone from his school days. He'd have to play along and pretend he recognized her. Otherwise the gossip would go around about how Tobias was high on his horse now that he'd been on TV. The usual stuff.

"Well, you know, my father had an accident, as you probably heard. So I had to come out here for a while to help out."

She smiled.

"That was sweet of you. How's he doing now, your father?"

"Not too good. He's just too old. He should have quit a long time ago. I've never seen such a stubborn old Swede. He won't give up."

"Well, he's not all that old, and I think he looks like he has lots of pep. And he still looks young."

"If you say so."

"But how nice to see you again! It must have been a hundred years since I saw you last! Except on TV, of course. Oh God, there's an old friend from school right there! I thought, and I recognized you at once. You haven't changed a bit."

"Neither have you," he managed to say.

She chuckled contentedly and placed her arm in his. "Just think! We finally have someone famous from our own little village! No one would ever believe it!"

"Come on, you're exaggerating. I'm not that famous just because I've written a few books!"

"You think so? It's not just because. I read about you in *Allers* magazine, too, and they had a picture of your daughter. She's so cute! Klara, right?"

"Right."

"I've actually read all your books, just so you know. Well, not the last one, I just bought it when I went to town last. A mystery this time, right? Actually, I don't like mysteries. But then I thought, well, it's *you* who wrote it, and as a matter of fact . . ."

She put her hand in her jacket pocket and pulled out a copy of *The Night* in paperback.

"I thought I'd ask you to sign it. If you don't have anything against it, that is. Since it's a paperback. Maybe you only sign hard-covers?"

Just as he expected, someone from school. At least one little clue. He took his time reaching for the book.

"Of course, I'll sign it." His brain was working feverishly, he had to remember what her name was. "But I'll probably have to go inside and get a pen first."

"Oh, don't worry, I have a pen right here."

The woman held out a ballpoint pen.

"What do you want me to write?"

"Oh, something sweet."

Just then, Sabina came out of the house. The little puppy ran over to her at once, and she bent down. Her curvy, soft hips. She began to walk into the barn, holding the puppy in her arms. Sabina saved him.

"Hi, Ingelise! I didn't know you were here!"

Ingelise! Of course! She'd been a year ahead of him in school; he remembered that now. She had often come over to their farm, too, in order to help his mother with the horses. How had he forgotten that?

"I wanted to have my book signed, now that we have such a famous writer visiting us. Have you read it, Sabina?"

"It's on my nightstand, but I haven't had time to read it yet. If I ever dare read it, that is. I imagine it's really gruesome."

Tobias thought for a moment and was about to write, when Ingelise grabbed his hand to stop him.

"I write my name with a zee, now. I-n-g-e-l-i-z-e."

"Why do you do that?"

"Why not? It looks cool. Not so everyday boring Swedish."

"All right, just as you want." *To Ingelize with friendliest wishes,* he wrote. *From the Author and your friend, Tobias.*

"Do you want to buy some meat?" asked Sabina. "We had to slaughter a steer on Shame Island."

Ingelize shook her head.

"You know I'm a vegetarian."

"Oh sorry, I forgot. Well, we'll find someone to take it."

They heard the sound of a motor coming up the road. Sabina's old Opel swung into the drive. Hardy was driving and Adam sat next to him.

"I've got to hurry home," said Ingelize. "Drop in sometime, Tobi. I have a herd of Icelandic ponies now. We could go for a ride. Wouldn't that be fun?"

Tobias nodded. "Well, why not?"

"And you could sign the rest of your books, too, while you're there. If that's okay with you."

"Sure."

Adam walked over, staggering in the mud. He held his hands in front of him, cupped together, and was making small gurgling sounds.

"Adam, what's wrong? Did you hurt yourself?" Sabina hurried up to him, eyes widened in fear.

The knotty backs of his hands were brown with blood. Adam even had traces of blood on his face.

"Jack the Ritter," he said, slurring.

"*Ripper*, you idiot!" Hardy had come up to them by now as well, his hat drawn low over his eyes.

"What's wrong with him, Hardy? Did anything happen to him?"

"He's been with me and I wouldn't let *anything* happen to Adam. You know that."

"Go in the barn and wash off with the hose!" Sabina said, giving her son a little push. Adam sneered, and his half-open mouth let saliva run down one side of his chin.

"He's got something to show you," Hardy said.

Adam stopped, his hands still roughly forming a circle around something that couldn't be seen. His nostrils flared.

"Show Tobias!" Hardy commanded. "Go on, show Tobias what a fine thing you've got there!"

Adam was doubtful. He stood, rocking on his feet, a smothered, gnashing sound coming from between his teeth.

"Come on, just show him!" Hardy repeated in a friendly way. "Show Tobias what you've got!"

Slowly, the big man began to move. His tongue swept over his lips, ran over his discolored teeth. Suddenly, his face twisted with disgust and he stretched out his arms as far away from his body as he could.

"What's all this about?" Tobias straightened his back, feeling the taste of metal in his mouth. "What does he have there?"

Adam began to sob, and then retch. He threw up without bending over, so it fell straight down his chest and covered his jacket. His arms were still rigidly in front, far away from his body.

"Cut it out, now, Adam." Hardy was laughing. "You were so cool out on the island."

"What do you have there, my son? Show me. Open your hands and show me!" Sabina was right next to her son, beginning to wipe his face with her handkerchief. "Show me, come on now. Open your hands and show Mamma."

Adam's hands had frozen in their cupped grip. Sabina had to stroke his back, pet him, gently soothe him for over a minute before Adam was able to relax. His fingers jerked open, and they were able to see what he had. In the sticky palms of his hands was a large, staring eye. It was still embedded in a bloody mess of jelly-like membranes. They could easily make out the veins and muscular attachments, cleanly cut by a long-handled knife. A small bit of eyelid was left, long lashes sticking to the edge. The iris had lost its original color and had turned into an indistinct gray.

Adam breathed noisily, his whole body shaking. Then he threw the eye away from him, gulping with dry sobs.

No one could act fast enough to prevent Frett from reaching the eye. She sniffed it and then ate it in one gulp.

"Would you look at that!" Hardy exclaimed. "Talk about gone in the blink of an eye!"

"What were you doing out there?" Sabina whispered. She had finally managed to soothe Adam and was helping him wash off most of the blood. Adam was in the barn, pouring water into his hands from the hose and letting it run over and over again. He was no longer crying, but there was a hurt look on his face.

"What do you think? He was helping me do the butchering," Hardy said with irritation. "Wasn't that the whole point?"

"I mean the eye. What was that about? You know how sensitive he is!"

"What the hell? It was just a cow's eye."

"It was thoughtless, Hardy, that's what it was."

"He was interested. I tried to explain to him all about anatomy. He was really interested. I showed him the heart and the intestines and a few other great details. It's as interesting as hell. Everybody should know this stuff."

"Where is the meat?" she asked finally, stiffly.

"In the car."

"Why don't you drive it over to Johansson's at the restaurant? We'll have to keep it over there for now."

Hardy swept off his hat. His hair was sweaty and matted down.

"Right now?"

"Do you have time?"

"Yeah, but I need my money."

"Tomorrow, Hardy, you'll get it tomorrow. I have to go to the bank first, and they're already closed. It's too late for today."

Hardy raised his hands.

"That'll make things rough for me."

"Are you in that much of a rush?"

"Oh, hell, it can wait then."

Hardy put his hat back on and turned to leave.

Tobias looked at Sabina. There was something different about her, a bit of fear, which was new. He'd never seen her like that before. He had an impulse to take her into his arms, to hold her close, to protect her.

But Sabina was already on the way into the barn.

"Stop using the water now, Adam," she was yelling. "Stop now! That's enough water!"

8

INGELIZE HAD FORGOTTEN HE WAS SO GOOD-LOOKING. She mostly remembered him as a quiet, nerdy boy, with black, stringy, totally straight hair. She'd never seen such straight, black hair on a human being, neither before nor since. And it looked like he wasn't turning into a baldy, either. How old was he now? Had he turned forty yet? He must have, since he was a year younger than she was and she was going to be forty-two in just a few weeks.

Ingelize turned into the road which led to East Kvarnberga, where she had her own farm. She glanced at the new sign. She'd ordered it from a company in town. *Ingelize's Icelandic Ponies* was painted in the center of a frame of bluebells and horseshoes. She'd had the idea herself, and the sign looked completely professional.

It'd be nice if Tobias wanted to go out riding. He knew how to ride, or at least he used to know. Actually, she had his mother to thank that she'd gone into horses in the first place. Svava had awakened her interest. She didn't remember how it started, but before she knew it, she rode her bike to the Elmqvist farm and helped muck out the stalls and was able to ride the horses. Svava had two half-breed, large horses. One was a Northern Swedish called Trolle, who was the incarnation of security. Ingelize took care of and learned to ride on Trolle.

"You have good horse sense," Svava had praised her. "Not everyone has that talent."

Ingelize burned with pride.

As an adult, Ingelize had made her dream come true. Her parents had been older when they had her, both over forty-five, and she'd been their only child. When they'd died a few years ago, she took over the farm. She started with two Icelandic ponies, but within half a year, she'd expanded, and now she had a herd of fifteen. Riding had become extremely popular. She took on companies as well as individuals. In the summer, she organized camps and, a few evenings a week, she gave riding classes. There were more than enough young girls who wanted to help out, just as she'd once helped out Tobias' mother.

Svava had taught her a great deal. Svava had been raised with horses. Ingelize remembered how Svava would describe the horses in her Icelandic homeland, their special temperament and character, a touch of melancholy in her voice.

"I would have preferred horses like that here," Svava had explained. "But I don't think they'd be happy. I've heard of Icelandic horses which came here and to Germany and to Denmark. They're tortured by the insects and get summer eczema. They really suffer. I wouldn't want to subject them to that."

Sometime later, Svava left the farm, and Tobias disappeared, too. One afternoon, when Ingelize had biked over, there was a truck in front of the house. She didn't see a single person. Carefully, she pulled aside the cover which lay over the back. She saw some chairs and the white chest of drawers which had usually stood in the hallway. She felt sick as she went over to the barn. The horses were in their stalls, and she climbed in by Trolle and began to curry him, but with the same sick feeling that something terrible was going to happen.

After a few minutes, she heard voices. Someone yelling, a man. She became frightened and pressed up against the wall, dropping the currycomb in the process. Usually calm, Trolle startled and stamped his hooves, one coming down right on her foot. The truck drove off as she stood there, fighting back her tears. Tobias' father was screaming after them and he sounded strange and mean. She didn't hear what he was screaming; she wanted to scream herself and throw herself down into the straw. Something had ended for sure now, she realized, never to return.

Then he was there in the barn and, for the first time, she heard a grownup man cry. She held her breath and tried to make herself as little as possible. He howled, yelled, sighed. Eventually, he left, got up on the tractor and drove out somewhere into the fields.

A small bone was broken in Ingelize's foot, and her foot swelled until later she could barely take off her boot. Even now, thirty years later, her foot was slightly deformed and she had difficulty finding shoes that would fit.

A few weeks later, she screwed up the courage to bike back to the farm, although she'd already heard from her parents what had happened. Svava had gotten tired of her husband and moved to Södertälje. She took the boy, Tobias, with her.

Of course, there'd been a great deal of small town gossip about the whole thing. That was the drawback of living here. Ingelize had gone to live in Gothenburg for a while, but she never really felt at home in the city. The whole time, she'd yearned to be back in the country.

Once her husband, Jens, made it into Parliament, she decided to strike while the iron was hot. Her parents had recently died. Jens was often gone, but now she had something of her own. She was no longer bored with nothing useful to do.

She'd bought all of Tobias' books and read them as if she'd hoped to find something in them that she would recognize. Maybe a person, a scene, a detail. She liked the way he wrote. She felt she'd gotten closer to him by reading his books. One of them had a love story with a great deal of erotic detail. She'd never thought about him as a man before. He'd always been that little boy who jumped on a horse, kicked its sides with his heels so that it leaped and galloped away just like those boys in Gothenburg's backyards would spur on their bicycles and mopeds.

Her mother had told her about Tobias' wife. Were they divorced now? Probably. That woman had been so strange. Görel, that was her name. She wore thin, white dresses in the middle of winter. Even in a summer heat-wave, her fingers were weak, chilly and damp whenever she shook hands.

"She must have a different metabolism than normal people," her mother had said. "The opposite, in fact: when it's cold, she's warm; when it's warm, she's cold. And you should see the hats she wears, the kind with wide brims, as if she's stepped out of a film from the golden era. No woman wears hats nowadays, at least not the kind you had to pin on with hatpins. Once I met her on the way to the beach. She'd broken off a rose which she was trying to fasten on her hat brim. She asked me for help. She said she kept pricking her fingers on the thorns. Well, I didn't know her, not well enough, anyway. And the look in her eyes—you should have seen her, Ingelize. I don't think that Tobias is all that happy with her."

When she'd read the article in the magazine, there was nothing about Görel there; but in one of the photos, there was a picture of Tobias at his computer with his daughter Klara. She also had black hair, as if she were a young Inuit.

Ingelize took out her paperback book and opened it with expectation. She read what he wrote. Felt proud. Which horse would she let him ride? Maybe Hábrók? Twelve years old, a clear tölt, with a bit of a temperament. Or maybe the calmer Bleijka? Something for her to think about.

But deep inside she felt she really did want to see him again.

9

"**LOOK WHAT I FOUND IN THE WOODSHED!** Take a look, Carl Sig-vard!" Sabina had come into the room; he'd been dozing for a while. Now here she was, and it was still light, and a fly was buzzing against the window pane. Heavy and wide-awake. The sun was starting to set.

"What is it?" he said, though his voice wasn't clear.

"I don't know. I think it's an old bed tray. You know, the kind you put over you when you're in bed so that you can have a food tray on it."

Yes, he remembered it. He'd carved it himself for Svava, if she would have to stay in bed for a while after the baby was born. He thought she'd rest and have her meals on it. But as it turned out, she didn't really need it. She was up and about in just a couple days.

But he also remembered she'd felt touched.

He'd then painted it red and Tobias had used it during his long periods of illness. He remembered how Tobias had lain in bed, all his crayons on the tray, Tobias' tired, fever-filled eyes.

He was about to ask, *do you remember how often he was sick?*

No, it wasn't Svava, it was Sabina, and she wouldn't remember anything about it. She had her own stuff to deal with.

"Yeah, that old bed tray," he muttered, and let her place it on the bed over him, over his aching hips.

"You can use it. It'll work."

He grimaced.

"I don't plan to lie here for the rest of my life, if that's what you think."

"I don't think that, either."

She walked over the floor, swaying. She was moving in a different way than he remembered she usually did: she was walking like a pregnant woman, although her times of the month had stopped—that much he knew.

"What happened with the meat?" he asked.

"I was able to store it at the Johansson place for now."

She left him to start dinner. The tray still stood on the bed. She had promised that they were going to gather together to eat up in his room. Now he heard a different tread on the stairs, not her usual ones, but quieter, more hesitant—had to be Tobias.

The door was wide open and Tobias came right in, carrying a tray in his hands; there were plates and utensils on it.

"Hi," Tobias said, almost shyly.

Carl Sigvard nodded in greeting.

"Maybe you can put it on the table over there."

"Sure."

"So you think I'm all washed up, huh! To make you come up here and eat with me."

Tobias shook his head, his neck so thin, his wisps of hair falling forward.

"No, not at all. I imagine it's lonely up here."

"Move the table closer. And the chair there. You can put the clothes on the other bed."

The clatter of porcelain and stainless steel.

"Are you hungry?" Tobias asked.

"Hungry is as hungry does. Those who do not work also should not eat. You know that."

"Pappa!"

"But that's the way it is, isn't it? Right?"

"You've sure as hell worked enough in your lifetime."

"Come over here. Come here so I can look at you."

Tobias reluctantly came closer, his arms dangling at his sides, his long fingers, those writer-fingers.

"I just want to tell you one little thing: It was good of you to take the time to come out here."

"Nah, of course, you got to help out when you can."

"That's not always so clear. You have to know that I appreciate it."

Now he had to turn his head away; tears were coming again, warm and wet. What a cry-baby he'd turned into. Why, he was probably just one step away from a stroke himself! His neighbor Erik Malmfeldt had gone the same route. Bleeding in the brain. Sounds like that'd be the end of it all, but it didn't have to be, though in Erik's case . . . Carl Sigvard had gone to visit him at Kastaniegården's old folks' home. That damned big old man had burst into tears like a baby! Did nothing but sit there and try to catch his breath; he wasn't able to speak. Sat there with his big naked feet stuck in his slippers.

Was he going to turn into someone like that? A day when he no longer had any use for his farm boots?

Damned if he would!

His boy was hanging onto the bedpost as if he needed the support. Looking at him from this angle, Carl Sigvard could see features that clearly were from Svava—her profile, her body. If Tobias had been a daughter, would he then have been Svava's perfect image?

Carl Sigvard cleared his throat.

"Um, by the way, Klara called earlier."

"Oh, she called here, did she?"

"She said it was nothing important."

"Uh-huh."

"How often do you get to see her?"

"Often enough. At least once a week."

"She's getting big now, isn't she? A real little lady, I imagine."

Tobias snorted.

"Lady is as lady does. But it's true she's entered puberty. And she has a wicked moodiness about her."

Svava had that, too. A wicked moodiness. She'd slam the pots down onto the stove; sometime a glass would smash on the floor. Once she threw out the entire Sunday steak because she was so angry.

And what would she be doing now? She was probably singing in the slushy snow, her usual *ridum, ridum.*

Out loud he said, "Have you heard anything from your mother?"

"We call each other up sometimes. Everything seems to be fine."

Did she have anyone new? Well, that didn't really interest him, not anymore. That he could say with honesty: *not anymore.*

His sheets were warm and filled with wrinkles and crumbs. He tried to turn, change position. His leg had fallen asleep, it tingled and prickled. Tobias leaned over him.

"Can I help you with anything?"

"Nah. But I want to ask you something. Can I? Are you really happy with your life up there in the city? Can I even ask without you getting angry? Are you content with your life?"

Tobias leaned back again, but remained standing, pulling at a loose thread from his sweater.

"Sure. I'm content. I have a great life."

"Great?"

Tobias swallowed and nodded.

"Of course. Your life is *great.*"

"Dad, I chose my life like you chose yours. And you have to make the best of what you've chosen."

"Chose! Right! In my day, it was a question of taking responsibility."

Tobias stomped over to the window, turning his back on him, his shoulders raised and tense.

"We've talked about this before," he said dully. "I thought we'd finished discussing this subject."

"Of course, that we have, that we have."

Sabina called from the kitchen, and his boy slunk out as if he were fleeing. "I've got to help her; she's finished making dinner."

You should be able to talk about things. He was so touchy, Tobias. Quick to take offense. He had that from his mother. You could never reason with her either. Her fox eyes, her nose up in the air, not a single word for days on end. She'd disappear to the barn with her horses and sometimes she'd even sleep out there on the bench with the rag rug. Letting him sleep alone in the house.

How could he have gotten her to be nice again? Was it his fault that she was who she was? Right in the middle of taking in the hay, he drove to town and bought her gifts—nightgown, a flower vase, the kinds of things women loved. All to placate her. She could keep a grudge, she could. And was unbelievably quick to take offense.

Sabina sure wasn't like that. So, really, he'd gotten a better deal in the end. If it wasn't for that monster of a son she dragged with her wherever she went.

He started to doze, even though he wasn't all that tired. He'd been lying there so long that he no longer had the strength to stay awake. His body was wasting away. It wasn't created for this; it was meant to be moving around, full of life.

Svava astride one of the work horses, the boy in front of her, embraced by her shining knees.

"Be careful! Hold on to him properly!" How he stood there in the wind, calling out to them.

The horse's hooves banging on the wooden bridge. He was standing there, wringing his hands.

"Look, Pappi, look what I can do!"

10

THE AIR WAS THICK AND LACKED OXYGEN up here underneath the roof. Long before Sabina had divided the food onto their plates, Tobias lost the desire to eat. His father was half lying in the bed. She had plumped up pillows behind him and together they had lifted him by his underarms. He had a glimpse of his father's body from a gap in his nightclothes. An old man's sick body. Now he lay there, his eyebrows grown together; they'd become bushy, too—rough, bent hairs. Tobias had noticed the same thing happening with himself, those first signs of age. His hair, too, had those white streaks in the mass of black.

Brown beans and Falun sausage. Was that such a good idea, with the old man's intestinal trouble? Well, maybe it would get the works going again. Tobias had gone to the outhouse to see if there was a way to help his father down there. Clean and well-ordered with a rug on the floor and a faded picture of the royal family, cut from a magazine years ago. The royal children were still young; the youngest sat in Queen Sylvia's lap. In one corner there were a few sacks of quicklime, which removed both the smell and maggots.

His father would go here to take care of his business while he thumbed through old copies of *Land* magazine. It was his father's oasis. But it would be impossible to get a wheelchair through here.

Sabina had spread a napkin over his father's chest.

"How's that?" she asked.

Then she sat down with a bent back and her hair coming out of her braid. Her little gold necklace dangled.

"Help yourself, Tobias!" She passed over the serving plate of beans toward him, but he declined.

"This is good Swedish food!" his father said.

"I know, but I'm not hungry."

"You're not?" His father chewed loudly. "But it's food for the day. We have it. You shouldn't despise it."

There was a loud sound from Adam's room. Sabina got halfway up, but since there was no more noise, she sat back down.

"Isn't he going to get dinner?" asked Carl Sigvard.

"He's already had some sandwiches. He said he was tired. He's not really himself."

"It's that Hardy," Tobias began.

The old man stopped in the middle of lifting his fork to his mouth.

"What's wrong with Hardy?"

"Well, I don't really know."

"Tobias doesn't like Hardy so much," Sabina said, a tenseness coming over her mouth.

The old man gave her a cunning look.

"There's probably no one on earth who's all that fond of Hardy. And as long as I was lying here thinking about it, he sure as hell could have waited to shoot the beast until we got the vet out."

"I think Hardy made the right decision. And he's helped us before."

"What kind of guy is this Hardy, anyway?" Tobias asked.

"He's Ann-Mari's son, if you remember her," his father said. "The woman who was living with Gustav. She was a big, fat woman, at least in those days. Don't you remember her? She'd come out here when your mother needed her. She was good at taking care of horses, just like a real man. But once old Gustav came into the picture, well, then he taught her other things that men do, that they're best at."

"What? Have sex?"

His father gave him a look of distaste.

"No, drink alcohol! And the boy had a hell of a time because of it, let me tell you! He got beat all the time. And then he grew up and started doing some petty crime and that led to bigger things as well, which led him to being locked up. In fact, he's just served time for fraud."

"Would you like some milk?" Sabina interrupted, and held the pitcher up to the old man's glass.

"The truth is, beer would taste a lot better!"

"I don't think that beer would mix well with your medicine. Oh, by the way, we shouldn't forget it. I'll go get the bottle."

Later, in the kitchen, Tobias picked an argument with her.

"Why would you defend that crook Hardy? There's something wrong with his head. Can't you see that?"

"Tobias," she said, trying to avoid the subject.

"That thing he did with Adam, or made Adam do! That was just to get at me! He doesn't like me, though I sure as hell don't know why. He's sick in the head."

"Let's not talk about Hardy now."

"Why not!"

She turned toward him, a glass in one hand, the dish brush in the other. Water dripped from her hands.

"Do I really have to explain it to you? He is the only person Adam looks up to. I've told you before and I thought you'd understand. He is one person who respects Adam, however strange you think that sounds. Adam turns into another person when he's with Hardy. For once, my son has the feeling of being valuable!"

"Yeah, building self-esteem by carrying cow eyes around! Didn't you see how that made him feel, Sabina? Didn't you realize?"

"I don't want to talk about Hardy any longer." She interrupted him and returned to washing the dishes.

He had to get out of there. The roots of his hair felt sticky, and his armpits as well. He had to get out, had to get some air, breathe! He couldn't stand one more second of this slow aging, Sabina and

his father, their life together. He had to go home, and soon, back to
his own life.

"I'm going outside for a while." He made an effort to sound
calm. "I'll just take a walk."

"You go ahead," she said tonelessly.

As he stood in the yard, he found he had a hard-on. He looked
around quickly and then headed toward the barn, turned the corner, and went into his father's secret little house.

What was going on with him? What the hell was wrong with
him?

He carefully closed the door behind him and hooked it. The
royal couple smiled at him as he pulled down his jeans.

Sabina, the voice in his head said, *this felt strange, wrong. Sabina.
Not right. It shouldn't be you. Helllll, not you!*

But it was her face he saw as the flood finally released and that
lovely spasm came washing over.

11

HE HAD A BAD TASTE IN HIS MOUTH. He wanted something sweet, a honey drop, something that would take away the staleness. He had cleaned himself off and thrown the toilet paper down the hole. He scattered a few scoopfuls of quicklime over everything. Nobody would notice anything.

There's something wrong with me, he thought. *I'm going fucking crazy.*

In the darkness, he had felt her lips, moist openings. He had seen her white teeth and the necklace dangling between her breasts. His fingernails had dug into her flesh so that it hurt both of them. She was standing there with her back against the wall, but then she turned and leaned forward, with her hands gripping the bank and raising her wide, light ass toward him. And he, in his thoughts, he thought she was wearing a skirt with her sausage stockings half fallen down, roughly knitted like rag socks, knee-length, and his hands were under her skirt and she did nothing to stop him and he raised it over her hips, and there was her round ass, like an animal's. His breath quickened like small spear-heads in his lungs and he pressed and aimed and made her rise up even more till he found the entrance and then, there in the tight warmth, he stayed as long as he could, but it wasn't long at all, like a red, flowing piece of cloth, and if anyone had come, he wouldn't mind, because right then he was in her and nothing else mattered, nothing could stop him.

Afterwards, he was freezing. His sweater was damp on his back. He shuddered and fastened the buttons. Then he began to walk. The dogs stood like statues as he passed; they didn't howl at him any longer. They'd seen him so many times they were used to him and didn't see him as a threat.

A threat.

I have to go home soon, he thought. *This whole place is not healthy. Something is sick throughout this whole place.*

He walked quickly along the main road. He had put on his large rubber boots, and realized after a while that he was going to get blisters on his heels. His socks slid down underneath his arches, bulging into small rolls. He had to repeatedly stop and pull them up again.

The sun had slipped below the horizon, and the sky changed color, pale rose with gray flecks. On the other side of the field, the ragged contours of the forest's edge were silhouetted. He thought about mushrooms. Marit often talked about going into the forest to pick mushrooms, and once they'd even gone to the forest around Gnesta and Stjärnhov, but other people had already been there and it was picked clean. Marit found four yellow chanterelles. He'd found nothing and his toes were frozen and he rapidly grew impatient. Right then, inspiration had come to him, or something that could be developed into inspiration, and he wanted to be by himself. Marit noticed that and seemed to feel hurt.

And the next book? Nothing yet, just some vague ideas. His pace slowed; he stopped and lifted his face to look at the sky. There was a knot in his brain, all drawn into one clump. He imagined how his brain lay inside his skull, shrunken to the size of a walnut. How could he force inspiration? Sometimes he could force it to appear, at home, in his living room which was also his work space, his back to the window and some great music coming from the speakers, either Handel's *Messiah* or *Christmas Oratio*, how his fingers could suddenly run over the keyboard of his computer. At those times he had to have peace and quiet. He refused to answer the telephone, refused to stand at the window and watch the school grounds next to the apartment building in which he lived, the kids in their down coats, their yells and shrieks. That was hardly the peace he needed.

Once long ago, he wrote poetry, went to poetry slams and read his poetry aloud in those dark basement bars where wax candles were stuck into bottles and the listeners rated the poems with numbers. Sometimes he washed out, but other times he was loved and was made the winner. First prize in poetry! How absurd!

In the future, however, he had to concentrate on more useful things, not all that wishy-washy stuff. He'd have to keep going with his crime-solving main character, Leo Pullman. This creation of his would have to find something to sink his teeth into. Tobias would have to go home soon and get going for real. His publisher, Titus Bruhn, was on his back: *We need to know for our planning. When do you think you'll have it, approximately?* And he'd lied and said it was already moving right along, so Titus Bruhn looked pleased. *Maybe you already have a working title?*

He saw a sign by the side of the road, *Ingeliza's Icelandic Ponies,* and a sign pointing toward the right.

"Ingelize's Icelandic Horses," he said to himself out loud, hissing the s and z sounds: "Ingelizzze."

She was standing in the yard as if she were waiting for him. She was wearing blue overalls and a bright red cap. She swept it off when she caught sight of him.

"Wow! You stopped by already!" She sounded happy and enthusiastic.

"Hi, again."

"Are you done working for the day?"

He nodded.

"Well, come on then, I'll give you the guided tour."

The stable had freshly whitewashed walls. Two teenage girls were mucking out some of the stalls. He saw just one horse, which looked gloomy.

"That's Álfkona," Ingelize said. "She's got something wrong with one of her hooves, and we're trying a warm, wet poultice. All the other horses are outside."

Tobias went over to the stall and the mare carefully came closer and stuck her head out. He stroked her long nose and breathed in the smell of horse. It had been a long time since he'd last been out riding. A few times he'd gone to Iceland to visit his mother, who had taken him on a number of short rides, and a few longer ones as well.

"Do you want to go out for a short ride?" Ingelize asked.

"Isn't it a little late?"

"Nah!"

He shrugged his shoulders, feeling uncertain.

She seemed to notice.

"You can borrow a helmet and some riding boots. Take Bleikja if you want. She's gentle, good if you haven't ridden for a while."

They got halters with lead ropes and went out to the meadow. A clump of horses were grazing far away on the other side. After a few minutes of cajoling, they were able to catch two of them. Bleikja was a dun mare with dark mane and tail. He led her back to the stable, where Ingelize brought out saddles and bridles. She was getting a dapple-gray ready for herself.

In the tack room, there were rows of riding boots and a shelf with helmets. He tried them out until he found the right size.

"We've got some good riding paths out here," Ingelize said, as she pulled the girth one hole further. "But now LRF is beginning to grumble. They want to limit the rules for everyman's right to the land."

"Why would they?"

"They're worried about wear and tear."

"Don't you have land of your own?"

"Not enough."

"What does Carl Sigvard say?"

"Haven't heard any complaints from him. But there are a number of real sourpusses around here. Like Fredriksson, for example. Remember him?"

"I have some vague memory."

"He's angry as hell. He's put up both bars and barbed-wire. Soon he'll lay landmines throughout the entire forest."

Ingelize had gone inside to change into riding pants and a short, mocha-colored jacket. She had a nice figure, he noticed. She sat smooth and easy up in the saddle and reined her whitish horse in a few tight circles around the yard. Tobias followed on Bleikja.

"Feel good to be back in the saddle?" She turned to smile at him.

"Yep!"

At first, they rode at a walk.

"You were a real riding demon when you were a kid," she praised him.

"Well, I don't know about that."

"Yes, you were, you were really good in the saddle. Your mom used to say you were born to be on horseback. Oh, I used to love being over at your place. Your mom was so nice. I was able to hang around in the stable as much as I wanted."

"Uh-huh."

"It was a real paradise. But you're always cast out of paradise sooner or later."

"That sounds dire."

"But there's some truth to it, don't you think?"

"Maybe so."

A few minutes later, he asked her if she was married.

"Yes, I am. My husband, Jens, is a legislator in Parliament, for the Center Party. Talk about a party that's dying out. But he keeps up the good fight as best he can."

"No kids?"

"Not in the cards."

"Well, you have your horses." Tobias mentally kicked himself at how clumsy that sounded.

She was quiet for a while. They rode along the side of the main road, and every once in a while, a car passed them. These horses weren't afraid. Not like a half-breed. A half-breed would have shied nervously every time a car came past, and jumped at every fluttering piece of paper.

Ingelize turned toward him.

"Tobi, where did you two go, when you just took off like that? When you and your mom moved, I mean, without saying anything to anyone."

"Södertälje," he said.

"We didn't know anything. One day, everything was just like normal, and then . . . bang! It really was a shock for me."

He didn't know what he was supposed to say. Maybe she noticed she'd blundered into painful territory because she clucked her horse into a trot and Bleikja followed automatically. They entered the forest. There was the strong scent of decay here, and in spite of the darkness, he could see the color change in the leaves. The dapple-gray broke into a gallop, his own horse following like a shadow.

The path went steeply upwards and he remembered the mountain he'd played on so many times when he was younger. He hadn't been there since those days. He never showed Görel or Klara this place. He hadn't wanted to bring them here. It was dangerous. There was a spot where the cliff went straight down to Mörkviken's waters. A shiver of fear went through him. What if they couldn't stop the horses? Of course, the horses instinctively avoided dangers, but they also could become hysterical and, out of fear, jump straight into death.

The mountain was called Precipice. In the distant past, the old folks had dragged themselves here once they were no longer able to work so they would never be a burden to their families. They'd jump right off the edge. Eighty meters below, Mörkviken's black deep waters swirled. As they fell, they would be battered by rocks, and finally, then, they drowned. So it was said. Probably just an old wives' tale like the one about the naked women on Shame Island. Still, there was something frightening about that cliff and that water. Tobias remembered one early spring when a man riding a kick-sled had gone through the ice. He'd been found much later by a diver, taken out of the water and placed on the gravel. The man was named Berggren, and he was the brother-in-law of the shopkeeper. He'd been a happy, loud man who often played the accordion at the local outdoor dance floor. Tobias had been in the first grade when it happened. He still remembered the nightmares he'd had afterwards, the face of the drowned man, fish-eaten, gnawed off. The kids would talk about it during recess, competed with the most gruesome details.

At the top of the mountain, they got off and let the horses blow. There was still some twilight left. Far away, they could see the lights go on, the clear red lights of the radio towers.

"It's great to be living out here!" Ingelize made a sweeping gesture over the shining still water. From up here, they could see Shame Island and all the other small islands dotted around.

"Easy for you to say," he answered.

"Don't you ever miss all this, Tobias?"

"Maybe sometimes, but I live a different life nowadays."

"Are you still living in Södertälje?"

"Yes, I have a condo, two bedrooms, kitchen, peaceful, a good neighborhood. And it's centrally located, so it only takes me five minutes to get to the train station."

"Do you live by yourself?"

"Well . . ."

"Well what?"

"I spend a lot of time with someone."

"But you're not living together?"

"Is this a game of twenty questions?"

She laughed with embarrassment.

"No, no, sorry about that."

He saw that she'd turned red and felt he'd been overly brusque.

"We don't live together," he said, trying to smooth things over. "She'd want to, but I'm not ready for that."

He instantly regretted saying so. She scraped the toe of her riding boot in the moss. Her horse pushed her from behind.

"Don't stand so close to the edge! People have fallen off before."

"Yes, I know. But still, isn't it wonderful up here? I usually take my groups up here. Do you know about my riding tour operation? People come here from Linköking and Västervik as well. We usually bring coffee and sandwiches to picnic up here."

"What do they pay for it?"

"Depends on how long we're out riding. For you, it's free, though. Just so you know. You are free to come and ride here whenever you want."

"I see. Well, I ought to say thank you, then."

"For old time's sake. How do you like Bleikja, by the way?"

"She's great." He turned around, stroking the mare's muzzle. She nosed around his pockets to see if he had any sugar. He wished he had some to give her.

"You can come back and try out other horses, too, if you want."

"I'm going back home in just a few days."

"Already? That's too bad."

"You think?"

"Yeah, it's been great to have someone to talk to. Someone I share a bit of my childhood with."

She asked him into the house. He'd never been inside before. As a child, he stood just outside the threshold when he sold May poppies. He remembered thinking her mother was old. It still surprised him that he had not recognized Ingelize, but her appearance had really changed. There actually was no resemblance to the tawny girl who once had helped them with the horses.

She took out a bottle of wine and a plate of small, hard cookies.

"So," she said, "feeling sore after riding?"

"Not really."

"Let's see what you say tomorrow. I ride every day, of course. But if I ever take a break, you can bet your life that I'll be sore the next time I ride."

He looked around the room. One wall was covered by a bookshelf. He noticed some popular titles. Maybe she was in a book club. Otherwise, she mostly had factual books, binders and public reports. In the window, there were some lacinated plants, the kind where if you touched their leaves, they'd give off a strong aroma. Görel had had such plants. She called them *old lady farts*.

Ingelize raised her glass.

"*Skål,*" she said. "Welcome to the middle of nowhere."

"Thanks."

"You still know how to ride at any rate. You were racing like a speed demon there at the end."

He laughed out loud. "Well, it's like riding a bike, I guess. Once you've learned, you never really forget."

She drank quickly. Her glass was almost empty by the time he'd swallowed more than a mouthful of the wine.

"I was thirsty," she said as she noticed his look. She got up and walked barefoot over to a transistor radio, pressed the on-button and music started. Took some dance steps on her way back.

"By the way, have you ever heard that boy, Adam, sing?" she asked, as she ran her fingers through her hair. "He's fantastic. You wouldn't think a kid like him could pull it off."

"Yes, I've heard him. He's a good imitation."

"He sounds just like Elvis. You should have been here on Midsummer's Eve. He sang some Elvis songs at the outdoor dance floor. God, he was fantastic! It's just too bad that he's so . . . ." She pointed at her head.

"Speaking of Adam, do you know that guy Hardy?" he asked.

"A bit. In a tiny village like this, everyone knows everyone. You can't keep a secret around here. You know that yourself."

"So what kind of a guy is he?"

"Well, things haven't gone so well for him. But now he's trying to get back on his feet again. No, I really don't know him all that well. Sometimes he comes over and helps me with a few things here and there. Right now he's helping me build a paddock. Maybe you noticed it outside. You certainly remember his mother. She's really huge and hunch-backed. She walks like this."

Ingelize bent over, walking with mincing steps.

"She used to go around shoeing horses; you must remember that. But nowadays they say she's getting dementia. I think that she's drunk so much alcohol that there's nothing left of her brain."

"He was in jail, wasn't he?"

"Hardy?"

"Yeah."

"What about it? We all make mistakes sometimes."

Tobias drank another large sip of wine, which was cool and good.

"Hardy doesn't seem to like me," he said carefully.

"I think he's just trying to keep up his tough guy act. He probably just has low self-esteem. You are well-known, famous even. And he is what he is. You understand that. In some way . . . you're a threat to him."

By now Ingelize had come to his chair, sitting on the armrest.

"How does it feel to be famous?"

"Cut it out. I'm not famous."

"But you were on TV."

"Tons of idiots have been on TV."

"Still. By the way, I've been wondering about something. Where do you get all of your ideas? Do you just think them up yourself?"

"I use my imagination."

"But the people in your books, they seem so alive."

"Thank you. Nice to get a good grade in writing."

"You really invent them from your imagination, too?"

"Of course, I do."

"Tobias, couldn't you write your books here?"

"Here?"

"I don't mean right here in this room. Here in the village."

"Why do you ask?"

"It's just something I thought of. I could use a partner, some-one who knows horses. There's an empty house out here, belongs to Maria Vesterberg and her husband. You could move in there. At least you could try it out and see if it would work. You could work out here part time and write part time."

12

SHE SHOULDN'T HAVE BEEN SO CLUMSY, so direct. He looked as if he'd turned to stone in the armchair. Certainly he was the kind of person that you had to be careful with. The atmosphere changed immediately. It was almost as if she'd asked if he would move into her bedroom.

"Well, gotta get going now," he said, jumping up like a steel spring. His hair hung in his face, matted down after wearing the helmet.

"Aren't you going to finish your glass first?"

He stuck out his hand to shake goodbye, and she took it and held it tight. She had no idea what to say.

"It was nice to go riding," he said, while turning his entire body away so that she could not meet his eyes. "Bleikja is a nice horse."

"If you have time, we can do it again before you leave," she said and realized that the wine had started to take effect: her tongue was not keeping up with her words.

She followed him into the entryway. Watched him sit on the chair to put on his boots. He was barefoot and his heels had red marks where skin had rubbed off.

"I've got to get you something to put on that," she said. "See, all your skin is gone."

She did manage to keep him sitting there as she ran up the stairs and rummaged through the entire bathroom, where she finally found a package of bandages and a scissors.

She fell on her knees in front of him like the sinner at Jesus' feet. "Does it hurt?"

"Not really. It's just I'm not used to these rubber boots, that's all."

"It wasn't the riding boots?"

"Oh no, not at all. I just was walking too much in these, that's all." He pointed at his rubber boots which looked brand new.

He had long, veined feet. She measured the bandage and pressed it down. She couldn't help massaging his feet a little.

She looked up at him.

"How thin your skin is. Strange, isn't it? Feet are supposed to be so strong, so that they can carry us through life."

He kept sitting and she reached for his rolled-up socks, straightened them, and pulled them over his toes.

13

RIGHT AFTER TOBIAS LEFT, Jens called. She heard voices and laughter in the background.

"Everything all right on your end?" he asked.

"Right as rain!" she replied cheerfully.

"Do you have to use clichés?" His stuffy tone made her want to hang up on him immediately.

"Everything's fine," she said curtly.

"Have you been drinking? Or is something wrong with you?"

"Someone stopped by. Tobias Elmkvist, an old friend from school. Sigge's son, by the way."

"Oh him. The author."

"Exactly."

"So you two sat around drinking wine."

"I asked him to have a glass. Before then, we were out riding. He's going to be moving here soon. I was talking to him about taking him on as a partner. You know I need one."

"Yeah, yeah."

"Are you coming home on Friday?"

"No. That was one of the reasons I'm calling. I still have to go through a great deal of paperwork. Why don't you come up instead?"

She knew he knew that she was going to say no, that she had the horses to take care of. So he could appear to be generous.

"No, I'm going to stay home."

"Well, good night, then," he said, somewhat warmer and friendlier now. "I'll call again in a few days. Kiss, kiss. And, sweetheart, put away the rest of the bottle, please."

She stood at the window looking over the garden. She fingered the downy leaves of her scented geraniums. People also called them Doctor Westerlund's Health Flowers. They had a wonderful scent. Keeping them in the house was supposed to insure health. People said they kept away colds. It was probably true; she was almost never sick.

Night came earlier every evening now that it was autumn. This past summer had been unusually rainy since the beginning of July and had stopped only a few days ago when the weather turned cold. Everything became more difficult once winter arrived. All the practical chores. She had to put frost nails on the horses' shoes so that they wouldn't slip. Harnesses and reins became stiff and more difficult to use.

From where she was standing, she could make out the stables and the beginnings of the paddock she was having Hardy build. He was taking his time. She could understand his aversion to Tobias. Hardy Lindström was an intense, emotional young man with many plans. They weren't always the best, and he seldom was able to achieve them. Certainly he was well aware of his faults. And then some fancy guy from the big city comes home playing the Big Shot. Of course that would have repercussions.

Hardy had been working on the paddock project for some time. First he'd driven a rotary cultivator over the area. The past few days he'd been busy breaking up clumps and removing stones. He'd only been over a few hours at a time; he said he had a lot going on. Sometimes she went out to help. She'd fill the wheelbarrow and dump the contents behind the outhouse. It would take a while before the whole thing was finished, but it wouldn't be long before winter arrived in full force.

She was fine without a paddock; that was not her real worry. People could still ride inside the stable, which had a large arena in the middle with the stalls on both sides. She usually gave riding lessons inside. But in the hot summer, the dirt would dry into annoying dust when the horses' hooves ripped up the surface.

The other day she'd asked Hardy to stay for dinner after his work as she had enough head cheese and red beets for two. He'd agreed. He'd sat in the kitchen with his long legs covering most of the kitchen rug space, watching her as she dished up dinner. She'd carefully started a conversation, and he was in a better mood that day so he'd actually talked to her instead of joking everything away.

"You're going to be staying in the village for a while now, right?" she asked. Hardy kept mum, stared in front of him.

"How many potatoes do you want?" she added quickly. "Four, right?"

He nodded. Then he said, "I don't know how long I'll stay. Things were different when the sawmill was here."

"More jobs, you mean."

"Yeah."

"That's for sure."

"I can't live off my mom forever. She's about ready to drop dead soon enough."

"Is that what you think?"

"Whatever."

"What kind of job would you be looking for?"

Hardy twirled a strand of his beard around his forefinger and laughed half-heartedly.

"Maybe Stockholm has all the good jobs. There is where I'd get a real break."

"I doubt it," she said insistently. "Look at me. I've been around the block a few times, believe me. But I came home again. Here is where you find real life. Animals, nature, everything!"

Hardy grimaced. "That's all relative."

"Get yourself a wife, Hardy. Have a few kids. Start a family."

"Nah, that's not important to me right now. First I have to, like, find out who I am."

"What do you mean by that?"

"I dunno. Nah, it's not a big deal."

Ingelize had the urge to ask him about his time in jail, what he'd experienced behind bars, what they'd done to him. This would be the right moment; he was beginning to open up. But just then one of the stable girls had phoned and by the time Ingelize could get off the line, Hardy had eaten his dinner and gone outside to smoke.

Eight o'clock. Ingelize had missed the news. Not a big deal, the news would be repeated tomorrow. She poured another glass of wine and moved the curtain further aside. Thought she saw someone out there. A change in the light under the lamp. Had Tobias returned? She leaned forward and tried to make out what she was seeing. Yes, indeed, there was someone out there, but if it was Tobias, why wasn't he coming to the door?

Maybe it wasn't him?

A cold feeling swept over her shoulders. These days she became afraid more easily, afraid of the dark and what could be out there. For unusual noises in the house, as if she weren't alone. She wished she had a dog, and at that exact moment, she decided to buy one.

She'd been tipsy from the wine, but all at once everything became sharp and clear. Was it really Tobias? She put down her glass, put on her coat and went outside.

The stable door was half-open. She should have brought something hard with her, like a hammer. She regretted that her hands were empty, useless, stuck down into her jacket pockets where there was nothing but some old tissues and a box of cough drops. She thought about Álfkona inside, and that gave her courage. She grabbed the door handle and pushed the door open all the way. It creaked and moaned. She'd thought about oiling the hinges every single day, but no. She heard the pony in the darkness, how it was chewing and breathing evenly. If the person had been a stranger, it would have been silent, listening. She quickly snapped on the electric lights. Faint, dusty light fell over the stalls. Álfkona gave a low neigh, and Ingelize saw someone next to her, someone large and crooked, the light illuminated the wrinkled face. Ann-Marie, Hardy's mother.

They observed each other for a moment. Ingelize swallowed, not knowing what to say. Finally, the old woman limped over and held out her hand. Ingelize took it, surprised at the strength in Ann-Marie's handshake.

"So you're the one visiting at this hour," Ingelize said. "I wondered who was out here."

The smell of dirt and stale alcohol reached her nose. The old woman's chin waggled as if she were wearing dentures that didn't fit.

"I came because of the horse," she said, although her words weren't clear.

"Álfkona?"

"I heard she had a problem."

"Who told you that?"

The old woman sniffed and used her sleeve to wipe her nose. A thin thread of snot remained, glittering on the cloth.

"I brought something," she said, and unwrapped a few pieces of linen which had been soaked in some kind of liquid.

"What's that?" Ingelize bent for a closer look.

The old woman turned her face up and grinned. "Devil's Bite, heh, heh."

"What's Devil's Bite?"

"That's what they call this plant, meadow rue. You chop the roots and boil them and then pickle them in alcohol for eight days."

"What? What do you plan to do with it?"

Ingelize opened the stall door to the horse, which was calm.

"It's a poultice." Ann-Marie slid her hand down the horse's leg until she found the swollen area. Quickly she wrapped the poultice and tied it with a piece of string.

"Nice horse," Ann-Marie said. "She'll be healthy and strong again soon."

"Can that harm her in any way?"

Ann-Marie gave Ingelize a wry look. "Not now."

Once she was by herself again, Ingelize thought that it was a pity that Ann-Marie was not younger. Ann-Marie would have been the perfect partner, though she drank, of course, drank like a sailor. She wasn't dependable, and her son was just the same.

Well, she would just have to hope that Tobias would fall for her offer. And if he did? Once he thought the matter over, he just might. He was from the village, after all, his roots were here.

14

MORNING. TOBIAS STRETCHED WHILE STILL UNDERNEATH THE BLANKETS. He gingerly straightened each limb. Yes indeed, his muscles were sore, especially in his arms and his groin area. He was not used to physical activity.

He held his breath. The back of his head was sunk deep into his pillow as if inside a bowl, the cloth covered his ears on both sides. It felt clean and cozy, like when he was a child, when his mother tucked him into bed when his fevers throbbed through his brain.

Right here in this house.

Thirty years ago.

Last night, he'd had difficulty falling asleep. He'd been on his back, hardly breathing. Against his will, he heard sounds from the room above his. Sabina's steps and murmurings, her gentle, comforting sounds. He heard the bed springs groan through the floor when she got into bed.

How did they manage their love life? Not now perhaps, but otherwise? Could Adam leave them in peace? How could they be sure that Adam would not suddenly be standing in the doorway? Or did they lock the door? But how would Adam deal with that? Tobias had witnessed at least two outbursts of rage that filled the overgrown boy whenever he felt wronged. His arms slammed like sledgehammers, he howled like an enraged bull. Sabina was the only person who could calm him down. She was the one who had brought him into the world.

People were insecure around Adam. They never knew how he would behave. Everybody except Hardy. That's why Sabina put up with Hardy and his loutishness. She could not afford to make an enemy of Hardy. Sabina was totally in his power.

Something was evil within Hardy Lindström. A true evil being, thought Tobias, the Devil's handyman.

Impossible to sleep. The sensations of riding were still within him, rocking him and moving him in rhythm as if he were a centaur. His father and Sabina were both talking the whole time up there, not loudly, but just a low cooing, as if she were making things very . . . nice . . . for him.

He sat up straight in bed, cursing himself as he did so, but he could not stop.

Stay in the village and write.

As Ingelize had suggested.

That way he would be able to help his father and Sabina now and then.

How long was his father going to be off his feet? Would he ever recover? Tobias closed his eyes and the cattle appeared in his mind, their lowing, the steam from their crammed-together bodies. The glimpse of scorn in Hardy's eyes, and the eye that stared gruesomely from the middle of Adam's hand.

In the end, he had to get up. It was only fifteen after eleven. No energy to write, no desire. But whiskey would hit the spot. A shot from the plastic bottle he'd bought in a tax-free shop, which he'd stuffed into his suitcase right before he came down. The whiskey burned his gums, a pungent, lukewarm taste.

Now he heard Sabina puttering around upstairs, her dry, wide feet. Was she wearing a nightgown or did she go to bed naked, her legs together, hiding the deep darkness?

His fingers started to sweat. He paced back and forth and then went into the hallway and searched among the coats, saw Sabina's good coat which she hardly ever used, let himself be engulfed in it, noticed it was lined with silk. He had to smoke, and he went outside, wrapped in his own coat, to smoke on the porch. A cold, clear night.

The stars had come out right above his head; it had been a long time since he'd seen the stars. You couldn't see them the same way in the city. He drew deep drags and listened for sounds from the edge of the forest, but heard no noise, no sound of life. If there had been an animal out there, the dogs would have reacted.

He closed his eyes and felt like screaming, like howling loudly, primitively, into the night. His heart was beating extra beats; this happened once in a while. The doctors said it wasn't life-threatening, but it always scared him. Maybe the whole thing would stop if he quit smoking. Klara usually scolded him about his smoking. He remembered that he was supposed to return his daughter's phone call. It was too late now. She was sleeping; it was a school day tomorrow. Görel was probably sleeping, too. The last time he'd talked with Görel, she was sinking back into depression. Usually in the fall she'd get melancholy and passive and was hardly even was able to call her doctor.

His legs began to freeze, so he put out his cigarette and went back inside. He saw a figure in the hall, as light and fluttery as a ghost. He swallowed and it stuck in his throat.

Sabina was standing there.

"Tobias?" she asked quietly.

"Yes, it's me."

"Everything all right?"

"You just scared me half to death."

"Sorry about that. Can't you sleep?"

She was wearing her yellow robe and her hair hung freely down her back.

"Did I bother you?"

"No, but I heard you go out."

"I just had to have a cigarette."

He felt her hand on his arm.

"Should I make you something warm to drink?"

"Oh no, no."

"We need our sleep, Tobias. Tomorrow we have a great deal of work to do."

"I know. Good night, Sabina."

He turned his back to her and went to his room.

Did he actually fall asleep? He must have been sleeping; he had fragments, pictures, of dreams. Razors digging through clumps of hair. Ridges on tight skin. Sabina, her face to the ceiling, her brown neck with white lines.

What time was it? He tried to find the light switch on the ridiculous little lamp, which was practically useless with its dancing cupids and pearl fringe. He found his watch. Six-thirty in the morning. He threw his legs over the edge of the bed, groaned; his whole body ached like hell. Once he stood, he saw the darkness had changed; it was gentler, no longer so deep. When he opened the window, he heard that the wind had started to blow again.

This morning they were going to finish the cattle. Just a few more days and he would be back on the train home. Sabina promised to drive him as far as Linköping.

He walked around the yard, smoking. The wind tousled his hair, but the weather was milder, no frost. He thought about the raft. It was this time of the morning that they had set out for Shame Island to bring in the cattle.

His cell phone rang. His daughter Klara.

"Hi. It's me."

"Hi, my girl. I was just going to call you. Are you on your way to school?"

"No, we have a study day today."

"And you're not sleeping in?"

"Nah."

"How's your mom?"

"As usual."

"What's usual right now?"

"You know. Depressed. Doesn't want to leave the house."

He sighed.

"I went to the store and then I made spaghetti."

"You're a good girl, Klara."

"How's Grandpa? He doesn't seem all that happy, either."

"Oh, that's right. You talked to him yesterday, and I was supposed to call you back. There was just so much going on."

"Don't worry about it."

"We have to be the strong ones now, Klara. I'll be home as soon as I can."

"Don't worry," she said again and he was struck with the longing to see her.

"Promise me that you'll call if there's anything going on!"

"Okay."

Inside the house he knew Sabina had made coffee and was busy running from room to room. Adam was still in bed, too, it appeared he had caught some kind of cold. If only he didn't get sick himself! He couldn't afford to be sick; he had to get home in a few days and get going on his book. Things would be easier for Klara when he was nearby, although he was never able to do much about Görel once she entered her down periods.

No one could.

He opened the barn door and stepped inside. The piglets ran in all directions, squealing with confusion. He stood there for a while watching them, how they eventually calmed down, how they slowly walked over and took a look at him. Sabina had already given them their food. How long ago had she actually gotten up?

She came up behind him; he saw her shadow, turned and smiled at her.

She looked tired, well, not really tired, she put her hands on his shoulders.

"Ready, Tobi? Ready to wrestle with our loveable critters again?"

Today it was more difficult to lure them into the shaving cage. The cattle had had the entire night to think, to suspect that something was going on. Could animals have intuition regarding their fate? Tobias remembered something he'd read about pigs that began to squeal as if they were about to die as they neared the slaughterhouse. They were able to anticipate their deaths; it was in all the strange things around them, in the sounds and the smells.

Sabina had once worked in a slaughterhouse. He wanted to ask her what it was like, but she was not eager to talk about her past.

He stood holding a tuft of hay.

"Come, come, little creature, come on."

The animals were not fooled. During the first hour, they only managed to get one inside, and right in the middle of the procedure, the razor stopped working.

Sabina climbed out of the cage, leaned against it, stretched her arms behind her neck. She was tired. He stood beside her; he'd smoked a cigarette and watched the jugular vein on her throat, how it pulsed underneath her skin.

She turned the razor over and over again, holding it up close to her eyes, inspecting it.

"This one is screwed up. It's fallen apart."

"So what do we do now?"

"We'll have to fix it. Are you good at fixing things, Tobias? There's a bunch of tools in the cupboard."

She started walking to the tack room, and he followed her.

The tack room was small with hardly any furniture. A bench was fastened to the wall with a rag rug spread over it. A rough, dusty desk. The door could be closed and locked. Tobias remembered that his mother had come here at times. She'd slept on a cot in this room whenever she felt ill or whenever things heated up inside the house.

There was a corner cupboard painted blue which his father had made. Sabina was reaching up to it now, opening the door.

"I thought that . . . yes, here it is. A screwdriver. Do you think it's too clumsy?"

He took the small, rusty screwdriver and compared it to the screw's notches.

"I can try," he said hesitantly.

She was sitting on the bench, feet propped on the desk. Her boots were tiny and dirty.

He walked right up to her, close so that she could not change her position.

"Sabina," he heard his own voice say, a light, different voice, and then he said her name again.

He saw a brief flicker of flight in her eyes, which vanished immediately. A moment later, the shine of water on her cheek.

His mouth, his tongue, on her cheek, licking away the salt, his hands to her throat, then past her necklace, onto her breasts, under her bra, how his fingers searched for the clasp, how they found it, opened it, her massive breasts falling into his palms.

"Tobias, what are you doing, what are we doing?"

Her breath was as sweet as a pastille, her tongue like a confused small animal. He pressed his own tongue to it, entwined it with his own, her smooth, white teeth, and she was crying, sniffing. No, she was laughing, yes, laughing, and she did not resist but reached for his neck, pulled him down to her breasts, her stomach. He pulled at her clothes until her overalls fell away, inside out. She came out of her blue shell and lay there naked on the bench.

Afterward, once they had put their clothes back on and he was kneeling on the stone floor with his head in her lap, Sabina was no longer crying but she did not appear all that happy, either. His head, his eyes were pressed into her hands.

"What have we done?" she said aloud, but there was no blame in her voice, only sorrowful wonderment.

"I'm not going to ask you for forgiveness," he whispered, "because I don't want it. You have no idea how much I have been longing for you, ever since the first time I saw you."

Her hands were calloused; he wet them with his lips, slightly bit them. Small calluses on her fingertips. Her tough, strong body.

"We have to forget this immediately," she said, but she did not move her hands, she did not move away from him. "We have to believe this has never happened."

He straightened his back, kissed her fingers, kissed her arms all the way up, saw her features soften.

"I've also thought of you," she said hoarsely. "God help me, I've also thought of you."

He placed his hands underneath her armpits; he stood and lifted her with him. She was shorter than he was; he'd never noticed before. She was only up to his shoulders. Her lips were on his chest, past the buttons on his skin.

"Tobias, he can't find out about this ever. He's the sweetest man in the whole world."

A movement, a sound at the door. A scraping sound, someone clearing his throat.

"Yes, indeed," came the voice, "it would be a pity to make Sigge Elmkvist unhappy, the sweetest man in the whole world. He certainly is worth better than this."

They leapt apart but it was too late. Tobias knew the moment he saw who was leaning on the doorjamb. Chin out, his rough, blonde beard. His eyes fixed on them through half-shut lids.

Sabina turned her back to them, pulled on her necklace, shoulders shaking. This enraged Tobias.

"What do you mean, sneaking around and spying like that?"

Hardy raised his upper lip, his face turning narrow and sharp.

"Me? Spy? I just came to get my money."

Sabina whirled around, too frazzled to completely understand.

"Oh, that's right, I was going to go to the bank."

"Right."

"It's true. But we've had too much to do with the animals."

"And other things, too, as I understand."

"Hardy!"

"I saw everything. You better get this, Sabina, I saw everything that the two of you did."

Sabina shrank and began to plead.

"Please, please don't say anything. You . . . you'll get everything you want. This just happened; we didn't intend it to happen."

"Didn't intend it to happen? That's not what it looked like to me."

"I'm going to go to the bank now. You can come with me if you want."

"No, I'll wait here."

"Hope that this didn't cause you any problems. If you really needed your money yesterday, that is."

Hardy laughed but did not answer.

"I'll be back soon. The bank's open now. I'll be right back."

She was folding her scarf over and over into smaller and smaller squares and then put it in her pocket. She had turned very white as if she had never gotten a tan.

They watched her start her old Opel and drive out onto the road. The car jumped a few times, as if it did not have enough gas. Tobias pulled out his cigarette pack.

"Want one?"

Hardy nodded and pulled one out.

Tobias leaned against the wall, his muscles softened, a fogginess in his brain.

"What you saw . . . ," he began.

"In there, you mean?"

"That."

"When you fucked her."

"Haven't you ever been caught up in something like this? When two people just . . . ."

Hardy let the smoke escape his nostrils.

"Doesn't bother me, but old man Elmkvist is not going to be all that happy."

"You're not . . . going to go . . . go tell him?" His stammering irritated him.

Hardy smiled, his pointed canines showed.

"In town you could manage an affair like this very nicely, but not here. There are no secrets in the country. No secrets at all!"

"Is it money you want?"

"Money?"

"You're going to blackmail us, aren't you? So I might as well tell you that I'm as poor as a church mouse."

Tobias threw down the stub and went back into the barn. It started to rain. His hands were shaking; his whole body was shaking. Sweat poured from his armpits. He walked into the tack room, picked up the razor and the screwdriver, tried to loosen the screw but failed. He trembled and shook. From the corner of his eye, he saw Hardy enter the room.

"What do you have against me?" Tobias said bitterly. "You've been on my back ever since I came here. It seems you hate me. Why?"

"I don't hate you, not one bit."

"Then what the hell is the matter with you?"

"Just that you're an asshole. A fucking snob who comes home and pretends to be something he's not. You believe you're even worth hating? Fuck you, asshole."

Tobias turned to face Hardy. Tobias' head was shaking; it kept shaking. He couldn't stop it from shaking.

"You were supposed to be so fucking special. And you come home and fuck the ass off your own stepmother. You're worse than a pig, you asshole, so all I have to say to you is *fuck you*."

The screwdriver was in his hand. Its short, yellow shaft. The screwdriver was in his stabbing hand. It sunk in, as if it hit butter, gurgling, thrashing, silence. Warm, red blood in his eyes, on his hands, on his clothes, as if from a geyser. Blood shooting straight up, hissing, the man weakly defending himself, no longer strength in his flailing arms. He'd fallen against the desk. The sharp corner hit his temple, and then the screwdriver again, how it sank into the soft throat, how the blood gurgled and bubbled as it slid in.

Then he found himself acting mechanically. He took off his overalls and wrapped them so that the blood was inside, the blood and the deep dark stains. Walked about in his underwear, barefoot on the straw. A cat ran from him, its tail in the air. The water in the hose was ice cold, but he didn't feel it. He rinsed his body, washing the present away. The door to the tack room was closed; his overalls rolled up over the blood was inside. There was some blood on his underwear, but now brown water washed away from him, away from his body, even his hair. There was a piece of broken-off old soap in the window and he used it to rub at his chest and his arms; he used it on his hands, a bit more gently. He rubbed and rubbed to get it right into every pore of his body, all the way in. He leaned forward and turned his head upside down, drawing the pointed end of the soap through his hair, hard and then gently, rubbing until he worked up a lather, and the water ran. It burned red and wet into dirty brown.

He was sitting in the barn in his wet underwear when Sabina returned. He was going to catch a cold after all; that thought went through his head. *Go, get dressed, you're going to get sick if you don't.* But he sat there, looking at his long, scrawny legs, goose bumps on his skin.

He heard the car turn into the driveway and the barking of the dogs, the slam of a car door, the wind blowing through the barn roof.

Her staring, empty gaze, the envelope in her hand, already held out as if to be rid of it, to get it over with. And then to forget.

Poor little Sabina! As if you would ever be able to forget what happened.

He was going to blackmail you forever, blackmail the life out of you.

Squeeze the last bit of juice out of your body.

Did she open the tack room door?

He heard no noise, no scream.

He found himself still sitting there, but new, clean overalls in his arms; they'd even been ironed. The gentle smell of laundry detergent.

Like a robot, he stood up and put them on.

'Til the End of Time

1

IF MARIT ONLY HAD A KEY TO HIS APARTMENT ON BELLEVUEGATAN, she would have gone there and cleaned the place up a bit. Bought some yogurt, some fruit. Aired out the old cigarette smoke. Maybe even vacuumed the floor. Tobias wasn't much for cleaning.

But the fact of the matter was that she had no key.

When she went to work, she often chose to go past his yellow, four-story apartment building. She sneaked a peek up at his window, but he often kept the curtains fully closed. Both rooms. Even when he was away, like now.

She missed him more than she thought was possible, and it was with happiness that she received his phone call telling her he was coming home sooner than he'd planned. He sounded tired. She promised to pick him up at Södertälje South Train Station.

The past few days had had variable weather. One day cold and frosty, the next mild, so that you never knew what to wear. This morning was especially cold. She walked swiftly. The chill made her eyes tear up; her mascara would start running. She usually did not wear so much make-up, just a bit of black on her eyelashes and some kohl. But it was going to be all messed up when she got to work, and that annoyed her.

She had gotten up late. She'd had trouble sleeping the night before. She'd lain awake, thinking about Tobias, evaluating their relationship. He'd called the minute she came home from work.

"I'm arriving tomorrow around lunch time. Can you come pick me up?"

"Already? I'm so happy. Are you really coming back so soon?"

Actually, it was stupid to reveal how much he meant to her. Any show of strong emotions made him draw back and get ready to defend himself. Strange, because when you read his books, you got an entirely different picture of the man. Especially the book of poems he'd published a few years back.

"Well? Can you pick me up or not?" His voice cut off her thoughts. It echoed in the receiver in an unusual, brutal way.

"Of course. I'll be there."

When she hung up, she began to cry.

Later that evening, after she'd eaten dry sushi that she'd picked up at the grocery store and watched the eight o'clock news, she pulled out his poetry collection. She spoke the title out loud, tried to return to a sense of happiness. He'd signed the title page, but there was nothing in it to suggest that he would have intended any of the poems to be for her. *Fall, 1999, to Marit, warm thoughts from the author.* Totally neutral.

Warm thoughts. Would he ever have any deeper feelings for her? She leafed through the book. It had gotten good reviews, she remembered, although it didn't sell well. At least the critics had liked it.

Who had been in his thoughts when he'd written these fiery poems? Not Görel. They were already separated by then, and she had the feeling that his years with her had been incredibly stressful. Who else would it be? Or was it possible to write love poetry without even being in love? She hadn't ever dared to ask him that.

While she poured herself a glass of juice, she thought about the time she'd met Tobias. It was connected to an interview she read in a magazine which had given him a prize for one of his short stories, and of course the magazine had written a long article about him.

Marit and her colleagues at the library decided to contact him. After all, he was a local author and that should be applauded.

The Blue Room Café was filled with people the Wednesday night that he'd come to give his talk at the library. As usual, mostly women. Tobias had not yet started writing his mystery novels. That evening he spoke about his earlier books and then read from the poetry collection. When he read out loud, his voice changed. It became soft and intense. Marit sat close to the door so that she could see how the other women reacted. To her great surprise, she noticed that she started feeling jealous.

A few days later, he stopped by the library with the bill for his speaking fee. It was just before lunch.

"Why don't we go out to eat together?" The words came out of her mouth before she could stop them.

He laughed.

"Now?"

"Sure. I thought . . . ."

"Can't, sorry. I've got to go to Stockholm today. How about this evening? If you're not busy, that is."

Expectation leapt into her.

"I can reserve a table if you'd like," she said hastily. "Do you like Greek food? Have you ever been to the restaurant on Ängsgatan?"

It had always been easy to talk to Tobias, at least at first. Before the evening was over, she'd practically spilled her life story to him —her marriage to Claes, her childlessness, which was not her fault but due to her ex's low sperm count.

Tobias observed her the entire time she was talking.

"Do you grieve not having children?" he asked in a serious tone.

She pushed her hair behind her ears. She felt warm; she felt her face flush.

"Well, I was fixated on it for a long while. I had a hard time whenever I saw pregnant women or baby strollers. I was fairly depressed about it. Yes, I grieved, but no longer. I've gotten over it. I'm turning forty in December, and there are other things in life besides children. Lots of things."

"Like what?" he asked.

"I have my health," she said with trepidation, and they both burst out laughing.

"I also have a birthday in December," he said. "The last day of the year. I used to celebrate by partying all night, but these days . . ." He shrugged. "You get older."

She was one year older than he was. He told her about his daughter Klara. He had a photo of her in his wallet. She had the same black hair, the same eyes.

"My mother is Icelandic," he said. "But she also has some Greenland Inuit ancestry. You can see we have a touch of it, both Klara and me."

She chose Torekällgatan this morning and practically had to half-run down the steep hill. This whole city was full of steep hills. That was the first thing she found out when she moved here a few years ago. Then she was a young newlywed. After the divorce, she kept her married name, Stenhägg, because it sounded better to her than her maiden name, Svensson.

Her marriage hadn't lasted very long. She and Claes were just too different. After Claes, she had had a few short relationships, none of them important.

Tobias' ex-wife also lived in Södertälje, but Marit had never met her, just seen her photo. Görel was not all that sociable, and often depressed; she was probably mentally ill. Marit had met Tobias' daughter Klara but Marit never felt any closeness. Klara had been at the library a few times, but she never said hello, just went straight to the children and youth section. She never checked out anything, but would sit there and leaf through a book. One afternoon, Marit had walked over to her.

"Hi, Klara, don't you recognize me?"

The girl's eyes were exact copies of his. She jumped as if she'd been caught doing something forbidden.

"You know, I'm Marit, the one with your dad."

"Right."

"I work here at the library."

"I know."

"I just thought I'd come over and say hi."

Marit felt incredibly foolish, as if the girl had dismissed her.

Marit turned left onto Storgatan. At this hour, the street was almost deserted. She perceived the flapping of wings and was able to glimpse a bird of prey, perhaps a sparrow hawk. It appeared disoriented and flew right into one of the windows of the Kringlan shopping center. A thud, and then it flew away, staggering, over the paving stones. She followed it with her eyes until it disappeared past the church far away.

The library was in the heart of the city, located in the so-called Luna Building. She'd been there ten years. She liked the contact with people, especially when she worked the check-out desk on the first floor. Not only people who wanted to borrow books would come up, but others, all kinds of people with various requests. Sometimes she had to answer the most incredible questions.

She neared the library and decided to go in through the main entrance; somehow she just didn't feel like going around back to the employee entrance. A crowd of people was already standing outside the glass doors waiting for eight o'clock. It was the same faithful group every morning. When the guard opened the door, they went right for the newspaper and magazine section, almost mechanically. They would pick up their newspaper and sit down in the exact same chair every day.

She dawdled a bit behind the group, not up to talking today. She was still sleepy and not able to follow a conversation. They were discussing some issue, how Björn Borg was such a millionaire, and the only woman in the crowd raised her voice to ask how could a person spend all that money, could it really make you happy?

One of the elderly men in a cap turned to her.

"He just went bankrupt," he teased her.

The woman looked amazed; her cheeks turned a slight rose.

"But . . . people sell his underwear," she said.

"How do you think the seamstresses feel?" the man continued, hunching his shoulders and refusing to meet her eyes. "They'd been sewing and sewing all that underwear and now they're not going to get paid."

Marit took a few steps to the side. She pulled out a tissue and dried the area around her eyes carefully. She felt a headache coming on. On the town square, merchants were setting up their booths. It was Thursday today, market day, and the merchants usually sold clothes and trinkets, and had a few tables of flea market items. She'd stopped being interested in market day a long time ago.

The bell in Saint Ragnhild's church tower rang eight.

The morning was stressful. People were not in a good mood. She had no idea why. Some days were just like that. Maybe they'd slept badly the night before as she had. A man wearing a winter coat was using the copier, trying to make copies of handwritten documents. Some pages came out well, but others didn't.

"Is this how they are supposed to look?" He leaned over the counter, his hands were thin and had spots.

"It's difficult to copy blue ink," Marit replied. "Try using the darkest setting."

His forehead wrinkled.

"That's what I've been doing!"

Marit went with him to the copier to help. The copies still didn't turn out well.

"Well, I don't know," she said. "It doesn't seem to work."

He gave her a dissatisfied look.

"Is that what you call service around here?"

Luckily, just then the telephone rang. A customer wanted to extend his loan on a butterfly book. She accessed his information on the computer and extended the loan, pretending the transaction was more complicated than it actually was. During all this, the copy man grew tired of waiting and disappeared.

At nine-thirty, she went upstairs to the food service area and bought a cup of coffee. Usually she'd also have a sandwich from home, but because she'd gotten up so late, she'd been in too much of a hurry. She bought a slice of rye bread with liver pâté and cucumber. Her colleague Hilda was already sitting at a table and looked worn out.

"Everything all right?" Marit could hear for herself how hearty she sounded.

"It's just all this rain," her colleague sighed. "It sucks the life right out of you."

"But today it's not raining."

"No, but I'm not on vacation today."

Hilda was a book page. She would get the book carts from the check-out counter and return the books to their proper places on the shelves.

"Well, that's true."

Hilda had spent her entire vacation in a rented cabin on Rindö, an island in the Stockholm archipelago. She had two kids going through puberty; her husband worked for Scania. It had rained every day they were there.

"It looks like it's going to be a fine fall," Marit continued. "Tobias is coming home today, so I took the afternoon off. I think I'll lure him to the forest on Saturday because there's hundreds of chanterelles."

Hilda gave her a bored look. "Where?"

"Don't know, but there's got to be a lot of them there."

"I don't think I'll get around to anything fun this weekend. I've got to do grocery shopping and the laundry and clean up the house. There's just not enough time."

"Huh."

"And I'm also working on Saturday, if my aches and pains let me."

"Well, then, I hope it rains on Saturday for your sake," Marit said. She always found Hilda difficult to deal with. Hilda was always complaining, always negative, always going on about pain in her shoulders and neck.

Who doesn't have pain in their arms? Marit thought. It was part of the job. Books were heavy and many movements monotonous and hard on the body, hard on the muscles. But didn't every job have risk for injury?

A few more colleagues appeared and settled around the table.

"You know what happened yesterday?" Molly said. "We were about to close but somehow I felt something wasn't right. I went to the genealogy section, and somebody was there who was suddenly in a great hurry the minute I poked my head in. Know who it was? That guy who cut out cat pictures from books last year, you remember, Eskil Hansson from Grusåsen.

"What!" Marit exclaimed. "We have a restraining order against him! He's not supposed to come here!"

"He seems to have sneaked inside anyway. Didn't you see him when you were working the counter by the entrance?"

"If I'd seen him, I would have raised the alarm."

"Well, anyway, there he was, and I don't know if he had enough time to do anything, though he looked awfully guilty. I asked him what he was doing since he wasn't ever supposed to come in here again. He muttered something about the order expiring."

Molly straightened her back and looked around the table self-righteously.

"He's wrong. It's a life-long order," said Hilda, "and he knows it. I can't believe how many beautiful books he destroyed with his damn scalpel before we got wise to him. He owes us a fortune."

"What did you do?" Marit asked.

"I told him to get lost. And if he ever stuck his nose into the library again, we'd call the police."

"Did he listen?"

"Yep."

Many strange things happened at the library. It was supposed to be the people's living room, and people took liberties that they wouldn't otherwise do. Like the schoolboy who wanted to photocopy his butt. Before anyone could stop him, he'd pulled down his pants and hopped on the machine. Maybe that's why it's not working like it should, Marit thought.

They'd also had a great deal of trouble with drug addicts who went into the bathrooms with their syringes and apparatus. Luckily, the police station is right next door.

Underneath the counter, they had a large notebook with a flowery cover where they kept a journal of everything that was going on. Funny episodes and episodes that were not so funny. Notes on things they had to keep track of, such as when the Turkish newspaper *Cumhuriyat* stopped publishing or a request not to put mysteries in front of other books just because there was no more room on the shelves, since the books would fall behind. They also taped in notes that they found inside the pages of the books, often written by adolescents. Mash notes and "Ask Fortune" squares.

At lunchtime, she went to Café Ark, which was in the parish house and run by the church. You could get a bowl of soup and a sandwich here for a reasonable price. And they were quick about it, too. She also had to run a few errands before she had to drive out to pick up Tobias. The Café had fruit soup today, not all that filling, perhaps, but she planned to make a nice dinner for the two of them that evening.

She bought tomatoes, fresh pasta, and ground beef at the grocery store, and on the way back, she sneaked into a lingerie store and bought a pair of lilac lace panties. The sizes ran small here, if she chose size 40, it was guaranteed that the panties would cut off her blood circulation, not to mention that they usually shrank in the wash. She took size 42-44.

As a rule, she wasn't much of a shopper. She felt weary whenever she went to the major chain stores in the center of town. The same kinds of clothes, made for teenage anorexics. At one store, there was a larger selection, but the racks were placed so close together that she would feel panicky whenever she shopped there. For the most part, she wore T-shirts and nice long slacks, and she would vary her outfit with vests and scarves if she had to fancy it up. Tobias wasn't one to be interested in what she wore, which was quite a relief. Nevertheless, she wanted to look attractive this evening. Maybe Tobias would be too tired after the trip for love-making, but just in case, she wanted to be ready.

2

CARL SIGVARD WAS NOT ABLE TO BE WITH SVAVA when she gave birth to their son. He was not allowed inside the delivery room. In those days, the soon-to-be fathers were never allowed inside. That's the way it was and nobody questioned it.

Would he have chosen to be with her?

He was used to helping new life come into the world. Many times he had to step in when a cow was giving birth and the calf wasn't sitting right. He'd push his arm right inside and carefully find the proper grip and turn the calf around. No, he wasn't the bewildered type.

So, yes. He would have liked to be there when his son was born.

She was so straightforward and courageous when she went into labor. She stood gripping the back of the sofa. The air puffed out from her taut lips: the time had come. He watched her through the door opening as he changed into his good suit. She moaned quietly, but as yet she had no fear; her knuckles kneaded the sofa back. Sometimes she laughed and let him brush aside the hair from her face.

They moved to the car in stages. He carefully guided her past the tricky patches of ice. Her pains were coming closer together now. She was single-minded and determined, but he noticed a slight panic in her eyes, and once she was seated in the front seat, she pressed her forehead against the side window and a gurgling sound escaped.

"Just remember that it's our child on the way, we'll soon have him with us. Or her." He was trying to give her courage, drive away bad thoughts, let her realize that it was a human being that would soon force its way through her legs, not illness or smelly blood, not a tumor or a kidney stone. He'd had kidney stones, so he knew how that felt. One had come straight out with his urine and the pain had made him bite a hole in his tongue.

But he didn't go to the hospital. He'd never gone to the hospital, never left himself in the hands of others, took care of his pains himself. Now he wanted to take care of her, but all he could do was press down on the gas pedal, and he risked spinning out on the S-curve by the store because her body suddenly fell against his . . . and her face: he'd never seen anything so bare.

It was the last day of the year and everywhere the farms were getting ready to celebrate. They hadn't bothered this year. She was already fourteen days overdue and they thought that it had to happen any time now. His neighbors Erik and Vanja Malmfelt had suggested that they could "stop in around eight and have a bite to eat, and maybe we could play cards while we wait for the bell to ring twelve," but Svava had declined the invitation. He called them and explained that Svava was too tired. Vanja was standing on her porch as they drove past. She waved her arm with a big thumbs-up.

It was afternoon and darkness had begun to fall, this deep December darkness. They'd had good snowfall the past few days, but today was milder and made all the roads slippery. He drove with the windshield wipers on. The roads were empty and silent.

He only heard Svava's dull moaning.

They took her in directly, took her beyond his sight. He had wanted to say something to her, something definite. That he would be with her even if it didn't seem like it. However, a nurse took Svava's arm and steered her away immediately. The door's glass windows shut right in his face.

He remembered the way the light had been, white, ice-cold so that it made his brain ring. Another man was also sitting there waiting. They greeted each other shyly. There was a vinyl-covered sofa and an overflowing ashtray as well as a heap of magazines, including *Status*, the magazine for people with tuberculosis. There was a personnel callbox over the door. It peeped and blinked, and, for a long time, he kept busy by trying to figure out how many combinations you could get from the five different lights.

The other man finally went into the bathroom to pee. Through the door, an intensive gushing could be heard. When the man came out again, his upper lip was sweating. He smiled, embarrassed. "A pilsner and sausage would be really good right about now," he said. "There was a hot dog stand by the entrance, but they're closed today. I saw that when we got here. It's New Year's Eve, of course."

"Yeah, I should have brought something to eat, too," Carl Sigvard agreed. "But there was just no time for that."

"Is this your first time?" the man asked as he stuck out his hand to introduce himself. Carl Sigvard had now forgotten what the man's name was.

"Yep. First time."

"It's our third. My mother-in-law is taking care of the other two. They're now three and one. Now we're going to have another little one in the house."

Carl Sigvard would only have Tobias. Why no other children came along, he didn't know. He would have liked more.

At a quarter to twelve, a nurse entered the waiting room.

"Mr. Elmkvist?"

He stood up, rocking on his toes, his entire body faint and weak, his eyes stingingng from the tobacco smoke. The nurse waved the smoke away from her face as she tripped over to him.

"Well, it's over and you have a healthy and active boy, at three thousand, nine hundred and eighty grams, length . . ." She had to open the paper in her hand. "Length: Fifty-two centimeters."

"And my wife? How is she?"

"You can go see her now."

The same minute he stepped into Svava's room, the church bells began to strike twelve. The sky was lit up by fireworks. She lay there with her head back. When he touched her leg, he could feel her shaking underneath the blanket.

He did not know what to say.

"Turn around," she whispered.

He turned and saw a woman in uniform holding an infant wrapped in a blanket. His son. A small, black tuft of hair, the wrinkled face, sharp fingernails which had already managed to scratch his face.

"Congratulations," said the nurse. "And Happy New Year."

That was the year 1960. He'd just turned thirty. As the year turned to 1961, his adult life began.

And here he was with a family to take care of. He remembered that Vanja Malmfeldt came knocking on the door the next morning. He had already gotten up and taken care of the animals. Vanja wanted to hear all the details.

"And I'll help you get the house nice and tidy before she comes home," Vanja promised.

Maybe he would have thought to do it all by himself, but he wasn't annoyed. Women knew more about this stuff. Certainly more than he did.

It was so strangely quiet in the house this afternoon. At times, he heard Adam cough in the room which had been Svava's sewing room, but Adam wasn't playing his music today. Maybe Adam had a cold. Did anyone mention it today?

Carl Sigvard looked at the clock. It was already late afternoon. Using all his strength, he managed to turn onto his right side. It felt as if all his inner organs were slipping down; it hurt, pressed the air out of his lungs. Outside it was twilight, Sabina should be coming indoors now, starting dinner. What day was it today? He didn't really remember. Sabina had indicated that the district nurse was going to look in on him. He wished the district nurse was entering the room right now, holding her bag, and he would show her that maybe the crutches weren't so bad after all. "Look what I've learned," he'd joke with her, and she would joke back in the way that younger women teased older men, bantered with them, almost like bickering. And he would heave his ass off this mattress and stand on his own two feet. Certainly he'd sway a bit, but what the hell. And they would help him, Sabina and the nurse. They would place the crutches under his armpits, and he would stomp off.

"Now I'll go outside for a while," he would declare, and with great effort he would make it down the stairs and out onto the bridge toward the outhouse. The wind would blow through his thin hair and right through the gaps in his pajama jacket, because the button holes were too big for the buttons, which always slid out.

Sabina would call out from behind him. "Can you manage by yourself?" and he would nod. The two of them would go in to drink a cup of coffee because they knew he needed to have his peace and quiet for some time, because that was the way he was.

His stomach was hurting like hell, all that gas. Sometimes he tried to pull the hams of his buttocks apart to lessen the pressure, but this didn't work any longer. He wanted to whine like a little boy, like Adam, when Adam didn't get his way.

He remained in a fetal position on his side, his kneecaps aching as they touched, lying the way a baby does when it's born, or a really old person while dying. His mother had died in this position, curled up with her arms over her flat chest and her legs drawn in to her stomach. You could only see the small twitches of her eyelids. She no longer recognized anyone. She could no longer speak. She just lay in place.

Was this going to be his turn now?

Like hell it was!

He heaved himself over onto his back, holding himself up by the elbows.

Sabina was leaning over the pillow. She held a bowl in one hand and a spoon in the other.

"I've made you some pudding, cherry pudding."

"Pudding?"

She nodded.

"Aren't we going to have real food tonight?"

She raised her upper lip and he saw what he'd never noticed before: her teeth had blackened near the gaps, like cavities.

"Sabina?" he asked, uncertainty in his voice.

"Eat the pudding now. I'll make more food later this evening."

She moved the little bed tray until it was placed over his hips, but she didn't meet his eyes.

"How are things going for you?" he asked.

She started to nod. Her head kept nodding as if there was a switch she couldn't turn off.

"You know how things can get sometimes," she said, grimacing.

"Sabina, you're not working too much, are you?"

"Eat your pudding. I'll be back later."

There was something strange about the pudding. He put a spoonful into his mouth and waited for the sour taste of cherry, which would make him pucker but not keep him from eating it up. He was very hungry. Wasn't that a sign he was getting better?

There was something wrong with the pudding. He could tell immediately. Instead of putting in sugar, she'd put in salt.

Carl Sigvard lay on his back and stared at the ceiling. He couldn't make out much, it had gotten darker but he didn't want to turn on the light. He listened for any kind of sound. Hearing was the last sense that left a dying human, hearing and touch. He thought about that, as he'd read it in a magazine not too long ago. His neck was sticky, his stomach like an anti-aircraft balloon.

He remembered how he had brought Svava and the baby home. The tiny boy lay in a masonite box with spaces for handholds on the side. Erik and Vanja had given the box to them, "since we're not having another one." Svava had met him in the hallway and her maternity dress hung loosely over her stomach but it was tight over her larger breasts and the cloth had dark, round milk stains.

He carried the box with his son up the stairs and into the house. What a ceremonial feeling! And then, once Carl Sigvard had taken his spot in the corner of the sofa, Svava lifted up the little one and placed him on Carl Sigvard's lap so that she could have a moment to get used to being at home again.

Now, so many years later, he missed that warm weight in his arms, the dent in the cushion where the baby had slept. At first, the baby had cried a great deal, but Carl Sigvard figured out how he could stick his finger between the toothless jaws. What strength that sucking had! The same strength as the nursing calves!

Sometimes at night he would wake up with a start and search through the sheets to find the baby, because they usually took him with them to bed when he was fussy. They were told not to do this by the experts, but they did it anyway. As he caught hold of the round, chubby baby leg, coming out of sleep, he realized that he'd been having such unpleasant nightmares that his heart was still pounding. Yes, he had many bad dreams during those days. He would lie awake in bed and stroke his finger over the soft, plump baby flesh.

May nothing bad ever happen to you, Baby Tobias, nothing dangerous in this entire world!

3

THE MOSS WAS SLIPPERY AND LOOSENED WHEN TOBIAS' FEET HIT IT, so that the stones were exposed. Many times he tripped and fell to his knees in pain from both sores and bruises. He felt disconnected from his body, as if he, Tobias, was no longer within it but hovering to the side and observing it. The long strands of grass captured his boots, tangled in his steps, made him sob out loud as he tore himself free with bursts of strength. Every single movement was large and exaggerated.

He took off running, past the small grove of trees, and he did not stop even though Sabina was calling him. Afterward, he reduced his speed and crept over the meadow where the ground sank underneath his soles, groaning as if it were an animal.

Now he was deep inside the forest. A gentle rain had started, mild, insistent; it fell in an almost friendly manner. He turned his face to the skies, and it ran down his throat and into his chest hair. He lifted his hands; they were familiar, chapped, dark circles under the fingernails. People said the dark circles came from sorrow.

How long had he been outside? He had no idea, at least no conscious one, but now the need for tobacco came over him, increasing, making him weary. His cigarettes were still on the windowsill, as was his cell phone. He'd stared through the fly-shit-stained window, waited for Sabina to go; he didn't move until he heard Sabina close the outside door up at the house.

Through pure desperation, he ripped a sticky pinecone from one of the trees and began to chew it so hard that it hurt his gums.

He kept standing next to the bark. The smell of damp lichen was incredibly pungent all of a sudden, and he pressed his tongue on the surface of the jagged bark until he tasted blood and iron.

Eventually he reached the outdoor dance platform, which surprised him, as he thought he was going in the other direction. The grass here was yellow and still hadn't been knocked over. Pearls of rain glistened on the spider webs as well as the rangy bluebells which had managed to survive the first frost. He climbed up onto the actual floor; the rain made the knotty boards shine.

Reason attempted to speak to him. Reason said: "Turn around!"

Instead he began to run across the dance floor and then slid, it was slippery; it was silent. *You have to turn around.* He found himself on all fours, his fingers spread out, no rings, broken fingernails—were these hands really his, were they his hands, these hands? He didn't usually do manual labor with them, no shit work. He used them to write; they were his fine tools. He still had to ask Sabina to give him a ride to the train station; she'd promised. He had to ask her right away. He had to go home and get writing even though his brain was mute and dry. He had to get over it. He had to get going.

How did he get back? He could not remember. Sabina was frying eggs in the kitchen and, without saying a word, she put a plate in front of him. He looked at her and his eyes filled with tears.

"I'm not hungry."

She was acting normal, the same position at the stove. She even managed a weak joke.

"Eat so that you'll be big and strong."

He cut into the runny yoke, but had to rush out of the kitchen to throw up.

He stood under the shower for a long time, until he was almost scalded. Then put on his jeans and sweater. Looked out his window. The barn door was open. He remembered his cigarettes and cell phone. He wondered if Sabina had brought them into the house. He went back to the kitchen to ask her.

"No," she said. "I didn't think of it."

Sabina had put on lipstick. He noticed how her mouth moved.

"Sabina?" he asked with a hoarse voice, but she had already left. He heard her footsteps go up the stairs. The kitchen stank of frying grease so he had to leave. Into the yard. He'd put his overalls over his head to protect it from the rain. Shouldn't have worn his shoes; should have changed to boots. Too late now. The dogs barked at him from behind their fence as if he were a stranger.

He had to stop for a moment next to the tractor so that he could vomit, but only scum and saliva came out.

He opened the barn door the rest of the way. A lamp burned inside, dim from dirt. He found himself standing in the hall, the pigs ran all around in their pens. They squealed and searched for the corners as he began to walk around the barn with the pair of overalls wrapped around his head.

There was a gap in the rough cloth, just enough to see where he was going, but not letting him see any more than he was capable of taking in. His cell phone was where he left it, as was his pack of cigarettes. Sabina had hung up the razor on a hook. Did she even repair it? The cattle were snorting and lowing. He only saw marked cattle now, no unmarked ones. Maybe those cattle were hiding. He stopped, stood, tasted, swallowed the thick slime in his mouth. There was fresh hay in the mangers, the crunch of grinding teeth.

. . . and he found himself drawn to the tack room.

. . . drawn to it.

. . . although no one was forcing him.

He lit a cigarette before he decided to go in . . . one drag for every step.

Four long steps.

No more than that.

The handle burned against his palm.

It wasn't locked.

He opened it with one jerk.

Empty.

The entire room was empty. He felt forced to take off the overalls and go up to each wall and look closely at the floor to inspect and make certain it was true.

Yes. Empty.

Not a stain, not a mark, not a hair.

Not a hair from the yellow-colored beard.

Dizziness returned and spun his brain around. His brain cramped and he had to sit down on the bench, and when he sat down, his pants got wet because the rag rug was thoroughly soaked. He touched it with his hand. It was clean, damp from water, nothing else.

He stood on the threshold and looked around one last time.

It did not happen!

None of it had happened!

Tomorrow he was going to be sitting in a comfortable train seat on the X2000, on his way home.

4

TOBIAS DID NOT SEE SABINA AGAIN THAT EVENING. He packed his suitcase and got ready to leave. He wrote a note which he left on the kitchen table.

Dear Sabina. I must leave tomorrow, Thursday. People need me back home. Please give me a ride to the train like you promised. A train leaves at ten. Tobias.

He drank the rest of the whiskey in his bottle, and then he fell asleep as if he'd been clubbed. When he woke up, Sabina was already busy in the kitchen. She was wearing different shoes from her usual ones; he could tell from the sound they made. At first he was not sure where he was. Then he remembered. His forehead began to throb.

She had dressed in a pleated skirt and a sweater. Her little necklace hung over the neckline.

"The district nurse is coming soon," she explained in a clear metallic voice. "She's going to take care of your father so his problem is solved."

"What about you? Do you have time to drive me in?"

"Yes, it's going to be nice to get away from this place for a few hours."

"How's Adam feeling about it?"

"I gave him some Valium. He'll stay quiet."

"Damn, you use Valium on him?"

"It's a good thing. It's very useful at times."

She poured coffee, and he saw her hand was shaking.

"Sabina!" he tried to get her attention, but she continued as if she did not hear him.

"I've already taken care of the animals. They've gotten everything they'll need today. They'll be fine."

"Sabina, I . . ."

"Go up and tell Carl Sigvard good-bye. He'll never forgive you if you don't."

"Does he know . . . ?"

She turned toward him and the skin under her eyes was puffy.

"Does he know what, Tobias?"

"That . . . I have to go?"

"Yes, I told him."

"Was he . . . ?"

"Hurry up, or we won't get there on time."

His father was lying on the bed in his underwear. Nice underwear, modern, boxers. His father's legs were gangly; his skin was off-color and ugly. He was fanning himself with a magazine. The room steamed from being overheated.

"So, you've had enough of country life."

"Yes, I have to go home now."

His father put aside the magazine and heaved himself into a sitting position.

"Too bad you had to go so suddenly."

"Görel is having some problems. I don't want Klara to take on all that responsibility."

"My sweet little Klara."

"She is that."

"She was such a cute little girl."

Tobias nodded. "Don't take me wrong. I've been here quite awhile already. I've tried to help out as best I could."

"Am I blaming you?"

"I guess not."

"I told you already that I'm grateful that you came. Both Sabina and I are extremely grateful. It's just too bad that you have to go so soon. It's like I've gotten used to having you around."

His father put his hands over his abdomen, which was tight and swollen, and kept rumbling.

"Are you having some difficulty?"

His father grimaced.

"It's just a small problem. A pretty girl is coming over today to help me with it. At my age you know . . . ." His voice broke and he had to clear his throat. "It's hell that I can't take care of my own basic functions on my own any longer!"

"Pappa."

His father coughed and raised his eyebrows so that his forehead wrinkled.

"Get going now. And hurry up and write your books."

"Sure." He took hold of his old man's bony hand, pressed it, and turned around.

"Oh, and one more thing."

Tobias stopped and held his breath.

"I'm proud of you. Maybe you don't believe me, but I am damned proud of you."

Tobias was waiting next to Sabina's Opel. He found he wanted to kick it, decided to do it, kicked the tire hard.

"Fuck it," he said.

"What's up?"

He hadn't heard Sabina come up behind him; she jangled the keys.

"Nothing."

"I didn't find my keys right away. I usually keep them in the . . . for a minute I thought I . . . but then I remembered that I drove the car yesterday."

"Where were they?" he heard himself ask.

"On the floor of the barn. Can you imagine anything so stupid? I could have swept them away if I hadn't seen them."

He opened the trunk and put his suitcase inside. He sneaked a peek at the house and the barn. Pain gnawed behind his forehead.

"Sabina . . . yesterday . . . what happened . . . ?"

"Nothing happened!" She cut him off. "Hop in the car. Let's get going!"

A horseback rider appeared on the side of the road. It was Ingelize. She was riding the same white horse that she had ridden on
the ride with Tobias. She gestured for them to stop, and Sabina
slowed down the car. Tobias wished she would keep going, pretend
they hadn't seen Ingelize. But it was too late.

Sabina rolled down the window.

"Hi there." Tobias could not see her face, just heard her voice
from above the roof of the car. "Where are you going?"

"Linköping."

"Why Linköping?"

"Tobias has to get home."

"I see. He's certainly in a rush." She dismounted. Her riding
boots swished past the car window and then her face looked in.

"Sometimes that's just the way it is," Tobias said quickly.

"I thought that you were going to stay another few days at least.
I thought we might go on another ride. I'd looked forward to it."

"It would have been fun, but there's stuff going on at home, so
I have to return and sort things out a bit."

Ingelize took off her helmet and ran her fingers through her
hair.

"Anything serious?"

"Not really, I just have to get back home."

"You haven't forgotten what we talked about. The offer still
stands, you know."

"Right."

"Don't forget."

Sabina said, "We have to get going."

Ingelize led the horse away from the road.

"Bye," she said. Tobias turned and looked directly into Ingelize's eyes. There was an expression in them which scared him.

"What kind of an offer was she talking about?"

"She wants me to help out with the horses. To move here. I
could rent a place, the Vesterberg place."

"Hell, that's what she wants?"

"Right."

"Are you going to do it?"

"Would you want me to?"

"You have your life up there."

"Yes, but . . . ."

"It would be a bad idea, Tobias."

They were getting close to Linköping. The buildings were changing, becoming taller, more uniform, and even though it was still morning, the traffic seemed heavy and aggressive. The drivers wore hard, mute expressions; they stared straight ahead and there was stress in their postures, stress in their grip on the wheel. Sabina did not let herself be ruffled. She turned in toward the center of town and found a parking place right in front of the station.

He had been sitting with his head turned toward the window, not daring to look at her. Now his neck was stiff and sore.

She pulled out the ignition key.

"Can you find your own way or should I come with you?" Her neutral voice, it was not her real voice, not Sabina's voice.

"Wait a minute," he said.

She was sitting with her hands in her lap. He lifted his left hand, placed it on her hands, felt her ice-cold fingers.

"You're freezing."

"There's something wrong with the heater."

"Sabina, I feel so . . . ."

She screamed, small, muffled, but still . . . . She pulled her hands away, stuffed them in her pockets.

"Get going. Now. I'll wait here in the car, but please, don't say anything. I can't stand to hear it. I can't stand what I might answer, so get going and remember that nothing happened. Remember that. Nothing at all!"

5

THE TRAIN WAS LATE. Marit sat in the waiting room and flipped through a newspaper, but couldn't read it. She couldn't concentrate. *Beloved*, she thought. *Beloved, my beloved.*

She felt slightly euphoric. At the same time, she knew she would come back down to earth the minute Tobias stepped off the train. He wasn't a romantic.

The word "beloved" was one she could only use in her thoughts and fantasies. It didn't fit the physical Tobias. He never used any love words with her. Well, in bed, the moment he came, he sometimes exclaimed he loved her, but not always. Usually when he'd had something to drink.

Still, she was always filled with expectation before her next meeting with Tobias. Expectation, she thought. How can a person live a life without expectation? Never having anything to look forward to, how did they manage to get through daily life? Like Hilda. May I never turn into Hilda! No lust for life, just bitterness; no joy left.

The speakers rattled an announcement, but it concerned the train from Gothenburg. She put aside the newspaper and went to the kiosk to buy a banana. Tobias would certainly want to go straight to his apartment. Should she make dinner there or should she try to lure him to her place on Täppgatan? Still, it was lucky they lived so close to one another.

When she and Claes separated, she bought a three-room apartment in the center of town. It was on the second floor of a rose-colored five-story building. Claes took most of the furniture. She wanted to start over with new furniture, pieces she chose herself. She stayed away from the big box stores and found hers at an antique store in Moraberg. She went to an auction and won an old-fashioned medicine cabinet, which she painted red. She kept her favorite books in it, everything from *Pippi Goes to the South Seas*, which she'd read until it was falling apart, to Sylvia Plath's *The Bell Jar*, Sigrid Undset's *Kristin Lavransdotter,* and Primo Levi's *Survival in Auschwitz.*

She was in overdrive the first year after the divorce. She read evening class schedules and took a number of courses. She learned how to renovate furniture; she took a seminar where she learned to read body language; she took one on improvisation and one on how to do weaving with pictures. She kept up the weaving; she even began to make her own patterns and pictures.

There was room for Tobias to move to her place. But the best thing would be to sell both of the apartments and buy a bigger one. Or a house. Maybe just out of town, in the suburbs of Mölnbo or Järna. They wouldn't be too far from the center.

They'd never talked about any of this. Tobias had never indicated that he wanted to move in with her. These were her own thoughts entirely.

After a twenty-five-minute delay, the train rolled into the station. Tobias was sitting in the last car. She saw him from a distance. He was walking slightly bent over and it looked like he was limping. She half-walked, half-ran to him, threw her arms around him, burrowed her nose into his jacket.

"Whew!" she exclaimed. "You sure smell like a barnyard!"

"Really."

"But I imagine it will disappear if you hang your clothes so they can air out."

He put down his suitcase so that he could light a cigarette.

"Did you have a good trip?" She babbled on, as she reached for the suitcase to pick it up. He took it away from her.

"Sure. Except for the delay. We were stuck on the tracks for a while."

"I noticed it was late. Did they give a reason?"

He blew out smoke.

"Don't know, maybe someone wanted to commit suicide."

"What!"

"Someone in the dining car said that someone had jumped in front of the train."

"How horrible."

She wanted to hold his hand, but both his hands were busy. He took deep drags on his cigarette.

"There's no smoking on the train," he said. "I could hardly stand it."

He didn't ask her any questions about how her life was going. Once in the car, he seemed to remember at least that it was a normal working day.

"Hey, aren't you supposed to be at work?"

"I took the afternoon off," she said, as she backed out of the parking lot.

He became quiet, drumming his fingers on his leg.

"Hope I didn't cause you any problems at work."

"No, it's all right. I had a few hours of overtime that I could use. But now it's your turn. Tell me how it went. And how is your poor father doing?"

She followed him up into his apartment. There was a heap of mail on the entryway floor. He pushed it away with his foot.

"I could have come over and watched your place for you," she said.

He took off his shoes and walked into the living room.

"It's fine."

She walked up to him and embraced him.

"Tobias!"

"Yes?" he answered, as if from a distance.

"You have to know that I've really missed you!"

He carefully pushed her away.

"Don't come too close to me, Marit. I think that I'm getting sick."

"That's all right. We can be sick together."

"Marit, listen to me. I have to have some time to myself. I have to lie down and take a nap."

Disappointment hit her like a hammer.

"Do you really have to?"

He nodded.

"But I can stay here and make dinner and take care of you."

"I'm not hungry, Marit. Please don't take it the wrong way. I just have to be alone for a while."

"I've bought food that I was going to make for dinner." Tears came to her eyes, and she turned her head away so that he wouldn't see them. She heard him light a cigarette; the smoke began to waft around the room.

"All right," he said at last. "I'll come over to your place sometime this evening."

"You're just saying that because you feel forced."

"No one can force me to do anything that I don't want to do."

"What's the matter with you really? You're acting so strange. Did something happen? Is it something about us?"

"Hell, no. Nothing like that. I'm just extremely tired. It could be nothing more than I'm coming down with a cold."

Tobias sank down further into the sofa and put his legs on the coffee table. He stretched his toes. She could see that there was a hole in one of the socks.

"All right then. I'll get on home for now."

He nodded.

"Don't be sad, Marit. I can't help feeling this way."

"I understand. What time do you think you'll be coming over?"

"Around seven."

"You'll certainly be hungry by then, and by the way, you have to have something in your stomach. You just can't smoke those awful cigarettes."

He forced a laugh.

"Okay, Mommy."

So nothing turned out the way she'd imagined. Tobias wasn't acting like himself. Of course, things could get better once he had the chance to rest. Yes, they'd probably be much better. She went home, decided to read for a while, but couldn't concentrate. She put on some music, Leonard Cohen, but she still felt restless. *She said, I see your eyes are dead. What happened to you, lover?* The song gave her the sudden primitive urge to throw everything she owned—books, chairs, cooking implements, everything—off the balcony. Well, now, what would that look like? The well-behaved assistant librarian has a nervous breakdown.

No one would care, she thought. This is crazy. Having a thought like that happens now and then; it's only natural. *And since she spoke the truth to me, I tried to answer truthfully.*

She went into the bathroom and stared at her image in the mirror. During her entire childhood, she'd heard that she was cute. Her mother had encouraged her to be feminine, dressed her in fluffy dresses, kept her from testing her limits. Her mother had her reasons. Marit's older sister had been born with heart problems and only lived to be four. *What happened to my eyes, happened to your beauty.*

She bit her teeth together, watched her jaw muscles tighten, harden. She bit so hard that it hurt down to the roots of her teeth. She had clean, fly-away hair. It had always been thin, hard to style. Now she had a part and often pushed her hair behind her ears, a reflex pure and simple. It annoyed her because she felt it made her ears look big. She picked up her hairbrush and gave her hair a few strokes; it crackled with electricity. *What happened to your beauty happened to me.*

She formed her lips into one word: "To-bi-as."

What if he left her?

If this was the end?

Who would she be then?

She lifted her hand and then hit herself in the nose so hard with the hairbrush that it left a red mark. "Stop it!" she hissed. "You're sounding just as negative as Hilda! Why would our relationship come to an end? Stop these destructive thoughts!"

It was too early to start making dinner. At least to start the meat sauce. Marit opened the refrigerator and took out the salad ingredients. She began to slice the cucumbers and mushrooms without paying them too much attention.

The doorbell rang. She jumped, as she wasn't expecting visitors, and very few people dropped in to see her. Residents in her building kept their distance. She didn't know her neighbors; she would greet them while passing them on the stairs, but that was it.

She dried her hands on her apron and went to see who was there. It was Tobias. Her happiness exploded, and with fumbling fingers she opened the door to let him in.

"Great, you're here early and everything!"

He nodded and hung up his jacket. He was wearing a different jacket. She'd never seen this one before.

She hugged him and he let her, but she felt the coolness and distance stiff in his body. She pushed away his bangs from his face. His hair had gotten longer; he probably should go get it cut. His eyelids were light and swollen.

"How are you feeling?" she asked.

"Do you have anything to drink?" he asked.

"I have wine, of course."

"Nothing stronger, like whiskey? A strong shot would hit the spot."

"Actually, I think I do have a bottle." Marit opened the kitchen cupboard door and took out a bottle. "I've had this here for quite awhile. I hope it hasn't gone off."

"No risk of that." Tobias found a glass and poured some whiskey. "Want some?"

"No, I have to go to work tomorrow."

"Me, too."

"You're starting a new book? Great!"

"Yes, I'm starting one."

"Fantastic! Can I ask what it's about?"

"Not yet. Too early."

"Oh, sorry!"

"No problem. How are things going with you?"

"Just fine," she said. "But sometimes I just get antsy. I need to do something. Something different! Maybe take a trip somewhere, go someplace far away. Maybe go to Thailand, wander around there. There was a couple that came into the library with that plan. They were our age. They'd saved many weeks of vacation and now they were going to finally take off."

She was surprised when he didn't dismiss the idea. "Thailand you say?"

"Doesn't it sound wonderful?"

"Of course, you'd have to have enough money to do it," he said, thoughtfully.

"Would you really want to go? Seriously?"

"Why not? I could leave tomorrow if it came to that."

"Tomorrow? Weren't you going to start your book tomorrow?"

He laughed and pulled out his pack of cigarettes.

"I assume I still can't smoke inside. You haven't changed your rule?"

"That rule is still in effect. So please go out on the balcony."

Tobias headed over to the balcony, but she stopped him.

"You haven't said a thing about your father. How is he really doing?"

"It's tough. Damned tough. He was a strong man and now he's just lying in bed, not able to do anything."

"Is he going to . . . ?"

"Kick the bucket? Not yet at least. But he's never going to be the same. Just think of how many meters he fell! Right onto the stone floor. If he wasn't such a strong man to begin with, he would not be here today."

"Was he happy that you came to see him?"

"Thankfully, yes. Nothing he would want more than to have me move back again."

"Move?" she asked, uncertainly.

Tobias opened the door to the balcony. He lit a cigarette. The smoke was pulled into the apartment anyway. Marit decided to cut the onions and begin to fry them. She turned the kitchen fan on full. It rarely helped; there was probably something wrong with it.

When Tobias came back inside, he came close to her and gave her a short hug.

"You're very sweet," he murmured.

"I like you so very much. I missed you. I longed for you to come back. The time you were gone seemed like forever."

He poured some more whiskey. "Too bad we're not always the ones in charge of our lives."

Marit held her breath, then plowed ahead. "Have you decided to move to Kvarnberga?"

Tobias then looked at her for the first time, looked her straight in the eye.

"No," he said.

She dumped the ground beef into the frying pan and began to squish it.

"I was thinking about your dad. He seems like such a good man in many ways."

"A good man? Yeah, I guess he is."

"It's good that he has Sabina."

"Yes, it is."

"I'd like to go with you to the farm one of these days. I'm very curious about how things look there. It would be fun to meet both your father and Sabina."

"Sure."

"You never told me what happened when you were little. When you and your mother moved out just like that. Why didn't your mother want to stay with him?"

He opened his hands. "She was hit by the great passion of her life."

"I see."

"He lived here in Södertälje and was also working with horses."

Marit wished she hadn't turned on the kitchen fan, but also was afraid that he would stop talking if she turned it off.

"And what about you?"

"No one asked me what in the hell I wanted," he growled. "Don't think that they thought about me! Just whoosh! Here's a new fucking city. I would have never . . . ."

He interrupted himself and walked back to the balcony. Marit set the table. She noticed that he came back inside and was pacing in the living room, back and forth, slow, tired steps. She regretted that she'd asked him about his childhood.

Carefully, she walked up to him and put a hand on his shoulder.

"Time to eat now."

Afterwards they sat on the sofa together. She snuggled right next to him and pulled his arm over her shoulders. The barnyard smell was gone. He now smelled like tobacco and fried onions. She burrowed her nose under his ear; his unique odor, she'd longed for it. It usually made her feel very sexy, but not now. She'd had a lot of wine and was extremely tired, but she couldn't really relax; he'd changed, but she didn't know why. Maybe the stress of seeing his father so broken and ill, guilt for not being enough. She stroked him over his leg, put her ear on his chest. She thought of the new panties she was wearing—well, nothing was going to come of that now; no one had the desire. They'd just sit here and try to find their way back to each other.

Don't move back, her thoughts churned. *Don't move back or I'll die.*

After a while, he leaned his head back and fell asleep with his mouth open. If she'd had the strength, she would have put her arm under him, lifted him, and carried him to bed. Instead, she sat there with his arm weighing her down, almost making her feel ill; but in fear of waking him, she didn't dare change her position.

She must have eventually fallen asleep as well. From far away, she heard the sounds of a siren on the street, stronger and stronger, more intensive. Tobias jumped up, let out a half-swallowed scream and was suddenly in the middle of the floor.

"What's wrong?" she called.

He didn't react to her words. He seemed still asleep although his body was awake. He swirled his arms around and started pounding away as if he were trying to do battle with an unseen enemy. His mouth stretched wide, exposing his teeth. She had never seen such an expression and she started to scream.

"Stop it, Tobias! Stop it!"

He reeled toward her, his pupils still turned up and in. He shuddered and shook as if he were having a fever. Then he suddenly snapped back to his senses.

Marit wailed, "What's wrong with you? You scared me! What was going on? Were you dreaming, having a nightmare?"

He swallowed and licked his lips, stared around the room as if someone were going to jump out and attack him.

"Yes," he said hoarsely. "That was what it was. The most horrible nightmare you could ever imagine."

6

THERE WAS A KNOCK AT THE DOOR, HESITANT AND CAREFUL. Carl
Sigvard was waiting for it. He was amused by her clumsiness, the
sound as she revved the motor of the car when she wanted to turn
it around in the yard. Her fearful respect.

"Come in!" he roared, and all at once she was at his bedside
with her bag.

"Good morning, Carl Sigvard. Since there was a note on the
door I just came in."

"A note? Did Sabina go out?"

"Guess she did."

"Nurse, uh, I always forget your name."

"I'm sorry. I'm Eva, Eva Persson."

"You don't have to apologize for your name."

She turned bright red all the way down her throat. She busied
herself with her bag.

"How is everything with you?" She said a few moments later.

"Didn't Sabina explain it to you?"

"Well, she did, but . . . ."

"Well, then!"

"It's your bowel movements, isn't it? Nothing's happening?"

"Yep," he said brusquely.

"If you have to keep lying down for a long time, the intestines
slow down, too. When you're up and walking around, it stimulates
the intestines, but . . . ."

"So Nurse Eva thinks that I should get out of bed?"

She bit her lip. He noticed her front teeth were large and gapped, like those of children. He felt a pang of shame.

"Nurse Eva is absolutely right. I will get out of bed!"

"There is another way," Eva began, but Carl Sigvard put his finger to his lips and wrinkled his brows. Blew air out of his lips.

"Hand me my trousers from over there and then help me stand up."

She was on her knees in her thin stockings, slipping his feet through his trouser legs, one at a time. She'd also found socks in a drawer. He was worried she'd smell his foot odor, but she gave no sign that she had. He heard ringing in his ears, which seemed to come from inside his head. He sat up fully on the edge of the bed, while his feet touched the boards of the floor. When he tried to shift, the pain almost took his breath away.

She found a shirt and buttoned all the buttons except for the ones on the cuffs, which she rolled up. His shirt hung over his trousers, but that would just have to stay there. He pointed to his sweater and she pulled it over his head, which almost made him pass out. He grabbed her hips and had to count to three; then he pulled himself up along Eva's slim body. She stood there sturdily, legs bent. Didn't help him, but just stood there.

"All going fine?" Her delicate high voice sounded far away, and the room was spinning, both the walls and the floor. "All going fine?" His hands curled around something hard; she'd somehow finagled the crutches over to him, only God knew how, and now he threw all his weight on them and let the supports bear it. He stood there swaying until the room stopped moving.

"How's it going?" she said and he knew that she wanted to say more, the rote phrases of praise, the usual encouragement, such as *You've been so brave, Carl Sigvard! Time to take care of your tummy!*

She didn't dare, must have realized it would be better for her if she kept quiet.

"Fine!" he said sharply. "And now Nurse Eva will help me walk to the outhouse."

He did it. With her help, he made it the entire way outside. First they went through the bedroom, one step at a time, and she bounced back and forth, clearing obstacles in his way. He finally came out into the hall and it seemed to him that his previous life had happened a long time ago. He stood swaying for a minute, feeling like he had to duck down. The hall had never seemed so small and cramped before; his memory was of a much larger area.

Then came the real hard work, the stairs. And now the delicate girlish figure was no longer doubtful, but stood facing him as she walked backward down the first step, her arms out against the walls, as if she could block him. She really wasn't much of a block since if he did trip, he'd knock her down with him, all fifteen steep stairs, and what would happen afterward was something he didn't dare imagine. Although he was the one walking, he was totally dependent on her trust.

With the last of his strength, he reached the bottom of the stairs and he seemed to notice a smile come over her childlike mouth, where respect seemed to have softened; but right then he needed a chair to sit down on—quickly—because the blood was leaving his brain.

She never asked, never said a single word about why he didn't use the bathroom inside the house. She bent her head closer to his chest and put on his shoes while he sat. She even went to the trouble to tie them properly.

The weather was gray and still outside with a barely noticeable mist. The dogs began to bark; they were greeting him, and he wished he could give them some kind of sign. He took a deep breath. He'd forgotten the smell of fresh air; he tightened his grip on the crutches and began to walk.

Afterward, when he finally reached his bed again, he lost consciousness, but it didn't really matter. It happened as he was trying to lie down, and when he came to, the nurse had taken the pillow from his head and placed it under his feet. She'd been a great help to him, Nurse Eva Persson. He owed her his respect.

While he was in the outhouse, she'd gone over to the chicken coop, far enough away to not bother him but near enough to hear him if he needed to call for help.

There had been a wheelchair in the downstairs hallway. He had a dim memory that he'd been brought back from the hospital in it. She'd stopped by it and looked at him, but he waved away the sight, and it wouldn't have worked anyway, as it turned out. The path to the outhouse was too narrow; in fact, it was too narrow for two people to walk side-by-side. So she walked closely behind him, making sure his crutches were being properly placed.

When they reached the outhouse, she sneaked past him and opened the door, and then made sure that he got inside properly. Then she closed the creaking door and went away. It was cold inside, but he was sweating so much his shirt clung to his back.

"Go away until I call you!" he commanded, not with great strength or dignity, but she understood and he waited until he could no longer see her through the cracks. Then he opened the lid and put his crutches aside.

It was only after he'd done his business that he noticed something had changed. The bags of lime were gone. He was absolutely sure he'd put two bags there. They were supposed to last for years. Now they'd disappeared.

For the time being he was not able to think it through. He poked open the door and called for the nurse.

"You can come and help me now!"

And she came.

She was still in his bedroom, patting his forehead with a washcloth, and he heard the water running.

"Please take this pill," she said and it was no longer a test of wills, no longer a fight. He swallowed the pill and drank the glass of water. His body felt light; his intestines were empty, scraped clean, and right in the middle of his exhaustion, he felt a sense of happiness and well-being, which made him want to be kind.

"I think I'll keep my clothes on for now. So Sabina can see them later on."

"The proof!" the nurse giggled.

"Yes, indeed, the proof!"

She opened the window slightly and picked up her bag to leave. "I'll get going to the next place, then."

"Thank you very much, Nurse Persson," he said, and didn't notice right away that he'd actually used her last name.

7

ONCE THE DISTRICT NURSE HAD LEFT, Carl Sigvard felt like a lump
of jelly, maybe even a stranded jellyfish which was driven onto land
with sand and shell fragments stuck in its fine threads.

I've gotten ahead of myself, he thought. *I shouldn't have done this.
It was much too early.* The gnawing pain was slowly dissipating after
the pill; he lay there and waited for the pain to be stilled. At the
same time he felt fulfilled, almost touched, by his own effort, which
had been borne from his fury. Nobody was going to treat him like
an idiot! He had his pride and now he was finally on the way to
getting better.

As he lay there, his ears were trying to pick up the sound of
the Opel, Sabina coming home. He wanted to demonstrate his com-
petence, be happy from her happiness. A few times he heard the
rooster, the well-endowed Leghorn that he decided to name Clin-
ton. He smiled as he thought about her laughter. The outside air
was still in his lungs and made him strong and he would recover
come Hell or high water—even if he had a backslide now and
again.

Sabina was taking her time. When had they left? How long
did it take to drive to Linköping? She'd decided to wear her good
pumps and pleated skirt; he rarely saw her dressed up. She had sat
in front of the mirror and grumbled that her lipstick was too dry.
He felt sorry for Sabina; she was really working herself to the bone,
and not just now when he was out of the picture. This is not what

he'd imagined he'd be offering her when he asked her to move in with him. He could surely let her spend some time out of the house, have a few hours to herself, but she'd been gone for quite some time now and he was starting to become afraid.

Back when Svava left him, he'd been bitter at the entire female sex. Faithfulness was something holy as far as he was concerned. But Svava had gotten tired of him. Just that alone was an insult. He never realized what was going on until it was too late. Sure, he'd noticed she'd changed, but every woman had her moods, and how was he, a man, supposed to figure it out? When she constantly kept him away from her, when she would rather sleep out on the bench in the tack room than in their double bed, he finally understood why. She'd met her true love. Some horse seller from Södertälje.

How he tried to get her to stay. How he had even degraded himself!

And their son, Tobias.

A boy needs his mother. She had the gall to say that to his face.

"A ten-year-old boy needs his mother and I understand this to mean he wants to go with me. He has no future here, not in this village, which is dying out! You've got to see that."

She understood it to mean . . . as if he had no understanding!

He'd made a mistake that day, a mistake that he regretted ever since. He'd grabbed the boy and held him against the wall, shaking him.

"So you're betraying me, too! Going with her and leaving me here alone on the farm?"

That's not how anyone should treat a child.

Tobias had hung limp in his grasp, ugly and lank, and started stammering as well, and at that moment his bowels had released and there was the stench of diarrhea and bile. He got a look on his face like his mother, had bangs that hung in his face, mewing like a newborn kitten.

That kitten likeness . . . he'd actually imagined a bag of stones and the boy dangling in his hands, so that she wouldn't get him. If he couldn't have his son, neither would she.

That memory plagued him for many years.

He'd written a letter later on, but he never knew if Tobias actually received it. A letter asking forgiveness.

He also wrote to Svava and asked her to send Tobias home during vacation. *Home,* he'd written. Svava sent him a postcard in reply: *We're not going anywhere for a while, and Tobias does not want to come. Let him decide for himself later on.*

He heard the mailman drive into the yard and circle the flagpole. He heard the rustling of letters, probably just bills and junk mail. Sabina usually brought in the mail and put it on the night stand. He imagined that in a few days, he'd be able to go out and get the mail himself.

He'd noticed that being kept up here made his hearing more acute, the sense he depended on the most. And it wasn't all that hard to differentiate the various noises down there, from the four-wheeled tractor to Hardy Lindström's old raspy Vespa. The tractor was relatively new and Sabina loved to drive it. He'd bought it from Erik at a good price, since they were friends. Dumb old Erik who always lived above his means. Bought a John Deere turbo although he really should have phased out his farm while he still had the strength. Now Erik was drooling in the old folks' home, eyes filled with tears.

"How's it going, Erik?" he'd asked.

No answer.

How do you talk to a person you've known your entire life who can no longer answer?

Vanja was still living in the house. Soon she wouldn't be able to take care of it any longer.

"We're dying out, Carl Sigvard. After a while, our bodies just give out, and we can't do anything to stop it."

"Don't give up," he tried to comfort her. "If you give up, you'll end up sinking until they take you away feet first. When you give up, that's the beginning of the end."

"The Lord decides," she sighed, as she turned toward the wall while fumbling for a handkerchief. Vanja Malmfeldt, who'd never been religious, rather the opposite, she liked to offer her guests gin and a good card game. Now she was going on about the Lord and the power of Fate.

He heard movement in the bathroom, Adam's lumbering gait. Adam walked on his heels, and it was impossible to stop him. Now he heard Adam peeing; it sounded like a waterfall. How much did that boy drink? Carl Sigvard hoped Adam wouldn't come into the bedroom. He wanted to be peaceful to think about what he'd accomplished, the outside air, how autumn had come and that this, too, was good, because time was marching on and was supposed to heal all wounds. Or that's what folks said.

He heard some thudding in the hall, and then the door opened with a creak. Adam stood there with his stubbly beard and sloped shoulders. Adam was wearing green sweats that had drops of urine on them. He kept gasping and sniffling and had to hold on to the door jamb so that he wouldn't fall over.

"What's wrong with you, boy?" He couldn't help asking, even though he would have rather pretended to be asleep; *play dead*, he thought, *just play dead*.

The overgrown man walked over to the bed, weaving as if he were sleep-walking. He was holding a toilet paper roll.

"What's up? Out of paper?"

Adam stopped, held the empty roll to his mouth as if it were a microphone. He made a few cawing sounds; his eyes went wild and he threw the roll away. It flew toward the dresser and landed in the corner.

"What's wrong with you?" Carl Sigvard raised his voice. "Act like a man! Don't come in here and pester me!"

Adam's puffy face became suddenly distorted; his lower lip stuck out and a mooing sound escaped his lips.

With difficulty, Carl Sigvard pulled himself into a sitting position. His lower body felt like a lifeless clump. He pinched his leg through the trouser cloth. Yep, it hurt. His legs had probably just fallen asleep.

He made an attempt to sound gentle.

"Are you sad about something, Adam? Are you not feeling well?"

The man sank to his knees and rocked.

"Maa-ma! Maa-ma!" he sobbed.

"Mamma has just gone to town for a little while. She was bringing Tobias to the train."

Adam burst out in a flood of nonsense sentences, and Carl Sigvard could only make out a few words. Adam raised his arms and then banged his fists on the floor, hard, banged, howled and sobbed.

"Calm down, boy, calm down."

He felt angry that Sabina had left him alone with the boy. She should have taken him with her. She knew how difficult he found situations like this.

"Cut. Kni-fe. Cut. Eye. Maa-ma."

"What kind of disgusting language . . . ? Could you stop it?"

"Cut. Kni-i-fe. Eye . . . cut knife!"

This was something that had to do with Hardy. Something that had happened on Shame Island. Sabina had mentioned it, but he'd forgotten what it was about; he'd just had his sleeping pill and was already on the way to sleep. Something about Hardy and Adam and an animal they'd had to butcher.

"As soon as Hardy gets here, you'll be able to sing your Elvis songs," he said loudly, and there was a stabbing pain in his ass. Had he overdone it? "You'll be able to sing Elvis songs. You're a good boy, Adam. You work hard. Why don't you sing something for me? Something really nice?"

Adam was still sitting and shaking on the floor. He roared and sobbed, pulling his fingers through his hair.

"Adam," he said, trying to tempt him. "Why don't you stand up and sing for Carl Sigvard? Then Carl Sigvard will be very happy." He didn't like talking baby talk. It was not good for Adam and Sabina didn't like it. *Treat him with respect, like any other grown-up; otherwise he'll always stay at the level of a child.* Well, what the hell, even Sabina used baby talk sometimes, especially when Adam was having a tantrum like a four-year-old, and he was dizzy and exhausted from his earlier test of strength. *Sabina, you better come the hell home soon!*

Late in the afternoon, he heard the Opel putter into the yard. The wind had picked up and was blowing hard; rain was lashing against the window. He was afraid that water would come in, and though he tried to get Adam to shut the window, that didn't work. Adam had stopped his noise, but didn't want to sing, which was strange, because it was usually harder to get him to stop. Adam had gone off somewhere else in the house, and everything was otherwise silent.

Then came the light taps of Sabina in her pumps.

Sabina, I love you. Look what I've done! Soon you'll have me back to normal!

That's what he thought; he was filled with these thoughts, but he had no time to utter them. When Sabina stepped through the door, he saw she'd cut her hair.

He lay there mute and could only stare.

"You like it?" She whirled, looked at herself in the mirror. Then she took off her skirt and pulled on her jeans. It looked like her head had gotten smaller.

"I was so tired of that long hair. Not practical when you have to deal with shit all the time."

"Sabina," he said. His lips had gone dry.

"Mona Sahlin has a style like it. I was so sick of long hair, and then I saw a drop-in studio where the stylist was a guy, and they say the guys style better than the women, because they're, well, you know. They know how a woman is supposed to look."

"Come here," he whispered.

She took off her good sweater but she did not come closer. She found her old yellow sweater and as she lifted her arms to pull it over her head, he noticed a laceration under one of her breasts.

She was ready to leave the room when she noticed that he was dressed.

He heard her poking around downstairs, starting dinner, stomping around. She was talking to Adam, who wasn't crying any longer but was hiccoughing and whining.

She had never ever raised her voice to her son. But this time she was yelling so loudly he heard it clearly in his room.

"Now be quiet, Adam! I do not want to hear one more word about that eye!"

He would often have temper tantrums when things did not go his way. He'd throw his body on the floor and rip up the rugs, grab things with his big hands and throw them around so that you'd have to hide. But this time was different.

Adam became quiet. After a few minutes, he began to sing. First roughly and not so clearly, but then more clear and understandable.

Love me tender . . . I'll be yours through all the years, 'til the end of time.

8

THE THIRD DAY, THE FOURTH, OR THE FIFTH? Tobias decided not to count them, not count these mornings where he threw the blanket off and got up early. Usually he'd long for dawn, when his inspiration was strongest and clearest.

Now he could not write at all.

He wasn't sleeping well, but he decided not to drink, since the alcohol gave him artificial rest which did not rejuvenate. Instead, he would lie on his back and try to relax his body, one part at a time, and, although there were no lights on in the room, light streamed in through the windows from light poles in the schoolyard outside.

"I've got to start working," he'd told Marit. "I need a period of concentration, so please don't disturb me now." She'd nodded, but didn't seem to understand, since she called him many times to ask how everything was going.

He'd talked to Klara as well, and asked her to come over to visit, but she hadn't, which depressed him. Was there something in his voice which kept her away? He looked at his hands, his normal Tobias hands, the ones which had carried her and changed her diapers, the ones which flipped the pages of her picture books.

"I'll stop by one of these days," was all she said.

"How's your mother doing?"

"She's fine. We're going downtown today to shop our heads off."

"But didn't you say that she was . . . feeling down?"

"Well, she's not anymore."

Tobias looked at the clock. Five-thirty in the morning. He got out of bed and got the newspaper, flipped through it without interest. He heated water in the electric tea kettle, measured some instant coffee. In the school next door, only one window was lit on the ground floor. He saw a man in a striped shirt who always arrived early to start his routine. The man read the newspaper at his desk, went through a heap of papers and, when it was seven o'clock, he went to start the coffee pot for his co-workers.

He's probably the principal, thought Tobias. His workday is calm and secure; he sleeps well at night, a deserved rest. He probably goes home to a townhouse when the school day is over, and there his wife is waiting. She's probably a teacher at another school, maybe even Blombacka where I went to school one hundred years ago. They eat a properly balanced dinner, fish stew and a large salad, because his wife has reached the age where she's started gaining weight and decided to diet, so she counts calories and takes her husband on long walks, where they hold hands as if they were still young and in love.

Damn it, Tobias! You can imagine stuff! He thought to himself.

But when he sat down to his computer, nothing happened.

Leo Pullman. What a stupid name for the character of a book! It's so fake it reeks.

He stopped that line of thought and pulled his keyboard closer.

You are not going to lift your ass from this seat until you've done two thousand characters, not including the blank spaces!

Damn it, he had no idea of a plot.

He went to the bookcase and wondered how the other guys did it—Mankell and Nesser. Would their books give him the spark he needed to get going? Or his own book, *Night*? What did his Leo Pullman look like, what kind of life did he lead?

Titus Bell, his publisher, had phoned some time in the past few days.

"I don't want to bug you, Tobias, but how's it going? How far have you gotten?"

"Damn it, Titus, it's only September!" He regretted his tone of voice immediately.

"Actually, it's October," Titus corrected him.

"Sorry. It's just that I haven't been sleeping well."

"I think I know what's the matter. You're having a culture clash and you're not able to get used to civilization again, ha, ha, ha!"

"Yeah." He tried to laugh.

They agreed to go to lunch but not right away, maybe next week. He'd written a note to himself which was somewhere around the house. *Call Titus re lunch.*

He couldn't stand being indoors. Around seven he got dressed and went outside but had to return immediately. It had snowed and everything was covered with slush. He put on his boots but he couldn't find his gloves or his cap. They were probably in the basement storage unit. He started back outside anyway, this time carrying his bag of garbage to stuff into the hallway garbage chute, and he ran into the young woman from the apartment next door. She was an assistant at the hospital and was always running late.

"How's it going?" she asked, but she was in too much of a hurry to wait for an answer. She thundered past him down the stairs and he heard the front door slam.

The air was damp and raw with that special smell of new-fallen snow. He lit a cigarette and immediately had a fit of coughing. These coughing spells were beginning to worry him, and he'd started to observe carefully whatever he coughed into his handkerchief. Klara was nagging him all the time with an anti-smoking campaign; they were studying that in school, and she'd written a report which she'd forced him to look at: *The Dangers of Smoking.*

Klara was right. Of course she was right. Smoking was hell—expensive and dangerous; but he kept it up. One month he tried using chewing tobacco instead, and Marit was especially enthusiastic about the change. This made him start smoking again. He could not stand her interfering in his life that way.

He crossed Oxbacksleden, which was filled with traffic, and threw away the stub. He stuck his hands in his pockets and kept walking.

He went past the grocery store which had been run by Björn Borg's parents. Behind it was the park and playground. Long ago, when he'd been a child, he could hardly wait to get outside the moment the snow began to fall. He remembered the giddy feeling when the snow touched his eyelids and how the gravel would sting his face when he and his friends started sledding down the hills.

Farther along Torekällgatan was the yellow brick house to which he and his mother had moved. The balcony had been covered in growing plants in Svava's day. She even raised potatoes, which they harvested in the summer; not many of course, but some. Pictures of his past came to him: he and his mother sitting at the balcony table, which could be folded up. The sun reflecting on her glass, making her wine light red. She would sometimes lean forward, try to talk personally, try to tell him about his father, but he would clamp his hands over his ears and run back inside.

The first morning after they'd moved, he went into the yard. A crab apple tree grew on a rise—that tree was still there. He had looked into a window, but nobody was home. He wanted to get used to all this newness at his own pace. Outside he saw a boy playing in the sandbox. The boy was actually too big to be playing in a sandbox, but still . . . .

The boy asked him what his name was, and Tobias replied using the usual pronunciation. This frustrated the boy, who shook his head in an exaggerated grown-up manner.

"Toe-bee-ass," the boy imitated. "What a stupid name, Toebeeass."

It really wasn't such a big deal. Classic, always reappearing in movies and books. Children are ripped up from their roots and teased in their new environment, then get over it and give back what they get.

Though sometimes they don't.

Svava had left the horses at the farm. There weren't enough stalls for them at Jörgen's stable. That was what the new man in her life was called, Jörgen. Later on, Tobias found it strange that she wasn't more concerned about them.

Leaving his dad was one thing. They weren't getting along, and couples broke up all the time. But to leave the horses? Carl Sigvard finally sold them. Tobias imagined that Ingelize was devastated.

His ears were freezing, but he kept going. Cars slid past him in the slush. He'd taken Klara up Torekäll Hill many times when she was young. Many of the city's old houses and buildings had been moved here instead of being torn down, and there was even a country store where you could buy candy in paper tubes. Animals were there, too. Goats, rabbits and hens. Animals that were easy to take care of and which children loved.

In the beginning, when they'd first moved here, he kept returning right here until his roots in the city began to grow. It was close to school, and instead of going down the hill and back home, he would go up. The goats would observe him with their strange, cool, almost scornful eyes. He'd taken some carrots from his school lunch. The goats nipped them into their mouths, chewed, and swallowed.

Finally one of the caretakers saw him.

"Don't you see it's forbidden to feed the animals? Can't you read?"

The shame of it shivered right down his back, and the man appeared to notice, because he softened.

"Come on, you can help me muck out their pen if you want."

He spent the entire afternoon there. The caretaker was called Sven. Sven was happy that he could show a city boy where eggs Really Came From.

Never again did he go up the hill by himself. Sometimes the class would go on a field trip there, and he'd stay in the middle of the crowd. He was worried that Sven would find out that he already knew where eggs Really Came From and Sven would feel embarrassed.

Tobias arrived at the parking lot. He stopped to catch his breath—he could feel he hadn't exercised for a while. Lighting a cigarette didn't make things any better. He looked at the city spread out below him; melancholy spread over him as if it were a pressure on his chest, as if his chest were being squeezed so hard that his ribs were pressed inward. He swore, blew his nose, took a few vehement drags.

Sabina.

Her name was fenced off, diffuse, and hard to reach, swaying like a dim screen-saver. He tried to forget her name; brusquely he forced it out of his brain.

Nothing happened.

Growing fear made him turn around and practically run home through the slush on the sidewalks.

Nothing happened!

Still, he had to hear her say it again. Her voice, her soaring laugh. "What are you talking about Tobias? You have a great imagination!"

But what about that event in his memory?

That *non-event*—which prevented him from sleeping, kept him from writing, kept him from living?

His forehead and ears were freezing. He got to his door, but he'd forgotten the entry code. Searched his pockets with numb fingers; found his keys at last.

In the kitchen he held his hands under the faucet until they began to tingle. It was hard to get warm. He rubbed his hands together and then put on the thick Icelandic sweater which Svava had given him the last time he visited her. Usually it was too warm inside to wear it, but not today. His wrists were tingling from his wet hands; he grabbed a dishtowel and rubbed everything dry.

It was only eight thirty. He found himself at the telephone, tapping the number on the pad, but he reconsidered and hung up. Ten minutes later, he decided to try again. He stayed on the line, but it wasn't Sabina who answered; it was Carl Sigvard.

"Hello, my boy, glad to hear your voice!"

'I th..th..thought I'd g . . . give you a k . . . call."

"Have you started stuttering again? I thought you'd grown out of that!"

"Ih . . . it . . ."

"Guess what I'm doing? Your old man is sitting at the kitchen table eating oatmeal!"

"Y . . . you're d . . . doing that much better?"

Carl Sigvard burst out in laugher.

"Better believe it! You can't put me six feet under yet!"

"Amazing."

"Miracles still do happen. Well, we finally got those steers off. Sabina's been like a whirling dervish around here, and Adam, well, you know Adam, you can't get much help from a guy like him."

"I guess now you're finally out of bed, you need to put on your overalls and get back to work," Tobias tried to joke, but Carl Sigvard wasn't listening.

"We were trying to get hold of that old devil Hardy. He was supposed to come over and help us out. It seems he's skipped out again, not dependable at all. Didn't say a word to anyone, not even to his mom Ann-Mari. She was up here yesterday evening asking about him."

Bile rose in Tobias' throat. He could not reply.

"You still there?" the old man raised his voice. "Hey, you still on the line?"

Tobias swallowed and controlled his voice again.

"I'm here. But there's someone at the door and I have to say goodbye now."

"Say hi to Klara and tell her that her old grandpa is going to make it in spite of everything."

Tobias lay on the bed with the blanket wrapped around him. He was so cold that his entire body shivered. His throat hurt, too, it had swollen so that he could hardly breathe. He was hit by a sudden feeling of panic and had to leap up and open the window.

It was recess and the schoolyard was filled with children. He stood at the window, panting for breath, feeling that his heart was going to explode.

A moment later he was calm again, so he went back to the bed, and this time he crept under the covers. Both his throat and his head were aching. He dozed awhile and was halfway into a dream. A noise woke him. Did someone come into his bedroom? He lay perfectly still. Sweat broke out, on his chest, over his groin, on his neck.

What if Hardy were still alive? And he was back to get his revenge?

That arrogant mouth, that beard, that hat sitting low over his forehead.

"What the hell were you trying to do to me, kill me? Was that what you were up to, asshole? Thought you'd get away with it, too. First fuck the ass off your own step-mother and then try and kill me?"

Tobias threw off the blanket, pulled off his Icelandic sweater, sat straight up in bed, breathing hard. No, no one was there; he was all alone. It was just a nightmare and nothing had happened.

NOTHING HAD HAPPENED!

What time was it? Damn, he must have dropped his watch. He got down on the floor and started to look for it. He crept on all fours, searched through the entire bedroom and then the living room and the hall. He crept wearing nothing but his underwear. The sweat had dried on his body; fear made him whimper. He suddenly yelled. A splinter from the wooden floor in the hall had gone right into his palm, into the fleshy part beneath his thumb. He began to cry when he saw it, began to cry like a baby.

He was still sitting on the floor like that when the doorbell did actually ring. He had heard the entrance door open and close, the usual dull thud, and heard someone walk up the stairs. He had noticed that and it was starting to calm him down. He pulled on his jeans as he went to look through the peep-hole, balancing on one leg.

He saw his daughter Klara.

She'd changed. She wasn't a child any longer. This unexpected insight hit him right in the belly. Klara was wearing black and purple clothes. He noticed the short, tight skirt and the leather jacket with rivets. Underneath the jacket was a fishnet top and around her neck she wore cords and chains. Her little, round Klara face was made up in white, and looked stiff. Her hair was a mess, clumped; it looked like she hadn't combed it in weeks.

He couldn't remember the last time he'd seen her.

"I hardly recognized you," he said as she was taking off her boots. She stared at him through heavily made-up eyes.

"So what? I hardly recognize you, either."

He attempted to hug her, but she was already on the way into the living room. He closed the curtains and pulled up a chair. He could still hear the sounds of children at recess.

"What have you done with your hair?" he asked. "Or maybe, what didn't you do with it?"

"Haven't you heard of dreadlocks?"

"So that's the style these days?"

She gave him an exasperated look.

"I can go back home if the only thing you can do is criticize!"

"Sorry, Sweetie, I didn't mean to criticize. I was just surprised."

She pulled off her jacket and he saw that she was wearing a bra under her top.

"I have to say hi from your grandpa. I just called him awhile ago."

"Okay. Is he all right again?"

"At least he's better. He was finally able to get out of bed."

Klara lifted his pack of cigarettes and he saw that her nails were short and gnawed on.

"Can I have one?"

"What?"

"Forget it, then."

"Have you started smoking, Klara? You haven't really started, have you?"

"Are you kidding? You smoke; Mamma smokes. Why shouldn't I smoke, too?"

"I've been thinking of quitting."

"That's your thing."

"Have you been smoking long?"

"Dunno."

"Well, take one, then!" He also needed a cigarette, and he couldn't sit there smoking and scold her at the same time.

When she took a few drags, he realized that she wasn't a beginner.

"Do you want some coffee?" he asked.

"Yeah, thanks."

He went into the kitchen and started to heat the water while she sat in the living room and waited.

"I don't have any cake or cookies."

"I don't eat that stuff anymore."

He brought in the two cups of coffee and sat down across from her. Thick red lipstick marks were left on the edge of her cup after she drank. She cocked her head and stared at him.

"So, Pappa, how are you really doing?" she asked. "I thought people get tan and healthy when they've been out in the countryside."

"Huh?"

"You look like a dead herring."

"Well, thanks for the compliment!"

"Seriously, that's what you look like."

"If you have to know, my throat hurts. I think I'm coming down with something."

"Hmm."

"And there's this!" He held out his palm so that she could see the tip of the splinter poking out.

"Poor little you!" she laughed.

"It really hurts."

"Poor thing, shall I take it out for you? Got any tweezers?"

"No."

"How about a needle?"

"God no."

"Well, you have to have something. What about a nail scissors?"

"Look in the bathroom cupboard."

She padded off and he saw that her skirt barely covered her ass. He thought about urinary tract infections, but decided not to mention it.

He shut his eyes and let her poke around with the nail scissors. It hurt in a hollow way. Finally, she was able to nudge the splinter out. She showed it to him and laughed.

"What a nasty little thing! But now it's out and you can start writing again!"

"Thanks," he said drily.

"Speaking of that, how is your writing going?"

"It's going."

"A girl in my class read your latest one, *Night*. She thought it was fucking awesome."

"Nice to hear."

"She was wondering if you could sign her book."

"Sure. Just bring it over."

"All right."

She leaned over and pulled aside the curtain to look out at the schoolyard. She leapt up and began to forcefully bang on the window.

"What're you doing?"

"A couple of kids started beating up a little one."

"Well, I don't want them to notice my window. I don't want trouble."

"But Pappa!"

"I need peace and quiet while I'm writing."

"But you can't just sit there! It's wrong! It's bullying!"

"You're right, Klara. Somebody ought to take care of it. Sorry, I mean that these things shouldn't be ignored, I didn't mean that it wasn't important."

"Yeah, right."

"It's just that I can't have any disruptions right now."

"Okay, okay, okay!"

"How's your mom by the way? You said she was doing better."

"She is."

Klara stubbed out her cigarette in the ashtray, dragged it around in the ashes to make a pattern.

"Shall I tell you a secret?"

"What kind of a secret?"

"She's found a new guy."

"Huh?"

"I'm telling you, Mamma found a new guy."

"Really?"

"A slimy one, if you ask me."

"What?"

"Just kidding. He's nice."

"Has Görel . . . ?"

"He's a little off, too, I believe. She met him while in therapy, so it's no wonder."

"Another patient?"

"No, a psychiatrist. But those guys are all a little crazy."

Tobias had to get up and stretch. He cracked his knuckles and she stared at him with distaste.

"This is just too much," he said quietly.

"Huh! Don't you want her to find a little happiness?"

"Yes. Yes, yes, yes. That's not it."

"Well, I can't see what else. It's a little late to say you're still in love with her."

The telephone rang. Tobias reached out to take it, but hesitated. Klara waved her arm toward the telephone.

"Go on, pick up. I swear I won't eavesdrop."

"I'll wait," he said, and pulled the cord from the jack.

"You are crazy! You never answer the phone, not even your cell phone! How are people supposed to get in touch with you?"

"If it's really important, they'll call back."

"Huh."

"Tell me more about that psychiatrist fellow."

"I don't know all that much yet. His name is Rickard. He used to work with people who were seriously mentally ill. But that was awhile back, now he's at Huddinge Hospital. And he really likes Mamma. You can tell."

9

TOBIAS HAD HARDLY REPLACED THE LINE INTO THE JACK, when the telephone rang again. A cultural organization from Jönköping was on the line. He vaguely remembered that he'd promised to go there and give a reading.

"I just wanted to make sure that you received your train tickets and that everything was under control," said the woman on the other end. He thought he remembered her name was Solveig.

"Um, tickets?" he repeated.

"I sent them a long time ago. Please don't tell me that they haven't arrived!"

"Wait just a moment, let me check."

He put down the receiver and went to search his desk. Shuffled a few papers and yes, indeed, there was a plastic file folder with a confirmation letter from the Author's Union as well as an envelope with the train tickets. He discovered that he was supposed to appear tomorrow evening.

"Yes, I have them," he said. "I've been out of town for a while and just arrived home, which is why I seem a little confused."

"That explains it. I tried to call a few days ago. You don't have an answering machine, do you?"

"I have my cell phone."

"I don't have that number."

"Ah, no. But I'll be there tomorrow, don't worry."

"We're looking forward to seeing you. I'll meet you at the station. Don't forget to change trains in Nässjö; you probably can see that on the ticket."

"Right.

"We've put an announcement in *The Jönköping Post* and put up some posters in the area. We're hoping for a good crowd."

He'd hardly hung up the phone when it rang again. This time Marit was on the line.

"Sorry if I'm disturbing you. Are you in the middle of writing something?"

"The phone's been ringing off the hook! I haven't had a chance!"

"Oh, I didn't mean to disturb you."

"I know."

"I was thinking . . . what if I came over with some food? I can buy something and bring it over on my lunch hour. You have to eat even if you're writing a book. We could have lunch together, I was thinking."

"Marit, I . . . ."

"I have to eat, too. And you know I don't have a long lunch hour, so I won't be staying very long."

"So when will you be here?" he said, giving up.

"In about half an hour. Is that okay?"

"That's fine."

10

HIS HEADACHE WAS A TIGHT BAND ON HIS FOREHEAD. He took some pain pills and lay down on the bed. Shut his eyes. Of all things, an author reading! What would he say? Something about the latest book. Leo Pullman's life and adventures? He couldn't think of any sensible introductory words. This was ridiculous! He'd given tons of readings before!

The story was set in Stockholm, in the wealthy neighborhood of Östermalm. An antique dealer was found with fifteen stab wounds to his heart. He'd spent some time with a forensic investigator to find out how blood would spurt and where it would really go. Talk about blood was usually popular. It made the older ladies blush and giggle nervously, almost hysterically. Usually only women came to readings. Middle-aged and up. Sometimes one of them would drag her husband along, and he would sit half-asleep and looking totally uninterested.

Afterwards, there would be time for questions, and in the beginning everyone would be shy, not asking much. But once it began in earnest, the questions flowed.

"What does your work day look like?"

"Do you get up in the morning and sit down to write? I mean, like an average office job?"

"Do you work at home or do you have an author's getaway?"

Why do they say 'getaway'? Why not just say cave or hole? He said it aloud to hear how it sounded: 'I sit at home in my author's cave and write.'

He opened his eyes and thought that the walls were falling down on him. The walls, the ceiling, and in the center of all the rushing and roaring was his fist holding the screwdriver.

Heat steamed from his body. He stank of stale body odor. He ripped off his clothes and went into the shower, stood under the water at least fifteen minutes. He opened the bathroom door to let the moisture escape. The bathroom was as hot as a sauna. Hot as hell itself. He put his leg on the toilet seat and dried his toes carefully. He'd pushed the rug aside, and there was a shine of silverfish. They seemed to have a nest in the bathroom.

The author's nest.

He had such long, thin legs. They were very white and the hair made a pattern all along his calves. He rubbed himself dry. He shaved his chin and cheeks carefully, but left his upper lip alone. He put on fresh underwear, the last pair, damn it all; he'd have to do some laundry, too. He'd have to go to the basement and see if there was a free hour on the laundry schedule, or he'd have to go out and buy new underwear. He was also out of socks, just a few pair left but well-worn and with holes in the toes.

He poured himself a glass of water. Water was good; you're supposed to drink a lot of water. As he drank, he closed his eyes and suddenly his hand with the screwdriver was there behind his eyelids. The yellow, turning handle. Then the feeling of warm blood on his skin, between his fingers, under his fingernails, into every crevice.

Nothing had happened.

Nothing had happened.

He'd seen for himself how empty and clean the tack room had been. No corpse, no dead body. Where would the body have gone? He'd closed the tack room door, and when he opened it again— nothing had happened.

I've got to call Sabina, he thought. I'm not going to get any peace until I talk to Sabina.

There was a knock at the door and he jumped, biting his tongue. The taste of iron. Why couldn't she use the bell like a normal person? Because of course it was Marit with two individual pizzas.

He unlocked the door.

She handed him the cartons, and they were so hot his fingertips felt burned. Marit set her Lovikka mittens on the hat rack. She gave him an uncertain look.

"Are you mad at me?"

"Why would I be mad?"

"You sounded angry."

"When?"

"On the phone."

"The phone was ringing all day. And Klara stopped by."

"Are you hungry?"

"A bit."

No, he thought. *I'm not hungry. This pizza smell is making me nauseous. Just seeing those greasy cartons is making me ill. I'm feeling so bad that you can hardly imagine it.*

Marit shrugged out of her coat and went into the kitchen, started to take down plates and silverware.

"So, Klara was here," she said impassively.

"Yeah."

"She's a self-confident young woman."

"Why would you say that?"

"Well, I . . . she seems to know what she wants."

"You saw her at the library?"

"That was a long time ago. But I just saw her again when I was shopping last week. She looks hot."

"Hot?"

"Yes, hot."

Marit opened the cartons and slipped the pizzas onto the plates. They seemed fairly large, or the plates were too damned small.

"I got us two. Cheese. I hope you like them."

"They're huge."

"Yes, but they'll be really good. I often buy them."

Whenever Marit ate an individual pizza, she started in the middle. He had often teased her about it. She would eat all the toppings and leave the crust. She was doing that now.

"Go on, eat!" she said. As she lifted her fork, a long string of melted cheese followed. She chewed, swallowed as if she were starving.

"How's everything going?" she asked. "Have you gotten started?"

He was instantly furious.

"Why can't you stop talking!"

Marit put down her fork. Her lower lip trembled; he'd made her sad. He cleared his throat.

"Forgive me," he said again. "Starting a book is the hardest part. It takes the life out of me."

"I see."

"This is what it's like when you're dealing with a writer. I can't help it."

"I guess not."

"It's just that I have to figure out the first sentence, and then the rest will start coming almost by itself."

"And you haven't found that first sentence?"

"Not a good one. Everything is going straight to hell."

"Well, I like you. I like you a great deal, in fact. Did you realize that?"

He felt ringing in the back of his head.

"I really don't want to trouble you, but you do have to eat, Tobi, otherwise you won't be able to write. You won't have enough energy. And I'm not trying to be a nagging mother, either, but it's true."

"Yes, I know, Marit."

"You're starting to look malnourished. Forgive me for saying so, but you're not your usual self."

"Hmm. Klara said that I looked like a dead herring."

A shade of a smile.

"By the way, I have to take a trip," he said hastily.

"A trip?"

"I'd totally forgotten about it. But there's a reading in Jönköping tomorrow."

"Tomorrow?" He could tell how disappointed she was.

"It's come at a really bad time! Now I have to concentrate on what I'm going to say there, as well. I'm so stressed, I'll soon hit the wall."

"Poor Tobias."

He pushed his hair out of his face. "Yes, things have really gone to hell."

"Why don't you try to write on the train?"

"Are you kidding?" He noticed he was echoing the tone his teenage daughter used.

"Buy some of those headphone thingies. They have a nice, classical channel on the train, and nobody will bother you."

"That's an idea."

She looked at the clock and jumped up.

"Jesus, look at the time. I've really got to hurry now." She walked around the table, and he stood up and hugged her. Her flyaway hair got into his nose and made him sneeze.

"There's nothing else you need to tell me?" she mumbled into his sweater.

"What are you talking about?"

"You haven't found someone else?"

He pushed her away.

"Asking a thing like that is just stressing me out more. I really can't handle any extra demands right now. You've got to understand me, Marit, this has nothing to do with you. Just give me some time!"

"Sure. Sure, I'll try." She turned her face up to him so he could kiss her. Her mouth tasted like onions.

"I've got to go. Call me later, all right?"

"Sure."

He gave her a pat on the rear; he wanted it to seem playful.

11

TOBIAS HAD TO THINK. When would she be indoors? Coffee and sandwiches midmorning. Lunch around one. Wasn't that the schedule? And what about afterward? She was taking care of everything in the barn as well as the household, of course, unless she has found someone to help her out. What about his father? Could he be up long enough to do the dishes or make dinner? No, she'd never ask him to do that. He was an old-fashioned man; that would be an insult to his masculinity.

What was the time now? Three-thirty? She'd probably be inside the house now unless she had to do some shopping. If she only had a cell phone! He was afraid that his father would answer the phone and wonder why he was calling so much. He'd have to figure out a white lie, something that would make it believable that he needed to talk to Sabina.

Maybe I could say that I've forgotten something, he thought. Maybe I could say that I've forgotten my watch.

As a matter of fact, he'd found his watch in his toiletries kit in the bathroom, but it could sound plausible that he'd forgotten it at their place.

For some time, he thought through scenarios in case his father answered the phone, or in case she did.

Finally he got himself together enough to dial, and Sabina was the one who picked up the phone.

"Hi, Sabina, it's me, Tobias." He could hear that he sounded out of breath.

"Hi. What's up?"

"How's everything?"

"Fine. Your father is getting so much better you wouldn't recognize him."

"That's great. I was beginning to think so because he was in the kitchen when I called this morning."

"He's getting his spark of life back. You can't imagine what a relief it is to me."

"Yes, I can. By the way, where is he right now?"

"I've just helped him back upstairs."

"Good. Sabina, I have to talk to you."

"What about?"

"I'm not doing too well, Sabina. I can't write; I can't function; I can't do anything. It appears that *my* spark of life has disappeared." He let out a frozen laugh.

"Tobias!" she was pleading.

"It was . . . when Hardy showed up. When we were . . . in . . . ."

"Well?"

"I must have . . . killed him, Sabina."

"No."

"You don't understand. I . . . I stabbed him in the throat . . . there was blood all over the room. I know I must have done it. And you have to . . . have to know it, too." He was raising his voice, almost yelling. "You saw the place. And you got . . . got me a clean pair of overalls."

He heard her swallow.

"Sabina, answer me!"

"Tobias, there's one thing you ought to know. You can't kill Hardy Lindstrom that easily."

Tobias closed his eyes so that his vision shimmered.

"Are you still there?" she asked.

"Yeah . . . yeah, I'm here. So you're tell . . . telling me he's still alive?"

"Don't believe everything you see. And remember one thing: Hardy is an extremely unusual person."

"Have you seen him? Have you talked to him?"

"He's keeping away. And that's just as well."

Tobias sat down on the edge of the bed. He started sweating again. He held the receiver tightly against his shoulder, pulled his sweater away so that he could get some cool air.

"What if he starts to blackmail us?"

Sabina didn't answer.

"What if he threatens to go to Carl Sigvard?"

"He won't," she said doggedly.

"How can you be so damned sure?"

"He'd threaten, but he wouldn't do it."

"How do you know? Do you know him that well?"

"Well enough. He's staying away. I think he's ashamed."

"Dad said that you'd tried to get hold of him."

"Your father is such a thoughtful man. He felt I had too much work to do around here."

"He told me that Hardy's mother had been there looking for him."

"Yes, but that's happened before."

"Are you telling me the truth, Sabina? It is the truth? If that's what really . . . . I'd feel so relieved."

"Life is full of ravines you have to crawl up," she said as if by rote. "But I don't have time to talk anymore. I have to start dinner. Take care of yourself, Tobias, and stop those meaningless worries. Talk to you later."

12

THEY WERE SITTING IN THE KITCHEN WHEN ANN-MARI APPEARED THE SECOND TIME. Carl Sigvard was able to handle the stairs by himself now, at least as far as going down was concerned. He would stand at the top of the stairs and throw his crutches down to the rug at the bottom, and then he shuffled down with the help of the handrail.

Once he was at the bottom, he needed assistance. He still had trouble bending over. It made him feel like his hips were breaking in half. If Sabina was in the vicinity, she would pick up the crutches for him. Sometimes, even Adam would give him a hand.

That boy wasn't feeling well at all. He was droopy and out-of-sorts, keeping himself in Svava's former sewing room. He would lie in bed and bang his head, giving out strange sounds. He never turned on his record player these days. Carl Sigvard had thought it might be nice to have silence, but now he was beginning to miss the music.

Sabina was worrying about Adam. Carl Sigvard could see it in her face even if she kept acting as if everything was fine.

"Isn't he usually a bit down when fall comes?" Carl Sigvard asked in an attempt to comfort her when she returned to the kitchen with Adam's half-eaten dinner.

"That's true, but it hurts me to see him like this."

Carl Sigvard had still not gotten used to her appearance. Her short hair gave her a coarse look, and her head seemed too small compared to her body. He couldn't stop himself from commenting on it, even though he knew she was bothered by it.

"Your beautiful long hair!" He'd just said it again, and as she turned to reply, there was a pounding on the door.

"Come in!" Sabina yelled, but the pounding intensified, so Sabina had to go open the door herself.

Ann-Mari Lindström had been drinking; nothing unusual, but it seemed she'd also taken a fall because her forehead was bleeding from a scrape.

"Hello, Ann-Mari," said Carl Sigvard.

"Mmmm," came the toneless answer.

Sabina pointed to the kitchen. "I'll get a bandage. You go in and sit down."

The old woman stepped out of her clogs and limped across the floor. Even though October had come, she was not wearing socks. Carl Sigvard could see mud on her dirty long johns underneath her skirt. When she sat down next to him, he had to turn his head from the overwhelming smell of alcohol and unwashed body.

"Did you hurt yourself?" he asked as he tried not to breathe.

Ann-Mari touched her forehead. "Eh! No big deal!"

"Would you like a cup of coffee? Sabina was just going to make some, weren't you, Sabina?"

"Yes, indeed."

Sabina's quick hands cleaned the skin over the wound and put on the bandage.

"Well, look at that!" Ann-Mari said happily. "Now people will think that I've gone to war."

"Yes, indeed," said Sabina.

"Has your boy turned up yet?" asked Carl Sigvard.

She turned her watery eyes to him and, melancholic again, shook her head.

Carl Sigvard tried to smile. "He'll be back, you'll see."

"He's not coming back."

Sabina put cups on the table. "Of course he's coming back; he's done so before," she said with some irritation in her voice.

The old woman put her knotty, misshapen hand over her heart and slowly began to rock back and forth. "He's not coming. I feel it right here!"

"Now, now, don't jump to conclusions," Sabina soothed. "You know what a gambler he is. Sure, he'll be back."

Sabina looked exhausted. Carl Sigvard felt increasing tenderness. If they'd been alone, he would have pulled her to him and stroked her short hair, kissed her forehead and the shadows under her eyes. He'd have to recover even faster so that she could take a rest. She was working herself to death.

"We've missed him, too," he said as he turned to Ann-Mari. "We could have used his help around here. When you see him, let him know that we could use a hand as soon as he can come over." He pointed to his crutches. "As you see, I'm not exactly back on my feet yet. But that'll change soon."

"Hardy did help you out," Ann-Mari said and lifted her coffee cup. Her hand was shaking so much that coffee spilled onto the table.

"Yes, he did, and he was hard working when he was out here."

The old woman stared at him helplessly.

"Sabina," he said, "put something stronger in Ann-Mari's cup."

Sabina shot him a disapproving look.

"I know, do it anyway. And I could take a bit in mine, as well," he added. "One thimbleful, that won't hurt us."

Against her will, Sabina got up and got the brandy bottle.

"*Skål!*" he said and raised his cup.

"*Skål*," replied Ann-Mari, sniffling, as she took a swallow. Then she grabbed the sleeve of his sweater and her fingers had strength despite her age.

"He said he was coming here to get the money."

"Yes? What money?"

Ann-Mari said, "He helped you with the cattle. He helped you bring them off Shame Island, and you were going to pay him for that."

"And he was paid," said Sabina. "I went to the bank and got his money."

Ann-Mari blew on her coffee, slurped and swallowed.

"Did he take off with the money?" exclaimed Carl Sigvard. "There's the answer! He took off to blow it all. The temptation was too much for him. What do you think, Ann-Mari? That sounds like something your boy would do, right?"

The old woman did not reply. She stared at both of them and shook her head sadly. It seemed as if deep despair spread over her body. Carl Sigvard couldn't help feeling pity for her.

13

EVEN AFTER ANN-MARI HAD GONE, her body-odor remained in the kitchen. Sabina opened the windows to create a cross-breeze. Carl Sigvard heard the dogs barking outside.

"Are you feeling tired?" Sabina asked him, but her voice was distant. "Shall I help you up to bed?"

"I'm not tired."

"You look tired."

"I just feel sorry for Ann-Mari."

Sabina nodded. "She's led a tragic life."

"She often used to come here—a long time ago now. She was good with animals. She was incredibly strong. You should have seen what she could do."

"Yes, I've heard a lot about her."

"She used to help Svava. She was such a happy person then, though she really didn't have much to be glad about. She was living with Gustav Åström who was run over by a bus. He was drunk as drunk could be, staggering over the road."

"She drinks, too. We shouldn't have offered her any."

"We could certainly comfort her with a drop of brandy."

Sabina turned on the faucet to start the dishes. Her back was straight, her movements sure.

"How much did you give Hardy?"

"Two thousand."

"Well, that money's all gone now. I bet he burned right through it."

"Probably."

"It's a damned shame that we need to rely on hired help like him."

"Well, that's the way things are now. We do."

"You're right. We don't have much choice, do we?"

"I know. I often hired him for Adam's sake, too. He's been like Adam's only friend."

Carl Sigvard reached for the coffee pot and poured some more.

"Friend!" he scoffed.

"Why not?"

"A person like Hardy doesn't know the meaning of friendship. He only thinks about the kind of money he can make. You always defend Hardy, but the only thing he wants from Adam is to make money. Don't you realize? Going on and on about taking Adam out on a tour. Do you think he's doing that for Adam's sake? Not at all! You're a bit naïve there, Sweetheart."

"Sometimes you don't have a choice," she sniffed.

"And one more point. Two thousand crowns! Just to help bring in the cattle! That really was overpaying him, I think."

Carl Sigvard didn't know what had gotten into him. He'd never reproached her or criticized her before.

Sabina dropped the brush into the sink and whirled to face him.

"You want me to move out? Take Adam and get out of here? Is that what you really want?"

His irritability vanished.

"Sabina!" he whispered.

She pulled at her apron ties but couldn't undo them. She jerked until the cloth ripped.

"Calm down," he pleaded. "I didn't mean to hurt your feelings. Of course Hardy should be paid for his work."

Sabina wasn't listening to him. She was already on the way out, and she slammed the door so hard behind her that the entire house shook.

14

RELIEF SWEPT OVER TOBIAS. He was not a murderer. Hardy Lindström was still alive. Maybe Hardy would go to the police and he'd be charged with assault, but he could always say he'd been acting in self-defense. Word against word.

What if Hardy went to Carl Sigvard? Told him what happened in the tack room? There had been greed in his eyes as he walked toward them. The same craving he'd seen when Hardy was telling the legend about the island of naked women.

Well, there was not much they could do about that. They could only hope. Sabina had sounded so certain when she said that Hardy was going to "lay low." She knew him better than Tobias. Maybe because of Hardy's supposed money-making tour for Adam's impersonations.

Tobias searched for a cigarette, but his pack was empty. He might as well go out and shop. He needed something for dinner and maybe he could swing by the state liquor store for some strong beer. He needed something to help him sleep.

The snow had melted and now there was a fine mist. He walked to the grocery store and bought some fruit yogurt, cheese, and a *pain riche*. On his way to the liquor store, he stopped by the bookseller. Before, his latest book had had a good placement in the window, but now it'd been replaced by the new fall books. The bookseller saw him and waved him in.

"Good day, Mr. Author! How's everything?"

"How's everything with you?"

"Just fine. A good fall selection. Many big names. It's really exciting."
Tobias nodded. "What about mine? Is it still selling?"

"Well, of course sales started to drop dramatically once the paperback came out, but we've seen some pick-up since then. Some
people wait for the paperback; they'd rather buy that."

"Hard for you, though," Tobias joked.

"Hard for you, too. By the way, anything new in the works?"

Tobias smiled as if he had a secret. "You never know."

"Is it a mystery, too?"

"You don't make a living with poetry."

"God, no! Poetry! Ha!"

The bookseller was interrupted by a woman wanting some sta-
tionery. Tobias waved good-bye and went next door to the liquor
store. There were so many people there he had to take a number
and wait a long time before he could buy a few cans of beer.

Once he got home, he decided he should go see Görel. He di-
aled the number and Klara answered so fast it seemed she was just
sitting by the phone waiting for it to ring.

"Hi. Is your mom home?"

"Yep."

"Is she alone?"

"Jesus, Pappa, I'm here, too!"

"Don't make fun of me. You know what I mean."

"*He* isn't here if he's the one you're afraid of."

"Listen up, I'm not *afraid* of anybody!"

"He's an expert on murderers and psychopaths!"

It took him a tenth of a second to realize that she was joking.

"I thought I'd stop by for a little while."

"Um, okay."

"If I may."

"Okay."

"Klara, stop saying ok!"

"Okay, I mean, sure."

"Do you think that your mom would mind?"

"Ask her."

"Why don't you ask her for me?"

"She's in the bathroom."

"All right, I'll just come over in a few minutes."

"You are more than welcome," she said with an artificial, grown-up voice.

He drank one of the cans of beer before he walked over. He took the wooden outdoor stairs down to Stora Nygatan, hurried past the library, and prayed a tiny prayer that Marit would not come out just then. Marit did not, but one of her colleagues did, the thin one with the unhappy expression. She greeted him in her usual anxious voice.

Görel was still in the townhouse on Nydalavägen they had bought just before Klara was born. The house was small but well laid out. Four rooms, perfect for a family with children. Tiny paving stones, usually found in gardens, were set both in front and in back of the building. Görel had immediately planted climbing roses as soon as they moved in. She had great ambitions. The entire front of the house was going to be hidden under a carpet of deep red flowers, and she'd described how it would look and even painted an oil painting so that he could see it for himself. But it hadn't happened. No matter what she did, the roses were not happy. The scraggly plants were always attacked by larvae that made the leaves turn black and curl. She gave up immediately. Typical Görel. She tended to give up at the slightest stumbling block.

He was relieved that Klara was able to live in the home she'd grown up in. It was a good neighborhood. People owned their own modest houses and it hadn't been all that expensive to live there. Even though Görel was on disability, she managed financially, and he also knew her parents sent her money every once in a while.

Tobias hadn't seen Görel in over a year. Whenever he visited, he always left feeling depressed. He still had a vague tenderness for the twenty-five-year-old he remembered while at the same time he felt guilty at not having enough energy to stay with her.

Right now he felt strong. He wanted to see how she looked and hear her tell him about her new man. He'd be able to take it. My God, a psychiatrist! It was probably what she needed. Maybe he could relax for a while and let the new guy take on all the responsibility. Wouldn't that be nice!

She was just too needy. Too delicate and ego-fixated. He'd met her at a party which some of his classmates were having. At the time she was into art; they called her the painter. Görel the Painter. She liked the name; it made her feel important. She was thin and always had a defensive look, as if people were threatening and persecuting her.

In the beginning she fascinated him and woke his protective instincts.

He'd been invited to her first show in one of the galleries in the Stockholm neighborhood of Södermalm, where all the artists hung out. He'd bought one of her paintings, too, though he couldn't really afford it at the time. The painting had the appearance of a vagina, warm and opening, and he felt desire whenever he looked at it, a pure erotic excitement.

Görel gave him a discount.

"I see that you want it," she simply said. "In fact, I was thinking of you when I was painting it, although I hadn't met you yet. I knew that you were there. You see, when I created this painting, I was calling you into my life."

She was totally serious when she said it, too. That should have scared him off right away.

When they'd been married for five or six years, he'd come home to find her holding the bread knife which she'd used to rip the canvas to pieces. By then, he already knew that he could not stay with a woman so mentally ill, but he'd managed to hang in there for a total of twelve years.

Her parents had turned their backs on him after the divorce, and that hurt him. He'd always thought they liked him. They had treated him like a son.

The name Elmkvist was on a ceramic plate attached to the door. Klara had made it in school and given it to them for Christmas. She'd painted a tiny ladybug on it, and he remembered how proud she'd been and could hardly contain her excitement when they'd opened the box.

There were lights on all over the house. Sudden uneasiness made him wonder if he should actually press the doorbell. Every inch of wall space inside, every bit of wallpaper held memories which seemed to rush over him, make it hard for him to breathe. At the same time, there was the old feeling of loss as if he'd lost his place in the world the day that he decided to leave her.

Twice Görel had been carried out of the house on a stretcher. Both times she'd swallowed pills and he'd come home to find her unconscious in the bed. At least she was thoughtful enough to do this when Klara was away visiting her maternal grandparents—at least he could give Görel credit for that.

Once she'd called him while he was working as a night guard at the post office. Although she spoke slowly and bluntly, she seemed fully ready to carry out her plan.

"I'm holding a nylon rope in my hand right now, Tobias. Do you think it will hold forty-five kilos? I weight forty-four point two. What do you think, Tobias, will it hold me? And there is a hook in the ceiling. Do you remember when you screwed it in? It was for the iron chandelier that you never liked. Where has that gone, Tobias. Did you sell it? Did you give it away?"

Sitting at work, feeling the rage rise within him. *Why don't you just get it the hell over with then? Stop all our suffering!* But when he got right down to it, he knew he could never say those words.

"Görel, listen to me now," he started, as the line of post office vehicles began to form in front of the gate he was supposed to be opening. "Don't do anything in haste."

He was a master at arguing with Death.

He'd taken down the hook in the ceiling a long time ago. That time he'd put Görel in a mental hospital for care, and he'd been alone to care for Klara many long months. He'd thought that his parents-in-law were on his side, but after the divorce, he realized they were not.

Klara took his jacket. "Come in, don't be shy!"

"I'm not shy."

"I've washed my hair."

"I saw that."

"You were the one who thought I needed to."

"Aw!" He gave her a little push.

He entered the living room and heard the sounds of birds along with rhythmic drumming.

"Have you gotten some parakeets?"

"No, it's a CD recorded in the Amazon. It's awesome, isn't it?"

"Yours?"

"Yep."

"You can buy something like that in this tiny town?"

"Rikard gave it to me. He's been to the Amazon, too, and he's told us about it. It sounds really cool."

"So he's an explorer as well as a psychiatrist?"

"Come on, Dad, don't be jealous!"

He heard someone coming down the stairs and turned to look. Görel, wearing a long, red velour dress, looked at him with surprised eyes. She appeared regal: her entire body had a new, self-confident bearing.

"Good day, Tobias," she said, holding out her hand as if they never had known each other, as if he'd never slept with her sharp spine against his stomach, as if he'd never dried away the snot and slime from her face after a bout of crying.

"Good day," he said, self-consciously.

"We don't see you here much these days."

"No, I'm often busy writing."

She studied him attentively. Her thin lips were pale and chapped. The ring finger on her right hand wore a huge brass ring with a runic inscription.

"I've already brewed some tea. Come, let's sit down and have a cup together."

The sofa was the same, covered in worn-out nut-colored corduroy. He remembered placing Klara sideways on it, right after they'd come home from the maternity ward. He'd wrapped her in a flannel blanket. She looked like she was wrapped in swaddling clothes, and he had held her close as he tried to get her to take a bottle.

Görel had been unable to breastfeed; her sore nipples were too sensitive.

"How are you?" he asked as he put his mug of tea on the dusty, cluttered coffee table. A heap of newspapers and a scissors were lying on the floor. A number of cut-out obituaries stuck out from underneath a copper bowl.

Görel stretched her arms in front of her knees.

"I'm fine," she said, inhaling.

"What's that all about?" Tobias asked, pointing to the obituaries.

"I'm making a collage."

"With obituaries?"

"There's so much symbolism in them. You, an author, should understand that."

"Uh-huh."

"What about you?" she asked.

"I've been down at the farm; my dad injured himself. Maybe you heard."

"Klara told me."

"He's doing better now."

"Glad to hear it. You know, I always liked Carl Sigvard. He had such calm about him, a sense of pride. He always reminded me of Sitting Bull."

"I see."

"You can't believe how sad I was when I heard he'd hurt himself. Nothing ought to happen to your dad; he's been hurt enough in this life."

Tobias nodded lamely.

"And how is Sabina doing?"

"Fine, I guess. She's gotten a new puppy."

"A puppy? How sweet!" exclaimed Klara, who was coming out of the kitchen with a plate of Swedish ginger snaps. "What kind of a dog is it? What's its name?"

"I don't remember. He's a regular dog. His name is Frett."

Silence descended. The CD with Amazonian music had ended. Tobias wanted to lift his mug of tea, but found that he couldn't. His hand was shaking so hard he wouldn't be able to drink. He also needed a smoke.

"Tobias, may I ask you something?"

"Yes?"

Görel leaned over the table and he was able to notice fine lines and wrinkles in the skin around her eyes. He waited for her to ask her question. She observed him without moving and did not take her eyes from him.

"What is it?" he asked at last.

"I just felt a sense of overwhelming sadness looking at you."

"Why is that?"

"I can't explain." She placed both her hands on the table, holding the edge. He thought she would touch him, place her hands on his, but instead she recoiled.

"You are not in harmony with yourself," she said softly. "That's what I see and it makes me sad."

Harmony. Something her idiot psychiatrist had pumped into her head. *You must be in harmony with yourself.*

"You're having a difficult time, Tobias. Something is torturing you."

He got up. "I have to have a cigarette. Be right back."

He stepped outside onto the gardening pavement stones. The garden furniture was still set up on the lawn, furniture that was not meant to be outdoors in the rain. He'd told her that many, many times: *The legs will rot, Görel; they're made of wood.* They looked like they would soon fall to pieces. When he'd lived there, the furniture was always put into the garage for storage. He'd put a rack under the ceiling where they could store a number of things. But now Görel had no car, so she rented out the garage to someone else.

He inhaled the smoke deeply and thought about the neighbors. He wondered whether they were even the same ones. They hadn't seen much of them; Görel had been much too unstable.

Harmony with yourself, he thought and shuddered. He was standing outside in his socks; he ought to have put on his shoes before he'd gone outside.

I'd better go back home, he thought. *It was stupid to come here.* He looked at Görel through the window. She appeared to be daydreaming. Klara was standing next to the CD player. *I've got to get away from here.* The thought leapt through his brain. *I have to get away!*

15

THE NEXT DAY HE LEFT FOR JÖNKÖPING. It was a cold, clear day and there was frost on the trees. He slipped and fell right in front of the train station, hurting his tailbone.

To his relief, he saw that he had an aisle seat. He hated sitting between some stranger and the window; he needed to stand up and walk around whenever he felt like it without troubling his fellow passengers. But once he got to his car, a woman his age was already sitting in his seat.

"Excuse me, this is my seat," he said, trying to be friendly.

The woman jumped and turned bright red in the face.

"Please, I have to sit here," she pleaded. "I'm somewhat claustrophobic. I asked for a seat next to the aisle, but they didn't give it to me."

It would sound stupid to say that he was also claustrophobic. He shrugged and struggled past her.

He'd brought along the novel his talk was based on. He hadn't been able to find his old notes, so he'd have to cobble together a new talk. He leaned back in his seat and watched how the frozen landscape opened up from his panoramic window. He tried to come up with a good beginning.

After a while, he noticed the woman next to him was looking at him.

"Excuse me," she said. "Aren't you that author?"

"This one?" he lifted it and pointed to his name on the cover. She peered at the cover nearsightedly, and then held out her hand to introduce herself.

"Åsa Sevedsson. I'm a teacher of Swedish. But we haven't . . . uh
. . . used any of your books in our classes."

"Well, I haven't written that many."

"True. And that genre . . . well, I saw you on TV, which is why
I recognized you. Do you write short stories any longer? I liked
your short stories."

"Well, you can't survive on those. Nor from poetry."

She looked at him over her glasses.

"What? I thought that writers wrote because of an inner drive,
because they had to."

"You're one hundred percent correct there."

"I didn't mean it quite like that."

"So what *did* you mean?"

"It's really not my business, but you seem to have sold out."

"Sold out?"

"That's right."

"You make me sound like a prostitute! Is the mystery genre
worse than others? Is that what you're really saying?"

"You will hardly win a Nobel Prize writing that stuff."

Tobias began to get angry. "I don't care about the Nobel Prize!
I'm trying to make a living by writing! Give the readers a good story
they'll enjoy! Why are mysteries seen as less than real literature?
Some works are just as good as Singer or Márquez. It's old-fashioned to look down on mystery novels. Times have changed. In your
field, you ought to know that."

She took off her glasses and began to clean them carefully.

"I haven't read your latest book," she admitted. "I remember
when it came out. I thought, 'too bad, another good author is falling
into the crime novel pit.' I thought it was a great pity."

"Shouldn't you read my book before you tell me what you
think of it? The critics were positive. And now, if you'll excuse me,
I have some work to do."

It was hard to collect his thoughts again after that. She was too
close; he felt her eyes follow his every move. He started to feel more
and more desperate. How was he ever going to get this talk to-

gether? He thought, *I can't just read a passage out loud; the ladies will be angry.*

He thumbed through his book, skimming here and there. He had an unbearable longing for a cigarette. He turned his head toward the wall and shut his eyes, but he felt the animosity streaming toward him from the strange woman beside him. He was not used to being recognized. Sure, a few times in Södertälje it had happened, but nowhere else. He'd never had anything bad happen to him because he was an author; rather the opposite. Though once a crazy person had gotten aggressive and asked too many personal questions. Right after the last book had come out, a letter had thumped into his mailbox from an anonymous antiques dealer, who'd felt insulted by its contents. Mostly people left him alone. But now this woman had hit a sore spot, made him feel split in two and disrupted his concentration even more than it had been.

The woman got off at Mjölby, but there was little time left to work before the stop at Nässjö.

Solveig was the name of the woman from the Stickvis cultural center, who had engaged him for the evening's event and had promised to meet him at the Jönköping station. He realized the intention behind the name of Stickvis. Jönköping had once been a center of matchstick manufacture, so stick-by-stick instead of step-by-step must have seemed a witty joke.

Well then, he thought, *let's get on with it, since there's nothing else I can do.* He lit a cigarette. It had been torture on the train without smoking. The train from Nässjö to Jönköping was already waiting for them at the platform, and he was only able to take a few puffs before he had to board.

Tobias was freezing. Behind the Jönköping train station, there was nothing but open space all the way to Lake Vänern, and the wind was sweeping from the north over the lake. He lifted his collar as protection from the icy wind and took a look around. He stomped his feet and walked around with his briefcase over his shoulder. A woman's voice came from right behind him.

"Hi, Tobias. That's you, right?"

"It's me."

The woman held out her hand. "I'm Solveig. Welcome to Jönköping. Did you have a good trip?"

"It was fine."

Solveig was in her sixties. She was wearing a bell-shaped skirt made of large-striped fabric, and she wore low shoes with silver buckles. Her hair was disheveled and straw-like. Once they sat down in the car, Tobias would notice the scent of musk oil, the same kind of perfume Görel used. He felt vague nausea.

Solvieg's tiny Golf had been parked farther down the street, and it was difficult to start.

"I don't know what's gotten into it," she groused. "It's starting to get old and rusty. And it's not the only thing around here which is!" She looked at him and laughed; her mouth was wide and happy.

Tobias tried to laugh too. However, a headache was seeping into his brain. He thought that he should have eaten something, a hamburger or whatever tasteless food they might have had in the bistro car.

The afternoon rush hour had slowed, if there even had been a rush hour in this provincial city. Once Solveig had gotten the car started, she peeled off at high speed, passing several cars with nerve-wracking moves before they got onto the highway. He had to restrain himself from grabbing her arm and begging her to slow down.

They arrived at last.

"Hope you're not hungry," Solveig said as she locked the car. "I had intended to have some coffee ready for you but our hot plate just broke. I imagine that you ate on the train."

"Yeah," he said, not wanting to go into it.

Stickvis was located in the basement area of a normal apartment building on Österängen. A piece of paper was taped to the door:

Night author *Tobias Elmkvist talks about his writing and his books. Come hear him! Thursday, October 4th, 19:00. Donation at the door: 30 crowns.*

Really inviting, for sure.

It was a long room with small rectangular windows high up near the ceiling. A table was placed in front to act as a lectern, and rows of well-worn chairs were set up before it. Tobias hung up his coat.

"Do you often have authors come?" he asked in an effort at small talk.

"Once or twice a year. We don't have much money. Typical for small organizations. So that's why we have to ask for donations at the door. Last year Elsie Johansson was here, and you can bet the place was packed. People were standing all the way to the door. Two hundred people! Good thing that the fire station didn't know about it." She laughed heartily. "We got six thousand crowns that night! Our all-time record!"

Tobias felt totally uncomfortable. Two hundred people! He was usually happy if ten people showed up.

Solveig chatted away. It was clear that she was the firebrand behind this outfit she'd helped found in the seventies.

"There were times when we were close to shutting down," she said. "And people were suspicious of us at first." She lowered her voice. "We have a great number of highly pious people here in town, so many that you wouldn't believe it! The Lord is in charge here and keeps his punishing hand held high over the people. You know they call Jönköping the Jerusalem of Småland. But we survived against all odds, and last year we even celebrated our thirtieth year. We had marathon readings here at our headquarters and also in the Courthouse Park, and they were terribly popular."

"Congratulations," Tobias said.

It was six-thirty in the evening. Solveig placed a glass of water on the lectern. "We can't offer much, but it's well-meant," she said.

Then she opened up the door, pulled a table toward it, and set out the ticket book and a battered green cash box.

She smiled encouragingly at him.

"How's it going? You look tired."

"No problem," he lied. "I am right in the middle of an intense writing period."

"That sounds wonderful! I've always wished I could write. I mean, write something big. An entire book. I've managed to scratch out a few poems and some of them even appeared in the *Jönköping Post*.

"How nice."

"Well, now we must just wait and see how many souls will turn out. It's a real lottery. Sometimes there are not very many. I think it depends on what's on TV. I'm not a big TV watcher myself. I can make my life interesting on my own."

She was almost a parody, a left-over hippie from the sixties. All she needed was a pair of granny glasses. Still, he felt warmth toward her as he watched her sit at the door and count her stash of change. He hoped that it would turn out to be a good evening for everyone. He'd have to make a true effort.

At ten to seven, voices were heard coming down the stairs and four middle-aged women shuffled inside. They said quiet hellos and found seats in the middle. Then, a female reporter from the *Jönköping Post* appeared. She was thin and bony, and she wore jeans and a light velour jacket with a teddy.

"I just thought I'd listen in for a while," she explained. "I hope that's all right."

Nerves overcame him all at once. His temples throbbed as if he were going to develop an ear infection. He slipped out to the bathroom and swallowed some headache medicine. When he got back, more listeners had arrived. He didn't dare count them, but perhaps there were a dozen. He held his book so tightly that he left fingerprints on the cover. Solveig glanced at him and looked at the clock. She let in one more woman. Not a single man had come. Then Solveig got up from the table and walked over to the lectern. Her hair looked wild, sticking out in all directions, stray tufts everywhere. She placed the palms of her hands together and the murmuring voices stopped.

"Tonight we have the honor of listening to the author Tobias Elmkvist. He will tell us about his writing and his books and we are looking forward to a pleasant time together. Please join me in giving a warm welcome to Tobias Elmkvist!"

He was standing next to her and while the sparse applause died down, he took a seat and placed his book in front of him. His voice was hoarse as he began to talk, so he swallowed and then took a large drink of water.

"I thought I would begin this evening by reading a passage from my latest book."

Tobias read the first and second chapters, which took about a half an hour. He knew that although they were listening, they were not totally pleased; this wasn't what they'd paid thirty crowns for. While he was reading, however, moments of inspiration hit him and he made a few notes as he read. Then he stopped reading entirely and began to talk freely.

"Can you imagine that there are some people who hate mysteries? On the train here, I met someone like that. She was so hateful, I imagined that at any moment she would pull out a revolver and pepper me with gunshot! Is there anyone here who loves mysteries?"

The women nodded, a few even raised their hands. At that moment he really hit his stride. From the corner of his eye he could see the young reporter suddenly scribbling notes. The audience had turned into a dark mass with white faces. He spoke whatever came to mind and let the words fall where they would.

"While I was reading did you notice my main character, Leo Pullman? Is there anyone here who's read the book and gotten to know him? Well, I didn't want the same kind of protagonist as the other mystery writers, you know, Wallander, van Veeteren, and Winter, the whole gang. No, my guy is a theologian at heart; imagine that, someone studying to be a priest! Instead, he chose police work, and the murders that he has to deal with are so gruesome that . . . well, you can imagine. It's hard to talk about a mystery without revealing too much. But evil deeds, that's what my books are about. Evil, think about that. What a terrible sound in just the pronunciation of the word! Evil attacks without warning. It's like going to the lake to take a swim. You start at the edge of the water and begin to walk in. It feels cool and pleasant on a hot day, but the waves are strange because the weather is about to change, and then you take one more step and the bottom drops away from you. Your feet are in the water with nothing to stand on, and suddenly you are surrounded by the depths and darkness. Evil comes all too quickly. It never comes when your time is up but right in the middle, when your life is in full swing. . . ."

All of a sudden the lights went out. The room was stifling and dark, and for a few moments, deadly silent. Maybe the audience thought this was part of the program. They stayed seated and although they moved, rustled in the darkness, they said nothing. Tobias had started to stand up, but slowly sank back into his seat. A spreading sense of unreality filled his body, his hands fumbled on the table-turned-lectern, searching for his glass of water.

He wanted to say *Hello there!* But no sound came to his lips. His heart started to pound. His throat was dry; he tried to clear it, reached again for the water, then he heard a click and trickle, and he realized he'd knocked the glass over. As if from a distance, he heard the audience whisper; someone yelled. He kept staring with wide eyes, and when the door was open and light streamed in, he saw who was standing there with his hand on the switch: tall, broad shoulders, his hat over his blond hair, his mocha jacket with the collar up, the chin sprouting a blond beard—Hardy Lindström.

16

CARL SIGVARD STILL SAT IN THE KITCHEN. The faucet dripped. Sabina had angrily rushed out of the house, which was so unlike her. Very strange. Using up a great deal of his strength, he got to his feet and hobbled to the faucet to turn it off. Her apron was lying on the floor. He poked at it with one of his crutches, then lifted it and set it on one of the chairs. Sabina had always had that apron. It was white with sunflowers although time had faded the flowers into blotches.

He wanted to go after her, but he didn't dare. The outside stairs were covered with ice, slippery as glass. He opened the door and yelled out into the darkness: "Sabina! Come back!"

The sound made the dogs start to howl in their dog run.

He'd experienced this before with Svava: her outbursts of rage and his meager attempts to make up. Up until now, things with Sabina had been so much simpler.

She'd come to the countryside from Västervik one evening when the pop group Göran Edgrens was playing at the outdoor dance floor. She came with two other women, friends from work. They were all the same age, around forty. He noticed her immediately, her straight posture, her spare facial features, something almost masculine about her, and he'd always liked that kind of woman. As steady and secure as a Swedish Ardienne.

She seemed happy when he'd asked her to dance. It was August, the time of the root vegetable harvest, and warm long into the night. In spite of her body type, she danced quietly and easily and followed his lead without mistakes.

When the night was over, she told him where she lived but that she was obliged to ride back with her three friends.

"Come and visit me if you want," she said, moving her braided hair near his nose. Shy but direct at the same time. He liked that.

So, a week later, in the evening, he went to visit her. She lived on the top floor of a house right on the edge of town. The house had asbestos cement sheeting. It was gray and shabby and there was no grass around it, just gravel and plantain. In her situation, she could not choose where to live. As a single mother, she had to take care of Adam. The boy's father had been a seaman and was long gone.

"The whole thing was a mistake," she told him later on. "I was head over heels in love with him, the kind of great passion where you don't think or see clearly. It only took a few months before I came to my senses. We had nothing to talk about. We were silent and it was clear it was over between us. But I'd already gotten in the family way and that was not so easy to get out of. So we got married. I agreed to that because what else could I do? It was a simple ceremony, not a big party or anything. I thought marriage would be best for our baby no matter what, but we hardly ever lived under the same roof. Of course, he came home whenever he was on shore, and he gave me money and brought presents for Adam. I have to say that he was a kind man. He drank a great deal but was never violent, just talkative and sentimental. No, it didn't work out so well."

"Is he still at sea?"

"No, he's been dead for some time. When they were loading cargo in Rotterdam, he was walking under a winch when something broke and the entire load fell on him."

"Did you ever think about abortion?"

"The pregnancy was too far along. I hadn't noticed anything. My periods continued the first few months, and I didn't suffer morning sickness at first, either. By the time I knew, it was just too late."

"You've certainly had your burdens to bear," he said. "Life is not always a bowl of cherries."

"No, very few of us receive our share of cherries."

"When you come to visit me, I'll take you to Marie's Comforting Spring," he said. "It's your turn to visit me. And I'll take you on a trip to Shame Island."

Sabina sent Adam to a summer camp for a few weeks to give herself some free time. Carl Sigvard did not know much about her son yet, but had heard that he was "difficult to raise" and "special." That was how she described Adam.

She came by bus one Saturday morning and this was the first time he had seen her in daylight. She had taken the trouble to look attractive. She wore her hair styled into one braid down the back. She wore a red dress with a wide skirt and she also had on a pearl necklace. She had red polka-dotted cloth shoes, tied with shoelaces. She loved things with spots, he learned, and it touched him to remember her shoes.

He'd gone to the bus stop to meet her that morning. First he took her to his farm and showed her everything. He bought almond cookies and made some coffee which they drank outside. She poked around in the barn, praised the pigs and the new pens he'd just built for them.

Then they went down to the lake where he kept his rowboat. He had a motor, too, but it wasn't working so he had to row, which didn't really bother him. She was wonderful, tanned, good to look at. After a while, they changed places and he watched her sit and row with her strong round hands.

The cattle were outdoors at their usual summer pasture. They were leery when the two of them rowed up, but he still took the opportunity to look them over. He could tell right away Sabina was used to animals. She found a stone to sit on and let the animals come up to her. He noticed that a long tongue had made her entire ear wet. Her delighted laugh made the young animals shy away, but they weren't really afraid, just gave some playful leaps.

He led her up the hill and down toward Mörkviken, the inlet between the island and the mainland. Marie's Comfort Spring was located there. The day was unbearably hot. Sabina bent down and cupped her hands in order to catch the water bubbling up from the ground. Her lips touched her palms.

As they relaxed nearby, he told her about the brutal legend of the women who were banished here if they'd been caught in prostitution or adultery.

"I don't know how true it is," he admitted. "I hope it isn't true, but on the other hand, people have always been cruel, filled with evil."

"So only the women were punished?" she asked.

He nodded. "You know how it was in the olden days. Other cultures are still like that today."

She filled her hands with water and cooled her neck and arms.

"I bet many of those women weren't even guilty, just victims of malicious gossip," he continued. "Therefore, people started to call this spring Marie's Comfort Spring."

She gave him serious attention. He had the desire to kiss her, and so he did, and then took her fingers, weaving them between his own.

"So who was Maria?" she asked.

"Maria was a servant girl on a large estate in this area. The mistress of the house developed a grudge against her, probably thinking that the girl was trying to tempt the master of the house. She decided to swear in court that she had seen the girl seducing the master. That was enough. So they rowed Maria out here to Shame Island. In those days people were harsh, even more so than now. She was not allowed to take any clothes and no food either, and the women who'd been brought here earlier were all dead. She was innocent of the charges, poor Maria, and they say that this spring appeared from the ground so that Maria could at least slake her thirst."

"That's a grim legend," Sabina said. She knelt and took another cupped handful of the bubbling water. He drank, too. This water was said to be life-giving and to have youth-retaining properties. They were alone on the island that afternoon with only the cattle there. They undressed and he observed how she folded and stacked her underwear and her red dress neatly, how she placed her shoes next to each other, how she undid the clasp of her necklace. He took her hand and showed her how they could climb down to the water without slipping. This was not a natural swimming hole. The water was colder and deeper than on the other side of the island as the inlet was almost always in shade from the high hill.

Sabina went into the water on her stomach and swam directly forward. Her braid flowed behind her like a shiny, supple snake, and for a moment, he was afraid. He turned and waded back to shore, then watched her turn around and swim back to him in a straight line. She was smiling; her eyes were sparkling. He held out his hand to her and then showed her the most secure rocks, and when she climbed out of the water, he stroked the water from her body, stroked her entire large, light body, letting his hands become acquainted with it.

Sabina's apartment was on the top floor of the asbestos-covered building. Below hers was the apartment of her landlord, an elderly confirmed bachelor. He was hard of hearing, which was a plus for them. Other landlords would have evicted them long ago, Sabina told him.

Meeting Adam was something of a shock. Sabina had never mentioned Adam's age, and he'd imagined a child of ten years. Perhaps, somewhere in his subconscious, was the image of his lost ten-year-old son, Tobias.

They walked into Adam's room together. He was sitting cross-legged in the middle of the floor with his forehead against his knees. Carl Sigvard was gripped by the impulse to turn and flee. Sabina hastily gave his hand a gentle pat.

"I did tell you he was like this," she said, quietly. "I don't know why. I've never gotten a real answer."

She went up to Adam on tip-toe and touched his shoulder. Adam stiffened, straightened his back, opened his slit eyes, and fastened his stare on Carl Sigvard.

"Adam," she said, cajolingly. Her voice had changed, tense and urgent. "It's time for you to meet Carl Sigvard. He is a nice man. He will like you."

Adam released a guttural, wrathful sound from deep within, leaned over and began to rock again. Sabina held him tightly, pulling his tousled head to her chest.

"He isn't used to changes. He can't handle them as well as other people. Everything takes time for Adam. Right now, he's just returned from summer camp. I think he's longing to return. Is that right, Adam? Do you want to go back to summer camp?"

Carl Sigvard later learned that the unusual thing about Adam was that he could change from the slobbering, rocking zombie into a person who could talk with an almost normal voice as Adam did then. He took hold of his mother's wrists, moved them, and stood up with surprising agility.

"At camp there was a girl who loved me true," he declared, and right after that he began to sing a song which Carl Sigvard recognized from the radio. That strange combination of man and boy stood beneath the ceiling lamp and sang with a clear tone and almost perfect pronunciation:

Love me tender, love me dear . . . 'til the end of time.

A few months after Adam was born, Sabina had realized something was wrong with her infant. Her husband had already gone to sea, and she was on her own with no one to talk to. She went to the state children's clinic, but no one was concerned.

"Children differ so much. He's just maturing a little late."

Her son slept a great deal and, although her breasts were filled to the bursting with milk, he appeared uninterested in nursing. It took many hours to nurse him and she had to pinch him on his feet so that he would open his mouth to cry, and then she would hastily place her nipple into his mouth.

"He didn't walk until he was almost two years old," she revealed to him, and Carl Sigvard felt that she had never told anyone about Adam's early years, not even her close friends. He was the first person she trusted with her story.

"Where did you keep him during the day?" he asked. "Didn't you have to work?"

"I brought him to a woman who did some child care, but it didn't work out. She had no patience with him and he is what he is.

Finally, I found a child care center. One person looked out for him. She'd had a little brother with Down's Syndrome. But Adam doesn't have Down's; he has something else. Still, what's the point of a label? These kinds of children are still children with individual personalities just like we have."

By then it was late in the evening. They were lying in her wide bed and they could hear Adam's rustling snores. They had an hour of respite. She was in the habit of giving Adam something at night to help him sleep.

"In many ways, he is just like a small child," she continued. "He can be so upset and unhappy if something doesn't work out the way he'd expected. It's actually not complicated at all to be with him. I want you to understand that."

In the beginning, Carl Sigvard used to worry about Adam's bouts of rage. He felt like he was walking on eggshells. It seemed that these bouts would come without warning, and then Adam would be uncontrollable and throw things around. At first, once Sabina had moved into the house, Carl Sigvard felt that things were almost unbearable and at times he regretted the whole thing, wanted to tell Sabina to take her son and move out.

But he got used to the situation. Adam became calmer as he learned his way around and got used to his new bedroom.

Ten years had gone by since Sabina had moved in with Adam. Carl Sigvard had bought her Frett the puppy as a ten-year anniversary present.

What should he do now? There was nothing he could do. He decided to sit back down and wait. Her intense moodiness was something new and made him feel helpless. He also thought about the wound in her flesh, as if from being ripped or torn, the one he'd seen underneath her breast. How could a person get a wound like that? Did it tear through her clothes? She'd been very strange the last few days. Was she starting menopause?

He heard footsteps on the gravel and the puppy's eager yelps. The door opened, a cold burst of wind swirled over the floor.

"Sabina!" he called out.

She entered the kitchen and she was just like normal. Frett was jumping around her legs. She got a bowl and ran some water into it. Frett drank, splashing water everywhere.

"I think that Frett can stay indoors tonight," she said in a normal tone.

"I'm sorry if I made you unhappy," he said.

"I've put it out of my mind; it's not that big a deal. I've gone to the barn and seen to the animals. I also wanted to make sure that Ann-Mari had left. I don't want people poking around our place, messing with our business."

"Forgive me for what I said about the money," he said.

She sat down next to him and took Frett onto her lap, holding the puppy's nose and shaking it whenever he tried to nip her.

"His teeth are bothering him. It's not so easy to be a little puppy."

"No indeed. And it sure as hell isn't easy being a human being either," he agreed.

17

TOBIAS LAY ON A STRANGE FLOOR. Heavy striped carpet was on a level with his eyes. It touched his forehead; he smelled dust. Tobias retched as if he were going to throw up. He couldn't raise his eyes, kept his eyelids half-shut and tried to remember. It seemed as if his life had happened a long time ago, his days, his nights. Had he begun this journey far away, his last journey?

Somewhere above him he heard the flash of a camera, the sound of a woman's voice.

"No pictures, leave him be, wait a moment."

He decided to open his eyes.

Everything came back. He turned his head, saw rows of bare chair legs, the dust and gravel on the floor, lights on in the room now, florescent lights. There was a man holding a camera, aiming it down, ready to click again.

The woman in the striped skirt was on her knees by Tobias and now she stood and marched over to the photographer.

"Please don't use those pictures in the newspaper," she said in a pleading voice.

Tobias sat up slowly and with great difficulty. His shirt was damp on his back. He shivered. He pressed his forehead with his fingertips, felt it inch by inch.

"Please . . . what happened?" The woman had come back to him. Worry made her face look puffy.

"I don't know. Everything turned black."

"It was my fault," said the photographer. "I was trying to sneak in and I knocked off the lights by mistake."

"Sorry," Tobias said. "Nothing like this has ever happened to me before."

"I know what's going on," said the young journalist coming closer. Her legs were thin in her jeans and the soles of her shoes seemed made of tractor tires. "You're burned out. This happened to me once. First you feel tension in your back and prickling in your neck and then everything disappears. Take it easy if you can. I imagine it's hard since you're a free-lancer; you can't take any sick days."

The woman in the skirt started to talk. Her name came back to him: Solveig. "He was looking tired when he got here. I asked him, and he said . . . ."

"Where did everybody go?" Tobias asked. He felt totally wiped out.

"It's well past eight o'clock. We usually break up about then. You seemed about finished with your talk anyway, though it was getting creepy with that talk about evil. Then the lights went out, an effective and dramatic end."

Tobias stood up and brushed at his clothes. He was given a new glass of water, which he drank.

"Can I take a few pictures?" the photographer asked. "I'm in a bit of a hurry, so I hope it's okay."

Tobias nodded and walked over to the wall by the door, stood there with his back braced against it.

The photographer protested. "Oh, no. That would only make the usual boring portrait. Please, at least hold up your book!"

Tobias went back to the table and picked up his copy of *Night*. He found it wet from the glass he'd knocked over and wiped it on his pants.

"All right, let's go," the photographer said.

A flash. Tobias tried not to blink. He tried to say *cheese,* tried to relax. Once they finished, he stopped the photographer from leaving.

"Earlier, when you got here . . . ."

"I'm really sorry about that. I was totally clumsy. I really didn't mean to cause a disturbance."

"Don't worry about that. But when you got here, I have to ask . . . were you alone or was someone with you?"

"With me? You mean Lotta, the journalist?"

"No, not her. A man, wearing a hat. A beard that appeared dyed yellow. A mocha jacket."

The photographer shook his head. "Nope."

"Are you absolutely sure?"

"Yeah, it was just me. Lotta and I were supposed to arrive together but I was running late. I don't know what the hell you're talking about."

"I thought . . . ."

"No way, man. No one was here but me. I wanted to sneak in without being noticed, and then I hit the damned lights."

Solveig placed her arm around Tobias' shoulders. The room was empty except for them.

"I was really scared," she said. "First I thought you were giving some kind of performance. When I heard you fall, though, I realized it was for real. How are you feeling now? Did you hurt yourself?"

"I'm fine," he said. "It's just that I've been really stressed lately. Maybe this is just the result. Sorry that things went crazy there at the end."

She laughed contentedly.

"That's for sure! The ladies aren't going to forget this for a long time! You can bet on that!"

Solveig turned off the lights and locked the door. Then she drove him to a small hotel in the middle of town.

"Thanks for coming. It was nice to meet you, but now my cats are waiting for me at home."

Once Solveig drove away, he felt really abandoned. His hotel room was simple and small: a bed, a table, a chair, and a TV which was hung on the wall so that you could watch it from the bed. There was nothing to do. He thought that he might be able to have a beer and a sandwich at the hotel, but there was no restaurant. Even the reception desk closed.

He decided to take a walk outside. Nervous and angry, he kept looking around. After a while, he ran across a hot dog stand, but when he decided to order something, the nausea and dizziness returned. *I can't faint here, I'd better get back to the hotel.*

The wind was chilly; he wished he'd brought his hat. He walked leaning forward. Then a sudden overwhelming dread overtook him. He whirled around to make sure that no one was following him. That image of Hardy Lindström in the doorway, that scornful expression: did his own overheated mind create it? Hardy appeared so real, so alive.

The wind made his nose run. Tobias stopped to pull out his handkerchief and blow his nose.

Stop it! he told himself. *Just stop it! How the hell would Hardy know that I was in Jönköping?*

Tobias saw a pub along the road. There was a crowd inside, a heavy layer of smoke over the round tables. He went up to the bar and ordered a beer. He drank it quickly and immediately ordered another. He was left in peace; no one seemed to notice him. Carefully he looked from face to face around the room. No, no Hardy Lindström here. He realized how unrealistic seeing Hardy would be. At that moment he decided what he would have to do. He would have to return to the farm and talk the whole thing over with Sabina. Life would be unbearable otherwise. He'd do it tomorrow. He'd get off the return train at Linköping and then rent a car to drive right there.

Back at the hotel, Tobias fell asleep immediately. At three in the morning, he woke up and had to pee. Dream fragments stayed in his brain. He was in a hammock, the same cloth as Solveig's skirt. He lay in it and rocked, was rocked, and he could not move, just lay there and felt ill. Solveig leaned over him. He saw the loose skin of her face, her wide red mouth; she laughed hysterically. A man came sneaking up behind her. His arms reached out from behind each side of her, reached toward him lying helpless as if in a cocoon.

"You're not going to get away, Tobias!" A man's voice. The hands reached. A wound in skin, a wound in the throat, a vein dark blue underneath the pale flaps of skin. The vein dark and clear, pumping blood and strength. He wriggled and tried to close his eyes, and that was when he woke up.

He could not go back to sleep after that, so he got up and took a shower. He let the water run, splash; he washed, scrubbed until his whole body hurt. While he dried off, he noticed that he had bruises on his left arm and hip. It hurt. And his tailbone still hurt from his earlier fall on the ice. He dried off carefully and then walked back into the bedroom leaving the door open and the steam to spread like fog.

'Please don't smoke.' A small sign on the table. He opened the window and lit a cigarette.

Sabina, he thought and he was overcome with a need to call her right away. He grabbed his cell phone, but the batteries were low. At least he'd remembered to take his power cord. It was four in the morning and, from far off, he heard a church bell toll the hour. He thought about what Solveig had said about the protecting hand of the Lord over the people, or was it the punishing hand? Was it the Lord who'd stricken him, knocked him to the floor in the middle of his talk? He felt his head begin to jerk, small, almost un-noticeable spasmodic movements. He took a deep breath and tried to keep still.

Klara, he thought. *For your sake, Klara.* He opened his wallet and took out an old black-and-white photograph where Klara stood with her hands clasped together and her mouth half-open as if she were saying something. The photo was taken outside, but he did not remember where or when. Behind her he could see the side of a wheelbarrow. The ground was wet with rain, but it must have been summer because Klara was wearing a little T-shirt and a short white skirt, and next to her was a speckled cat. Who'd taken that picture? Görel? Yes, now he remembered. The photograph was taken on the farm, and Klara was so soft and tender, like a leaf. And now? Now she was changing; he would no longer have his little daughter, *my daughter Klara*. No, she was changing into someone else, a stranger, someone who would no longer need him the way a child needs her father.

He wiped his eyes and realized they were wet. He was sitting there and crying, but no sound came.

At six in the morning, the employees began to arrive at the hotel. He heard the rattle of dishes and when he opened the door to look down the hallway, he smelled the aroma of coffee. He'd been sitting fully dressed on the bed—tense, fully awake— and now he picked up his suitcase and went to the breakfast area. A tawny girl wearing a black skirt and white shirt was setting the tables. She greeted him sullenly.

The *Jönköping Post* was packed into a newspaper rack, and he took one with him to the table and flipped through it. He saw a picture of himself inside. The journalist, Lotta Andersson, had written a short article. Thank God there was no mention of his fainting episode.

He took a soft-boiled egg from the egg bowl, but when he cracked the shell, it was hard and crumbling. He pushed away the egg cup, drank a few cups of coffee, and ate a slice of bread with a rubbery piece of cheese.

The weather was warmer again, and leaves swirled around his feet as he walked to the train station. He felt stronger now, and the spasms in his head and neck had stopped.

18

TOBIAS RENTED A CAR IN LINHÖPING. He chose the cheapest one available. He drove toward the farm without stopping and, just before two in the afternoon, he pulled up in the parking lot of the outdoor dance platform. The clouds were low, hanging right above the treetops, almost hiding them. The place was deserted and bare, and wet leaves had been blown across the platform's boards.

He locked the car and threw his briefcase over his shoulder. He wanted to get to the farm unseen and find Sabina alone. Water forced its way into his shoes and many times he was near to slipping on the muddy ground. Chanterelles shot up among the rotting leaves. For a moment he remembered Marit and her expectations, what kind of person he was, what they should do together, move in together, turn into a real couple, maybe even have a kid or two. It wasn't too late, biologically speaking. There were even some women who had children at fifty. Marit said she'd stopped thinking about those things, but he knew it wasn't true.

The rain picked up when he reached the edge of the forest. He stopped beneath a fir tree to collect his thoughts. Through the mist, he saw the buildings: the barn, the house, the garage, and the long dog run behind it. Sabina was home. He could see her car parked in the yard. Good, he'd find her sooner or later. The dogs would start barking; he couldn't hide from them. But he did not want a single human being to discover him, and he knew the paths, the ones well hidden, he'd grown up with them. Carl Sigvard would be in the house and hear the dogs start to bark, but he'd think they'd seen a moose or a fox, something they'd caught scent of.

Once, long ago, in the grove of trees, he'd built a hide-out. He'd dragged boards and nails and built a treehouse between two strong branches of a pine tree. It had a roof and a floor, and he'd used a jute sack as a rug. Tobias recognized the tree, but his hide-out was long gone.

How old had he been? It was over thirty years ago.

Before the catastrophe.

He remembered that he'd never been able to show his parents the tree fort. He had longed to hear their happy exclamations of surprise and their approval. He needed their recognition. But his parents had no time. They were busy with something big and threatening, something happening to them and between them, something they hid from him.

That was the worst part, that they would not talk to him about what was happening. But he sensed the danger like a rabbit huddling under tufts of grass from the hawk. He had no idea what was going on. They'd ceased talking to each other, stopped using their normal voices. Their movements changed, too; they walked in a different way.

Svava kept to her horses and sometimes a man came to visit her. After Carl Sigvard had driven his tractor to the fields, Svava and the man would disappear into the tack room. Svava's cheeks had a red flush to them when she told Tobias, "We have to go through some paperwork, Tobias. Go outside and play somewhere."

Tobias would go to his hiding place. One evening he decided to stay there. His parents would have to react, call his name, search for him. Finally hunger forced him to return home. He saw Carl Sigvard standing on the front porch. His face was empty and blank while his eyes searched.

"Where's Mamma?" Tobias asked.

"You don't know where your mother is?"

His father grew quiet. His lower lip shot out. He appeared to be an alien like the ones Tobias had seen in comic books. His father's glittering eyes scared him.

"I'm hungry," Tobias piped up.

His father blew out a lungful of air. He grabbed Tobias by the arm and pulled him into the kitchen. Made him some sandwiches from hardtack and cheese. They crackled like gravel when Tobias chewed them. He wanted to tell his father about the tree fort he'd built. He wanted his father to ask, "Did you ever make anything from those boards I gave you?"

He wanted his father to take his hand and look at the blisters, blow on them, put a bandage on the places where the skin had rubbed away.

His father did not even look his way.

"I think it's time for you to go to bed, boy. There's school tomorrow."

That evening he lay in bed and froze. His legs felt like clumps of ice. He held his breath and tried to figure out how long it would take before he died. Eventually, he dozed, but he woke again from a whining noise. At first he thought it was the wind blowing through the cracks, but within the whining he heard voices. His parents were hissing and whispering. He put his pillow over his ears so he would not hear them.

They seemed to stop being his parents. Rather they seemed to blame him as if he were the one who caused all their troubles. Nothing he said or did could reach them. And still he had no idea what would happen.

Not until he and Svava were sitting in the car driving away from the farm did he understand. They had a moving van behind the car with some of the furniture in it. She said, "You are going to grow up in a real city. It'll all be fine, Tobias. I promise."

He was in the back seat. There was something wrong with the seatbelt up front so she did not want him to sit there. He used his fingernails to pinch the thin skin underneath his balls. He said nothing. There was nothing to say.

As an adult, he thought of the months that followed as a kind of petrifaction. Svava took him to meet Jörgen. "We're not going to move in with him yet; this is just a test period."

Jörgen also had children, two girls, the same age as Tobias. The girls did their best, but he would not warm up to them. When they saw that, they turned spiteful instead. Jörgen kept horses, too, an entire stable, which was so neat and clean that it echoed. Finally Svava told Tobias her plans. She and Jörgen were planning to open a riding school together. Not the average kind of riding school for children, but a special one for elite riders who wanted to polish their skills.

"My little Tobi is an excellent rider," Svava boasted, using her new pattering voice. "He rides like a real man."

Jörgen laughed so that spit appeared in his beard. He was actually a fairly nice guy and he did his best to make friends with Tobias. "I've always wanted a boy. Those two . . . ," and he made a face at the girls who were sitting in the corner of the sofa. They were all in Jörgen's large living room.

Tobias was not able to speak. It was impossible to answer without betraying his father.

They gave him a horse, too. In a manner of speaking.

"His name is Dingo; he can be yours."

Dingo was lively and eager. At least they hadn't forced some old mare on him. Tobias rode a lot, first inside the stable with Svava and then outside. But he did not like the new landscape. It seemed strange and threatening. Even the trees seemed like enemies, keeping their distance from him.

He'd still been a nice guy, that Jörgen.

Svava and Jörgen were a couple for a number of years, but then they separated. He never figured out why. But Tobias began to realize as he got older that Svava wasn't the easiest person to live with.

He'd have to get closer now. The rain increased. As he expected, the dogs began to bark as soon as he left the cover of the forest. They threw themselves against the fence and howled.

"It's me, you idiots!" he muttered. "Don't you recognize me? I was here just a few weeks ago! You crazy mutts!"

Tobias did not see anyone. They were probably having their afternoon coffee break now. He realized how hungry he was. A cup of coffee and a cold meatball sandwich, or one with liver pâté and sliced cucumbers, would hit the spot. *Sabina will have to bring me something to eat later*, he thought.

He approached the barn from the back because there was a way in through a door that used to open on the manure heap. Next to the back wall there was a heap of trash meant for the dump a long time ago, but which had been slowly covered by overgrowth instead. He saw the usual stuff: an old-fashioned lawn mower, a bicycle, some rusty, used-up tools, a refrigerator, a crate of old bottles, a broken TV antenna. When he got closer to the pile, he realized that someone had been there recently and had shuffled the trash around. Some of the grass which had grown in and around was torn up. Something new was there, not just next to the rest, but pushed behind and between as much as possible so it would be hidden, well-hidden.

His mouth went dry when he saw what it was:

Hardy Lindström's scratched-up Vespa.

19

THE BOAR WAS HUMPING A SOW WHEN TOBIAS SNEAKED INTO THE BARN. They gave off a rank, pungent smell. They did not notice him. The enormous pig covered the object of his affection while balancing on his two hind legs. He grunted and panted.

The door to the tack room was closed. Tobias had no intention of going in there. He went over to the pens, and the piglets squealed and ran around as they usually did. Tobias' heart was pounding. Why was Hardy's Vespa hidden among the trash behind the barn? Who'd put it there?

His legs wobbled all at once; his whole body was exhausted. He felt as if he was going to break apart. A shadow started to move in the darkness, and Tobais jumped before he noticed it was a cat. The cat resembled Missan, the one who had lived on the farm over thirty years ago. Maybe this cat was her great-great-grandchild. He bent down and began to stroke the cat's soft, striped fur. The cat began to purr. Tobias picked her up and held her in his arms, dug his nose into that soft warmth. The barn odor was already creeping into his clothes and body; it would seep into the wetness from the rain. The smell would stay inside the rental car and passengers on the train would notice. People would turn their faces away from him and wrinkle their noses. Right now, he didn't care. He stroked the cat's head, felt the skull inside, small and sharp.

Then someone appeared in the doorway. A noise and a ray of light widening. He dropped the cat, and she leapt to the floor with a hiss. Tobias sneaked between the pens. Was Sabina finally coming? He tried to peek over the edge of a pen. Yes, someone was there, but it wasn't Sabina, nor Adam either for that matter. It was a little old woman wearing a long, rustling raincoat. Although he was not able to see her from the front, there was something familiar about her. He remembered her coming to the stable to help with the horses—it was Hardy Lindström's mother.

The old woman swayed as she walked up and down the aisles, peering into nooks and crannies. She walked to the tack room and opened the creaking door. She made a strange sorrowful sound.

What should he do? Should he go over to her? No, no good. He decided to hide farther back behind some sacks of grain.

The sound of feet on wet gravel and the lights went on in the barn. Tobias heard Sabina's voice.

"You back agin, Ann-Marie?" Sabina was using the local dialect, which Tobias had never heard her use before. The vowels were distinctly different.

The old woman did not answer, but began to sob.

"I told you he ain't here. Git it in your head. Ann-Mari. He ain't here."

"Where is he?" the old woman complained. "He was s'pose to git the money."

"He got his money. I went to the bank and I only went to git the money 'cause of him. Two thousand in five-hundred-crown bills. You don't believe me, go ask the bank yourself. I put it right in his hand. You gotta accept it, Ann-Marie. No reason to come running here every day and look for him. He ain't here. He probably went off to the big city and is amusin' himself. You know how your boy is. He ain't no angel. Maybe he got some debts, too. You don't know what he got when he was in jail, so-called friends that want some of his money."

Tobias watched as Sabina draped her arm around the old woman's shoulder, and then gave her a hug.

"Git along home; the weather's turnin' nasty. They said so on TV. A thunderstorm in the middle of October. Have you ever heard of such a thing?"

Sabina went into the tack room once the old woman left. She turned on the light. Tobias got up and walked into the hallway and said her name.

She screamed in fear.

Sabina was wearing her head scarf, but somehow the form of her head was different. He put his finger to his lips.

"Shh, Sabina, it's only me."

"You scared me to death!"

"Sorry, I didn't mean to."

She had been by the desk holding a sheet of paper. She set it down again and straightened her back. "I didn't see you."

"I didn't want anyone to notice. I rented a car and parked it by the dance platform, and walked here through the forest. I was in Jönköping to give a reading and I was on the way back home. But then I decided to hop off the train in Linköping and come here."

"Why would you want to do that?"

"I have to talk to you."

Pain appeared on her face. "What is it that you want, Tobias?"

"Can't we go outside?"

She shook her head.

"I don't want to step foot in there," he said.

"It's raining outside."

"Well, then, let's walk over to the pens."

"What happened . . . between us . . . . It must never happen again."

"It will never happen again." Tobias turned and began to walk away and he heard her follow him. He walked over to the grain sacks where he'd been hidden. Sabina was right behind him, but kept a lookout toward the door.

"I saw Ann-Mari here," he said. He rubbed his arms for warmth.

"She's gone now."

"You're sure about that?"

"Yes, she often comes. I've found her in the barn lots of times. Now she's gone home."

"What does she want here?"

"She wants to find her boy. He's still gone."

"He's not gone to see her at all?"

Sabina nodded. She fingered the edges of her scarf. Tobias had the desire to place his hand beneath it, just to see how it felt.

"I saw something outside," he said instead.

Sabina threw back her head. "What are you talking about?"

"His goddamn Vespa. It's in the pile of trash."

"It's broken. The motor stopped working."

"Huh?"

"He asked me to take it to the dump with all the other trash."

"Is that true?"

Sabina took a deep breath. "Yes."

Tobias took one step toward her and grabbed both her cheeks, squeezing them. "You're lying!"

She tore herself away. "What has gotten into you? Have you lost your mind?"

He couldn't bear it any longer. He pressed his knuckles to his eyes, slid to the floor and began to howl, a noise from deep in his throat, a sound he'd never heard from himself before. She squatted next to him as he sat on the floor.

"Dearest, dearest Tobias. What's really wrong?"

"I can't take it anymore, Sabina. I'm falling apart. He's dead. I know he's dead. It doesn't matter what kind of a game you're trying to play. I saw his body in the tack room. I killed him, I know. A person can't survive with his jugular vein slit. I know that, Sabina. I know and I think I ought to go to the police now. That's what I have to do."

She played with a tuft of his damp hair, wound it around her fingers.

"There's no body," she said, whispering right at his temple. Her breath was warm and sweet. "What are you going to confess when there is no . . . corpse?"

He hiccoughed, seated there, his chin on his chest, hands weighted against the cold floor.

"That's what I don't understand. I saw his body with my own eyes. I knew he was dead. No matter what you say, Sabina, you can tell when a person is dead. They have a strange expression around the mouth and he had it, but then I walked away . . . and I began to wash off and then you came and I ran away because I couldn't look at you . . . or anyone else either."

She cocked her head and the shawl slipped down slightly. She licked her dry lips.

"Would it . . . ," she began.

"Yes?"

"Would it be easier, for you I mean, to know there was a body?"

"It can't be undone!" he screamed. "I killed him and I can't undo it!"

"Shh, Tobias, shh. I'll tell you something if you think it would help."

Tobias moved, settled his back against the wall of the pen. He was so weary he felt he could fall asleep, but he had to pay attention and listen to her. She sat right next to him and stroked his knuckles.

"Well, Tobias, this is what happened," she said so softly that it was difficult to hear her. "The truth is, you did kill him."

Tobias had to close his eyes and take deep breaths.

"When I came back, he was on the floor and it was true what you said. It was clear he was dead . . . blood was everywhere in the room. You looked in shock, so I helped you. You were freezing and I went to get you a clean pair of overalls. Then I watched you run away, and I thought, let him run; let him get through this first part by himself, because I knew how you felt and I felt the same way. Now the end had come, the end had come for you and for me, and not just for us, but also for those we love, for Adam and for Carl Sigvard. How could Carl Sigvard survive something like this? His only son . . . the son he is so proud of. Yes, Tobias, he is proud of you although he could never show it the way you wanted him to. And then a thought came to me . . . yes, a thought appeared to me and I knew I had to act quickly."

"What did you do?"

"I . . . I took him apart. I cut him in pieces."

"Cut him in pieces?"

"Smaller pieces, small enough so I could move them. You know I can do these kinds of things. I've worked in a slaughter-house, and I was very quick once upon a time. And then I cleaned the room thoroughly so that no one would ever be able to detect anything. I can promise you that; no one will ever be able to find anything in that room. You went inside. Did you see anything, any little trace?"

"You . . . cut him in pieces?"

She nodded.

"And then . . . what did you do with them?"

"Remember the raft? The ones we brought the cattle home on? It has those large oil barrels to hold it up, remember?"

He held his breath.

"In them. I stuffed the pieces in them. No one will ever find them there."

"But the smell, Sabina! It's going to start to smell, it's probably already starting to smell!"

She smiled, but her smile was sorrowful. "I put lime over them."

"Huh?"

"I know it works. They used to use lime for mass graves and such during wartime. The lime kind of cuts down on the smell and rotting. Carl Sigvard used lime in the outhouse, and that's where I found some. I promise you, there will be no smell and no one will ever find him. It's a secure hiding place, Tobias. You can rest easy now."

20

SABINA ENCOURAGED HIM TO COME INSIDE.

"We'll just tell Carl Sigvard that you gave a reading and you decided to drop by on your way home."

"Seriously, I can't stay."

"You are completely soaked. You're probably hungry, too. And you look completely wiped out."

"I have to go home. I'll go back through the forest so that no one will see me."

"Well, what if you get sick? You might already be sick. You certainly look sick."

Sabina's hand came up to his forehead and he jerked away before he realized he'd done it. He saw she noticed.

"Why didn't you ever tell me?" he demanded. "Why didn't you say something? Instead you tried to make me think I'd imagined it from my own morbid thoughts."

Sabina said nothing.

"No one, no one can ever imagine something so horrible. Not even my worst nightmares have ever given me the terrible pictures in my head now. You swore to me, Sabina, you swore to me that nothing happened. How could you, Sabina, how could you?"

She stood up and bit her lip. "I thought it was best for us all. It was an impulse, not anything that I thought through. I thought your shock might pass away. I've read that you can repress certain experiences and then be able to get over them and live your life. I did it for your sake, Tobias. Can't you realize that?"

"You shouldn't have lied to me."

"It's not about lying. It's about getting along with life. Being whole people, strong people. We shouldn't feel any guilt and no one should make us feel guilty."

Tobias took a deep breath. "First I have to get used to the real person I've become. I am a murderer. I have to let that sink in and it feels so . . . horrible. How could I look anyone in the eye after this? Pappa? Klara? Marit? How can I look them in the eye and hide behind this secret? They love me. They treat me like the same old Tobias I was, but I'm not that Tobias anymore . . . . I am a man who has taken another man's life."

Sabina remained ram-rod straight.

"Don't accept such an idea! You must do the opposite! Forget that this happened! It's all over!"

"Sabina!" he yelled back."You never even asked me what happened!"

"I felt I knew. Hardy threatened to tell Carl Sigvard. Blackmail, right? That's what he was up to. If he wasn't going to get more money, he'd go straight to Carl Sigvard. Tell what he'd seen. Am I right?"

"That's pretty much it."

"He was a grim, calculating person. That's what he was. Psychopathic."

"I thought you liked him, I mean for Adam. You said he was good for Adam."

"Deep inside, I never really liked him. I pretended to like him; I tried to like him. But I was afraid of him. Even though everything was always so difficult with Adam that . . . no, it's best not to have anything to do with that kind of person."

"What about Hardy's mother? She's sneaking around all the time, you say. How will we get rid of her?"

Sabina grimaced. "Leave that to me. She'll finally give up coming here. It's just that she knew he was planning to come here. She's stuck on that idea, she's a bit . . . ." Sabina pointed to her head.

"What if she goes to the police?"

"Not Ann-Mari."

"Why wouldn't she?"

"A woman like her go to the police? When the police were the ones who threw her beloved son in jail?"

"Can we believe that?"

"Think it through yourself."

The rain was pouring down outside. The light patter on the roof had turned to a roar. Thunder growled in the distance.

"I have to go," Tobias said.

"Do what you want. I obviously can't change your mind. But I have to go back to the house now or Carl Sigvard will start to wonder."

Tobias got to his feet, took Sabina into his arms.

"What will happen to us?" he whispered. "What is going to happen to us, Sabina?"

As he started to leave through the backdoor of the barn, he remembered something.

"You have to get rid of his Vespa. If anyone comes poking around and sees it, there will be a hell of a lot of questions."

"Yes, you're probably right."

"So you lied about the Vespa, too. He certainly didn't ask you to get rid of it."

She looked him straight in the eye. "No, he didn't."

"What do you plan to do with it?"

"I'll find a better hiding place."

He had an idea. "I'll take it with me. I'll throw it in the trunk of the rental car and get rid of it somewhere."

"What if anyone sees you?"

"No one is outside in this weather."

"You're right. Sounds good. Do it, then. But I still don't like the idea of you out and about in all this rain."

He couldn't help laughing out loud. He realized how pathetic he sounded as he said, "A person like me deserves no better."

21

AT TEN IN THE EVENING, TOBIAS RETURNED TO SÖDERTÄLJE. He didn't return the rental car in Linköping but drove it the entire way home. Tomorrow he would take it to the nearest rental agency. It had been a rough trip. He had pushed the Vespa with him through the forest and it was heavier than he'd imagined and the pedals kept getting stuck in the underbrush so he had to keep stopping to pull it loose. The entire time the heavens poured down water, and he was sullen when he finally arrived at the dance platform, exhausted and scratched by branches. The car was where he left it. At first, he couldn't find the keys and for a few terrible seconds he thought he'd dropped them in the forest. That made him desperate. He zipped open his briefcase and dumped the contents out on the gravel, and there the keys were, thank God.

It was impossible to fit the entire Vespa into the trunk. A bit of the front tire stuck out and he searched but couldn't find anything to tie down the lid. So he was forced to drive slowly and carefully, which didn't matter so much in the low visibility of the rainstorm. Just outside Rimforsa, he stopped at a turnout for a leak. Then he took the Vespa from the trunk and pulled it well into the forest, threw it from him, returned and drove away.

He was freezing when he got home; the cold had gone all the way to the marrow of his bones. He'd been able to keep himself warmer in the car by turning the heat to full blast until the inside windows were covered with moisture. He opened the windows and kept driving.

By the time he reached Nyköping, the rain had stopped. He was dizzy with hunger and wondered if he dared to stop at a fast food place, but when he glanced at his face in the rearview mirror, he decided not to bother. Instead, he drove to a gas station and bought some cigarettes, some chocolate bars, and a soda. He stood underneath the overhang and ate the chocolate, one bar after another, and drank as much of the soda as he could at one go. While he smoked, he looked at the newspaper headlines, imagined what they might say: *Famous Writer Murders 27-year-old.*

How old was Hardy? Or had been? Hardy would never be any older than he was that day in the tack room. The flower of youth.

Tobias swallowed and put the can down on the pavement. There was a little left, but he was finished. He needed to pee again but didn't want to go back inside the gas station. The employees had given him funny looks. A man and a woman behind the counter. He could feel their inquisitive looks on his back. They would certainly remember him if the police came around and asked a few questions.

No, he thought to himself, Sabina is right. She knows what she's doing. Watertight. A watertight hiding place. He couldn't help himself: he started to giggle, his entire face twisting as he tried to keep from laughing out loud, the laugh inching up his throat, ready to explode and expose him. And if he could not stop it, he would be laughing hysterically, the way no person in their right mind laughs.

He hurried back to the car and he was freezing. His clothes were stiff and cold, his socks were soaking, his shoes completely trashed. They'd never look good again no matter how they were brushed or dried. You were supposed to stuff them with old newspapers and let the newspapers soak up the water and let the leather have a chance to dry. Who taught him that? Svava? Carl Sigvard? He was going to get rid of these shoes the moment he got home. He was going to wrap them in a trash bag and dump them down the garbage chute. After what these shoes had been through, they would never be the same again.

What a clever woman Sabina was. Clever? She was filled with good advice. And she'd made herself into a criminal, too. She'd decided to take part in his crime. Now there were two of them, and if the police found out, they would both be punished. Tobias thought about his father and felt like weeping. He was filled with tenderness toward his father. He did not want to do this to him; he did not want to cause his father any more pain. His father had had enough suffering in his life. He was the kindest man on earth, that's what Sabina said about him, and then that Hardy had to come along, that scum of the earth, and Hardy had to spy on them. How he'd watched them and decided to use that for his own gain. Did a person like that deserve to live?

Tobias was fourteen years old before he had the chance to go back to his father's farm. By then, he was old enough to ride the train on his own, and Carl Sigvard met him at the station. Carl Sigvard had a new car, a Volvo. He was so short, Tobias thought, as he watched his father on the platform looking for him but not yet seeing him. His father had such a thin neck, and he was wearing a cap that looked new but a few sizes too big.

Then his father saw him. The look in his father's eyes had so much sorrow that Tobias was never able to forget it afterwards no matter how hard he tried.

"Hi there, my boy. I hardly recognized you!"

His father's handshake was hard, as if it were a test. No hug, nothing that sentimental.

"You have any other suitcases?"

"No, just this one."

What could they say to each other after that? Nothing of importance. His father climbed into the car and went through the obligatory questions:

"How's school? You got any friends up there?"

His short obligatory answers.

All the rest, all the things bubbling in their hearts, burning in their heads, none of that came out.

Missan, the cat, was still there. By then she was very old and tired. They were able to talk about her, of course. They could talk about how the number of rats in the barn increased because her hunting skills were diminished. He'd had other cats which disappeared. Maybe a fox got them; there were so many foxes and deer these days. "They come right into the yard and eat the fruit off the trees!"

How Tobias had longed for the farm! During the last four long years, he'd longed for it, imagined it.

Nothing was the way he'd left it.

Later, standing on the platform waiting for the train back, Carl Sigvard had said, "Now you'll be able to come here a little more often. You're old enough to decide for yourself. And one of these days, the whole farm will be yours. Everything I'm working for will be your . . . heh, heh . . . paternal inheritance."

Tobias went right to the shower, clothes and all, as soon as he got into his apartment. After he stripped, he saw his body was covered with bruises and rips. Once he'd dried off and drunk a few glasses of wine, he called Marit. It was almost eleven at night. She wasn't asleep, as he'd feared; rather it seemed she'd been sitting and waiting for him to call.

"May I come by for a while?" he asked.

It seemed as if her nose was runny. "Of course, you know you can."

"You haven't gone to bed yet, have you?"

"No. I'll look out the window in about five minutes and throw down the keys."

As Tobias walked over to her place, he wondered how she would react if she knew who he really was deep down. Would she even consider opening her door to a murderer? Would she take him into her bed, cover him with her sheets?

Tobias no longer wanted to be alone. Maybe Marit could share this burden, even unwittingly. Maybe Sabina was right, maybe he should to try to forget. Especially since this might be the perfect crime. If you could call it a crime. It really wasn't. It was an unfortunate accident, manslaughter at best, not premeditated.

Could his own crime-solver character, Leo Pullman, find the killer in a case like this? No, Leo wouldn't solve this one. The perfect crime. No body and no suspects, either.

What a great idea for a book, he thought bitterly.

Marit had been crying. Her face was red and puffy, her eyes swollen and wet. She was wearing her robe when she opened the door. She threw her arms around him and held him tight right there in the hallway. She pressed her body hard against him. Tobias hated such a scene; he regretted he'd come.

"What's wrong?" he asked curtly.

"Nothing."

"So you're standing here crying for no reason?"

"I'm just sad, that's all. My period is going to start soon. But that's not it."

Tobias pulled himself away from her and stalked into the living room. A watercolor by a local artist hung on the wall over the sofa. The picture showed five women, round and fertile. Two of them were naked, sitting in a meadow, surrounded by naked small children who looked like cupids—chubby, roly-poly. The women were holding their arms out to the children.

Tobias stood in the middle of the living room with his hands in his pockets. He imagined she was hoping he would ask her what she really meant to say. Ask her what was really on her mind. But he could not.

"Well, I am glad you came," she said, though her voice was sad.

"Doesn't look like it."

"Tobias . . . ."

"I'm tired. I've driven a long way. The weather was goddamned awful."

"Driven?"

"I decided to go past Kvarnberga, so I rented a car."

"Why did you do that?"

"Because no trains go to Kvarnberga."

"That's not what I meant. Why did you go back? Did something else happen there?"

"Marit," he said, "my father lives there. He was in an accident. Do I need a reason?"

She didn't answer, turned away and wandered into the kitchen.

"And get out some more of that whiskey, okay?" he called after her. "Let's have a glass together and then let's go to bed. I am so fucking tired." He followed her.

They sat across from each other in the kitchen. She drank a shot of whiskey and grimaced. Tobias noticed a scrape on her nose.

"Did you hurt yourself?"

"Where?"

Tobias pointed to the bridge of her nose.

"Oh, that. It's fine now. That happened awhile ago."

"I see."

"Funny you didn't notice it before."

"Why would that be funny?"

"What about you, then? You look like you've been in a fight."

Tobias stared at his hands.

"So what did you do?" she continued. "Rape someone?"

Marit stared right into his eyes and he turned red.

"That's not the kind of thing to joke about," he said.

She drank some more whiskey. "So what happened then?"

"The dog," he said. He tried to laugh. "Sabina's new puppy. He got lost and we had to go into the forest to look for him. He'd gotten stuck in a thicket."

Marit was silent. He could tell that she did not believe a word. He kept silent, too.

"The rain was awful," he said after a while. "It was hard to drive. I couldn't see the road in front of me, but it finally stopped, thank God."

A watchful look came into her eyes. She said, "I've been thinking a lot."

"About?"

"About us."

Tobias took out a cigarette and rolled it between his fingers as he sat there.

"About how our future might be."

Tobias grabbed the lighter.

"Go out and smoke then!" she exploded.

When he came back from the balcony, she'd already gone in to the bed. She lay on her side, staring at the wall. He stood in the doorway, swaying a little, braced against the frame.

"Do you want me to leave?" he asked quietly.

"I don't know," was the answer from the bed. "No, I don't want you to go."

He slowly took off his clothes down to his underwear. He crept in next to her. She was stiff, chilly. He put his arm around her, but she did not move. She hardly seemed to be breathing.

"Shall we go to sleep now?" he asked.

"Sleep, sleep, sleep!"

"What's wrong with that?"

"Should we sleep our lives away? Is that what you want to do?"

"What are you talking about? We need to sleep just to get through life."

"Life is too damned short as it is."

She didn't usually swear.

"What's really on your mind?" he asked quietly.

"Sometimes I don't know if I am alive or dead. I am over forty years old. Is this all there is?"

Tobias wished that she would just shut up, relax, and go to sleep. Instead, the darkness seemed to make her more eager to talk.

"We've just got to live the best we can," he said, wanting to brush it all aside.

"I just wish that we could talk more. Yes, yes, I know you're too tired to talk right now, and your writing has to come first, and all of that; and your father, you have to think about him, too. I know all that. I get it. Intellectually. But I really wish that we could talk more to each other."

"I see."

"I'm starving to get close to you!" She began to yell. "I'm happy we're a couple, if you could call it that. At least you want to be with me, but, oh . . . Tobias, it just feels that sometimes it isn't enough!"

Tobias' mouth was dry and inside his head, as he shut his eyes, he heard the sound of the car motor, its roar, the car's movement. Tobias gave her hip a small pat.

"Let's go to Thailand," he said in her ear. "Let's start planning to go."

Marit snorted. "That will never happen!"

"Sure it will. We'll plan it later. Now try to go to sleep."

Marit said nothing, and Tobias started to relax. His eyes closed and he was drifting off to sleep when she spoke again.

"Are you asleep, Tobias?"

"Nooo."

"I'm thinking about something. Something totally different. Do you think there's life after death? That we exist, maybe in a different form, take on a new shape once we've died?"

He was wide awake at once.

"What the hell are you talking about?"

"Seriously, what do you believe?" she asked again.

"Why are you bringing this up now?"

"My sister . . . tomorrow is the anniversary of her death."

"Oh."

"No, don't believe I always think about it. But my mother called today. It must be the worst thing in the world, to lose a child."

"That was a long time ago, wasn't it?"

"Forty-three years. But she never really got over it."

Tobias rolled onto his back; his eyes were hurting.

"Mamma believes in reincarnation. As for me, I don't know. What do you believe, Tobias?"

"Believe, believe. It doesn't matter what anyone believes. No one can ever prove anything one way or the other."

"Don't you ever think about it?"

"When you die, you're dead."

"That sounds so final."

"Final is just what death is."

"When my sister died . . . she was only four years old. She had always had that heart problem, and both my parents knew that she might not be with them for very long." Marit stopped, losing her train of thought.

"Do you remember your sister at all?" he forced himself to ask.

"She died before I was born. But I remember one thing that my mother said. Mamma said that one evening, the same evening after Carina had died, a sparrow flew right into their kitchen through the open window. It sat on the kitchen bench looking straight at them, and they could hardly move. The window was open, but it stayed a long time, staring at them, before it flew back outside. Mamma said she could see Carina behind the sparrow's eyes. She said that she felt much better after that."

Tobias coughed. "People see what they want to see. Nothing wrong with that."

Marit turned toward him and laid her arm over his chest.

"Good night, Tobias. Sorry I was so angry before."

"Good night."

22

TITUS BRUHN, HIS PUBLISHER, CALLED MONDAY MORNING. Tobias
was already awake, woken by Marit beginning breakfast in the
kitchen. Marit brought the phone to him. She was pale, her hair
stringy and not yet washed.

"You'd better answer," she said.

Tobias picked up the phone and felt a clench of pain in his
stomach.

"Hi, Tobias here."

"It's Titus. You asleep?"

"No, not at all."

"Great. About getting together for lunch. Today would work
out for me. Tomorrow I have to head off to Frankfurt for the book
fair. How's today looking for you?"

"Fine, today will work. How about I come over around 1:00?
Okay for you?"

"Great, see you then!"

Tobias got out of bed and went into the kitchen. Marit was
standing at the window still in her robe.

"Marit?" he asked, and she turned around. "Aren't you going
to go to work today?"

"I took the day off."

"Why?"

"I just don't feel like going in."

"But sweetheart . . . ."

"I got my period and I haven't slept all night."

"Not at all?"

"Not one bit."

"Why not?"

"I was thinking. We've got to talk, Tobias. About us, our lives together."

Please don't start that again, he thought. He poured a glass of water and drank it up.

"You want to break up?" he said, knowing his words were cruel.

"No," she said, but she sounded half-suffocated.

What had gotten into her? Her period? She usually was in a bad mood whenever that came around. She'd get on his nerves. But all this intensity, this repetition, this was not like her at all.

"That was my publisher," he said to change the subject. "I have to go meet him."

"Right now?"

"It's important! It's about my contract!"

She seemed to shrink. Tobias took her in his arms; she didn't resist, but her arms hung loosely.

"I'll come back this evening. I promise. Then we can have a good dinner and talk. Go back to bed, Sweetie. Try and get a few hours of sleep."

Bladguld, Golden Pages, the name of the publishing house which Titus Bruhn ran, was located in an eight-story building on Industrigatan in the district of Kungsholm. Many other smaller publishing houses were located there as well as a few tiny tech firms. Titus Bruhn published only Swedish authors. He had wanted to name his house Blågult, Blue-and-Yellow, to honor his Swedish heritage, but of course that name was already taken.

After a few rough years in the beginning, Bladguld was doing well. One major reason was that Titus had managed to lure away a best-selling author, Sissi Nord, from a rival. Sissi wrote books in the same spirit as *Bridget Jones' Diary*. Her three books, about a single woman looking for Mr. Right, had sold in great numbers.

Posters of Sissi Nord and her books were prominently displayed in the front window. Tobias knew that Sissi wrote from real experience. Just like her heroine, Sissi Nord was thirty-five and single. Tobias had an inkling why she hadn't found a partner. He'd met her a number of times on the book circuit, and Sissi had appeared greedy and desperate. At the Gothenburg Book Fair a few years back, they'd shared a taxi to a bar after an authors' dinner. They were in the back seat and before Tobias could even say a word, Sissi had sneaked her hand into his pants pocket. Tobias hadn't wanted to embarrass her so he just moved closer to the window, fully aware this maneuver would find its way into her next book. Name and all. That was the fashion these days—female authors who were rejected by men they'd hit on would find revenge in their novels. In her books, Sissi's alter ego was called Lena Lind. The character was good looking and sexy, but so what. He did not want to become a laughing-stock in Sissi's book.

The publishing house was not very large. Titus had been the sole proprietor when he started the company, but he'd gotten a co-owner, a woman named Annie Berg. She'd left Carl Lüding's publishing house about three years ago, when Carl moved his headquarters to Norrland. Annie hadn't wanted to move to Sweden's northernmost province, understandably enough, since her extended family was in Stockholm.

Annie Berg had the reputation of being quick off the mark as well as hard-working. She had a nose for the kind of books which would become bestsellers. For instance, she'd persuaded Sissi Nord that they would take good care of her and treat her like the celebrity she had become. If she decided to switch to one of the Big Name houses, she'd be just another number instead.

Annie was the one who greeted Tobias when he came in. She was somewhere between forty-five and fifty, short, somewhat colorless. She had an air of melancholy about her, and Tobias imagined that he knew why. While Annie was still working for Carl Lüding, one of her colleagues had disappeared. One wintery day, the colleague had gone to tend to her parents' grave in Hässelby and was never seen again. The woman had been a close friend of Annie's; they'd worked together a long time. Titus had told Tobias the whole story. Annie was a private person who rarely opened up, not even at parties. He had a vague memory of the newspaper head-lines, now over three years ago. The journalists had made quite a bit of hay over the 'Berit case,' as they called it.

"Hi, Tobias," Annie greeted him. "Titus is in his office."

Tobias walked between rows of bookcases and boxes on his way to Titus' office, saying hi to Mimmi and Eva as he went past.

"Did you like the paperback cover?" Eva asked. "A little more gruesome than the hardcover, don't you think?"

Tobias formed his fingers into the OK sign and said, "Fantastic!"

The door to Titus' office was ajar and Tobias heard him on the telephone. Titus was leaning back as far as possible in his chair, his feet on his desk. The entire floor was covered by stacks of books. Titus was a plump forty-year-old with a mustache and a gap be-tween his front teeth. He was wearing a polo shirt, jeans, and a jacket. It didn't take a moment for Tobias to realize that Titus was chatting with his mistress, but Titus did not give off the feeling he wanted privacy. Rather the reverse.

Titus gestured Tobias in, and Tobias sank into the embrace of the guest chair. Titus' rough shoes rested on a heap of manuscripts, gum stuck on one of the soles. After a great deal of cooing and mur-muring, Titus finished his call. The entire book world knew that Titus was having an affair with a woman who ran a bookstore in Stockholm. Tobias wondered whether Titus' wife was as aware as everyone else. No idea.

Tobias and Titus walked to a sushi bar on Saint Eriksgatan. They found a small table by the window. Titus peered at Tobias over the frames of his glasses.

"You look tired," he said.

"Well . . . ."

"Have you been up all night writing?"

"Things have been rough," Tobias said defensively. "I was in the country to take care of my father. He's had a bad accident, you know. Fell out of the hayloft right onto a stone floor. It was lucky he sur-vived at all. He's not a young man anymore. I was there to help with the farm work, take care of the animals. Oh, it's hard to see one gen-eration give way to the next."

"And that makes you feel closer to your own end, doesn't it, as the generation before you disappears."

Tobias nodded. He picked up a piece of sushi with his chopsticks and swished it in the mixture of soy sauce and wasabi, letting the rice soak up the liquid. He put the piece in his mouth. It was so strong that tears came to his eyes.

Titus grinned teasingly.

"You never get used to it, but it does clear the sinuses!"

The restaurant was fairly empty as the lunch rush was over. Titus had brought over two cups of green tea for them, but Tobias did not like green tea all that much. He thought it tasted like straw. He also needed a cigarette, and he wished Titus had chosen a different restaurant, one where you could have wine with your meal and afterwards a decent cup of coffee with cognac on the side.

Titus started to drum the table with his fingers.

"Tobias, I need to know your plans, and soon," he said.

"If I intend to write another book?"

"Yes, though I don't want to pressure you. Still, I have to know how things are going. Will a book be ready for next fall?"

Tobias put his tea cup down.

"I'm not a machine, you know," he said.

"Of course not."

A moment of silence. Outside there was the sound of sirens, and three fire trucks raced down the street. People on the sidewalks covered their ears. Titus raised his arm and began to massage the back of his neck.

"Well," he said, slowly. "Shall we just say that you're going to skip a year? It won't be too bad. The paperback is out now, and people are not going to forget Leo Pullman if it takes an extra year for him to appear again."

Tobias sighed. "I don't know."

"It can't be easy to sit down and write when other things are pulling at you. I certainly understand that."

"What else is lining up on your fall list? What about Sissi, does she have another book in the works?"

"She's writing a children's book."

"What?"

"I couldn't really say no . . . ."

"Excuse me for asking, but what the hell would Sissi Nord know about children?"

Titus shrugged. "We'll see when she turns in her manuscript."

"And as for me, what do you need from me, at the absolute latest?"

"Well, as for the manuscript, you can get it to me sometime this spring. Right now I need a title and some kind of framework, at least enough to work up a cover. Nothing's critical yet, but I need some progress fairly soon, as I've said."

"All right, I'll give it my best shot," Tobias heard himself agree. "I've got to have some income, too. I can't be out of the loop forever."

"Need an advance?"

Tobias gave this some thought. "Not right now. If things change, I'll let you know."

"We'll scrounge something up if you need it."

"Are you talking about an advance or a plot?"

"A plot, actually."

"Any ideas?"

"Why not change the background? Something going on in the country, maybe. You have all the details already: cows, silence, darkness falling early . . . ."

Tobias stiffened. "You must be kidding."

"I'm just trying to shake something up."

Did Titus suspect something? Tobias felt ill suddenly, felt he had to vomit. He jumped up and ran for the bathroom. Small drops of sweat broke out on his face. He soaked his hands in the sink and splashed water on his face. It felt as if his whole body was burning up, but his fingertips were ice-cold. He started to shiver.

"You look sick," Titus said when Tobias returned.

"I must have eaten something that disagreed with me. How about you?"

"I'm perfectly fine."

"By the way, about your idea. Leo Pullman is a city cop. I can't just send him off on a wild goose chase through the countryside. But I have an idea I just need to develop. It's a good one, a damned good one, actually."

23

HE WAS LYING, TO TELL THE TRUTH. He had no idea at all what Leo Pullman was going to do. But he thought that he would force himself to sit down at his computer and try to pull something out. It had worked before. *Self-discipline*, he thought. *If I just get started, something will come.*

While Tobias waited for the commuter train, he decided to call Marit. He stuck his fingers into his pockets to search for his cell phone, but it wasn't there. He must have left it at Marit's place. Yes, he remembered he'd left it on the small table in the hallway.

Until he got back, he couldn't phone anyone.

When he got to his place, he called Marit from his land-line, and she answered immediately.

"How are you feeling?" he asked.

"Mamma is on the way over," she said.

"Your mother's coming over?" Tobias felt real relief.

"She phoned after you left. She'd called work and they told her I'd called in sick. So now she's coming over to take care of me."

Marit's parents lived in Norrtälje. Tobias had met them occasionally. They were both retired gym teachers. Marit's father had dementia and had recently been moved to a care facility, but he was often able to visit his former home.

"Is that what you want?" he asked.

"She won't give up. You know, it's hard to keep a secret from your own mother. She can tell right away if something is wrong."

"When will she be there?"

"In about two hours."

Marit seemed slightly more energetic now.

"It's a good thing your mother is coming," he said. "I really have to grind at this book. Titus was on my case, and I promised I'd have something for him. And, of course, I still have to earn a living."

He heard her take a deep breath.

"So you're not coming, after all?"

"Not right now. You're not going to be alone anyway if your mother's on the way. If she wasn't coming, I'd have hurried over right away."

"Would you really?"

She was silent but he heard her crying.

"Don't be so sad," he said, pleading.

"I need you."

"Sure, yes. Sweetie, I understand."

"Go and write, then. Make sure that you really accomplish something."

"I will."

"Promise?"

"I promise."

Tobias turned on his computer right away. He would stay there until something came out.

A taxi driver's body found on a forest road next to his car. The murderer pinned a note to his shirt. The note was written in the victim's own blood.

Didn't someone already write something like that?

Tobias remained in front of his computer. It was evening. The school playground was silent; the kids had all gone home. The kids were probably at home, eating spaghetti and meatballs, and then there would be the eternal scolding about homework, TV watching, and bedtime.

What would be written on the note?

The moms and dads would start fighting with each other, too, and the next thing you know, the dads would be slamming the front doors and heading to the pub to down a few beers, and the moms would be cleaning up the kitchen, crying in their beds later when the dads finally came home . . . .

What the hell would a note like that say?

. . . and all the kids would be in their beds listening, feeling their stomachs hurt, thinking it was their fault that their parents . . . .

What the fucking hell would that fucking note say?

I got what I deserved.

Yes, there's a start: something could come out of that. Something thrilling, something that would work . . . .

Tobias named the few lines *Pullman 2* and saved the file. Folded his hands and stretched them over his head. His knuckles cracked; it hurt. He clicked open the game files to solitaire, opened Monte Carlo. That was a hard one, almost impossible. Playing a round of solitaire could clear the head, Titus often said. Tobias played five games in a row and did not win a single round. He lit a cigarette, went to pee. Deep down inside his imagination, things began to stir.

Finally the first few real sentences were there:

Leo Pullman had just come home from jogging when the telephone rang. Damn it, he thought. He'd been looking forward to some time by himself this evening. He was exhausted, worn out, dying for a vacation.

Not a bad beginning. Tobias went back to his computer and opened the document and was just about to type in those lines when his own telephone rang.

Damn it, he thought.

The voice was a woman's and at first he didn't recognize it, but luckily she told him her name:

"Hi, Tobias, it's me, Ingelize Moberg."

"Hi, Ingelize."

"Am I bothering you?"

"Well . . . ."

"The thing is, I'm here in Stockholm. Visiting my husband."

"Yes?"

"And I was thinking, we should get together."

"Right now?"

"This evening or tomorrow morning."

"Well, actually, I'm right in the middle of work."

"I understand. But there's something I have to talk to you about, something important."

"If it's about that idea for me to move back . . . ."

"No, no, that's not it. Something else. But I don't want to talk about it on the phone." She lowered her voice. "It has to do with Sabina."

"What about Sabina?"

"It's really important or I wouldn't have bothered you. But I can tell you . . . . I'm frightened."

Pain bit his heart. Tobias had to place his hand over his chest, to try and press it away.

"Are you there, Tobias?" He heard Ingelize's voice as a distant waterfall. He swallowed, began to search for a cigarette.

"Where are you now?" he managed to ask.

"At the moment I'm in Jens' apartment on Kammakargatan. I can get to your place, if that's easier. It's not that far."

"There's a good commuter train connection."

"Can I come over right now?"

Might as well get it over with. Ingelize seemed really upset. He had to hear what she wanted.

"That'll be fine. Do you have your cell phone with you, Ingelize?"

"Yeah."

"Call me when you reach Östertälje. I'll walk over to the station and pick you up."

24

ALTHOUGH INGELIZE WAS WEARING A KNIT HAT OVER HER SHINING RED HAIR, Tobias recognized her from far away. She was wearing a short leopard jacket, a black skirt, and high boots. She was better looking than he remembered. Ingelize gave him a quick hug and started to talk in a strained manner.

"So this is Södertälje."

"Yep."

"See Södertälje before you die," she sang the line off-key.

"Huh?"

"Well, maybe the song said Sundbyberg instead of Södertälje. See Sundbyberg before you die. Meet spring in Söööödertälje."

He forced a laugh.

"How many people live here?"

"Seven or eight thousand."

"Do people commute in to Stockholm to work?"

"Yes. Lots of people do that."

They walked in silence for a while.

"It's really chilly," she said. "You don't know what to wear. I had to go and buy this fur at a shop on Drottninggatan."

"It's cute."

"Of course, it's faux fur. But it looks real. Don't you think so? You know I'd never buy a real fur made from killing animals."

"No, of course not," he said, but he had to bite his tongue from mentioning her leather boots. Weren't they made from killing animals? Wouldn't that be just as cruel? But he refrained.

"You said you were in middle of writing something."

"Yes, I am."

"I know I'm really interrupting you, but . . . ." Ingelize stopped and grabbed his arm. "Something truly awful has happened at your father's place."

Tobias' mouth suddenly filled with saliva and he had to turn and spit.

"We're almost there," he said. "That's my building. Up those stairs."

Tobias tapped the entry code and opened the door. Turned on the hallway lights. Walked over the black-and-white-striped floor. So far he was completely calm.

"A nice entryway, isn't it?" he heard himself saying. He saw his own gloved hand make a sweeping gesture toward the newly renovated walls. "This is a nice, peaceful neighborhood. A little different from some places in this city."

Ingelize didn't answer. He heard her footsteps behind him in the stairwell. He already had his keys out.

Once inside, he took her fur and hung it up on a hanger. It was lighter than it appeared. She was wearing a green sweater which hugged her breasts.

"Make yourself at home. Would you like a glass of wine?"

She nodded, looked around without curiosity .

"How could you leave the horses?" he asked, surprising himself. His hand was shaking and he spilled some wine when he poured it.

"I have a few girls who promised to come. Hard workers."

"I see. Want a smoke?"

Ingelize shook her head. She drank some wine. She'd put one leg over the other when she sat down on the sofa. She bit her lower lip with her upper teeth as if she couldn't find the right words.

Pain throbbed through his forehead as he glanced sideways at her, a slicing pain which seemed to cut through his entire head. Reflexively, he closed his eyes.

"Please, tell me what's going on," he growled.

Ingelize drank more wine, almost emptying her glass.

"I'm freezing," she whispered.

Tobias pointed to a plaid blanket on the back of the sofa.

"Wrap yourself in that. By the way, are you hungry? Do you want a sandwich?"

"I'm not hungry."

"Can't you tell me what the hell's the matter?"

She pressed her palm to her forehead.

"I don't know where to start. It's just that . . . a guy from our village has disappeared. You remember him, Hardy Lindström. You told me he didn't like you all that much."

Tobias nodded. He rubbed the tip of his tongue unceasingly against his teeth until he could taste blood.

"Hardy used to come over and help me out with some construction jobs. He used to help out your father and Sabina, too."

"Yeah, he did."

"Well, now he's just up and gone, disappeared."

"As I understood it, he wasn't the most dependable guy, that Hardy Lindström. He'd gone to jail, too, right?"

"Yes, but he'd never disappear like that. He's actually close to his mother. She's really worried. She has the feeling that something bad has happened to him. The other day, she came to my place and asked me to help her fill out a missing person report for the police."

"A missing person report?"

"Yes, she's desperate. Ann-Mari hates the police. Actually, she's probably got a record. But she's always been good with horses. She used to go over to your place . . . I mean to your mother's, back then . . . she shod horses, she took care of them."

"I know." Tobias answered mechanically, listened mechanically, but his irritation was rising. What was Ingelize leading up to? Why couldn't she just spit it out?

"So did you file a report with the police?"

"Yeah, we called the Kisa station."

"And? What did they say?"

"What could they say? They asked us some questions, but didn't seem all that interested. They're up to their ears in work, I imagine."

"How long has he been gone?"

"Since September 26th."

"I see."

"And then . . . ."

"Well?"

"And then I happened to think of something strange. That's what I need to talk to you about now."

The telephone rang and they both jumped.

I won't answer, Tobias thought, but he did anyway.

"Hi, Tobias!" A cheerful male voice.

"Hello?"

"Do you have a few minutes?"

"What for?"

"My name is Patrick and I'm a financial advisor."

"Financial advisor?"

"I've called to tell you how to improve your finances through investments."

"If I had private finances to invest, maybe I'd have a few minutes, but I don't, so I won't."

Tobias hung up before Patrick could answer.

"Fucking idiot!" he hissed. "Interrupting people at home!"

Ingelize smiled stiffly, but swirled her wine glass in her hand.

"That takes care of him," he said, and hoped that she would change the subject. Maybe chat about her horses, talk about her somewhat sad marriage. But she picked up right where she left off.

"You were at home at the time, remember? I wanted you to sign my other books, too, not just that paperback. I'd forgotten to ask you, and so I thought I'd just go over to your place since you were still in Kvarnberga, or I'd miss out. So, the day we'd gone riding, I put the books in a bag and rode my bicycle over to your house."

He was totally focused on her words.

"I heard someone in the barn, someone was spraying water. So I walked over, and . . . I saw Sabina."

She became quiet, drank the last of her wine, didn't look at him. Somewhere in the building, water began rushing through the pipes. Someone must be taking a shower, maybe the young woman next door. Sound from a TV came from the upstairs apartment. Tobias took a glance at his watch; it was twenty minutes to eight.

"And?" he demanded.

"Sabina was spraying water everywhere. It was like she'd gone crazy. She was holding the hose and spraying down the tack room, you know, where the desk is, and she was spraying on the walls and the ceiling and the desk and . . . everywhere. Everything was soaking, and I wondered what she was doing, and when I looked at the floor, it was . . . it seemed to me . . . a great deal of blood, and she was washing it toward the drain . . . and it was frothy and light red . . . it looked . . . ."

Ingelize suddenly got up, threw off the blanket, and ran to the bathroom. Eventually he heard her pull some paper off the roll and blow her nose. When she came out again, he saw that she had been crying.

"Sabina turned around and saw me, and she looked scared to death. She started yelling that I'd scared her out of her wits and what did I want and she was so angry that I felt really stupid for coming over. And I said, 'I just wanted to ask Tobias to sign these books for me,' and then she turned off the water. 'What are you doing?' I asked, though I could see that for myself, and then she looked even more angry and she said a steer had gotten loose, hurt itself. She'd had to slaughter it. It had been heading for the tack room, and it was the second steer in such a short time that had to be killed, and the other one had to be slaughtered on Shame Island, she said, and she was sorry that she sounded so impolite, but she was in a really bad mood."

"And then what?"

"And then she said that you weren't home but she'd tell you about the books, but I knew she wouldn't because she seemed so confused and so unlike herself."

"She was. The whole steer business was my fault. I didn't close the stall door properly." Tobias had no idea where the words came from. "She was angry at me. She had the right to be angry. I came to help out and I ended up making things worse."

Ingelize did not say anything.

"I wanted to help out, but I fucked it all up. I was no help at all."

Ingelize wasn't listening. "I wanted to get out of there as fast as I could and then I saw something on the ground. In the corner of the room. It was . . . Hardy's hat."

"Well, maybe he forgot it."

"He never takes off that hat. He wouldn't forget it."

"Maybe he was nearby."

She lifted her face to look at him and she was no longer crying.

"Maybe," she said. "But if he were nearby, he was no longer alive. I realized . . . it's so horrible, you see . . . I realized all that blood . . . it came from him."

Afterwards, Tobias had no idea how he'd kept himself together. He clenched his fists, let himself be carried into the fiction of being strong. Being able to take action, he was the leader. An unusual calm filled him. He went to the kitchen and got the wine, poured for both of them.

"So you're telling me that my father's companion Sabina is supposed to have beaten Hardy Lindström to death? Is that what you're trying to tell me?"

She laughed, embarrassed.

"Well . . . it's just I had such a strange feeling about it. And ever since that day, Hardy's been gone."

"That's a serious accusation."

"I don't want to accuse anyone of anything. I just had to come and talk it over with you. Can't you see? I couldn't carry around such suspicions. The whole thing is appalling, gruesome."

"Have you gone to the police with this?"

She swallowed. "No. But if Hardy doesn't turn up soon, I'll have to."

"Excuse the question, but . . . did you see a body in the barn?"

"No."

"Or an animal's body?"

She gave him a confused look.

"No, no body of any kind. Just blood."

"She'd probably put it in the freezer. Not enough room for everything. She had to give some to the guest house down the road. She was really angry about the whole thing."

"Well . . . ," she said hesitantly.

"Damn it all, Ingelize, Hardy will turn up sooner or later! You just can't go around talking like this! What will people think? This would be horrible for both Sabina and my father. If people started to talk . . . . Once a rumor like this gets started, it has a life of its own."

She kept silent.

"Did you tell this to anyone else?"

"No, I wanted to talk to you. Why do you think I called you in the first place?"

"You didn't say anything about it to Jens, your husband?"

"Jens? No."

He walked her back to the train. He was drunk from the wine and could hardly walk straight. At least he'd calmed her down; at least he could believe he did. She appeared so small next to him. When she was about to climb onto the train, he drew her towards him and touched the tip of her nose.

"Take care of yourself," he said. "I'll call you later this week. I bet Hardy Lindström will turn up soon."

The reaction came later. He was standing at the sink, rinsing their wine glasses. What Sabina had done hit him right in the stomach. With her own hands she had butchered a human body.

How did she do it?

What tool did she use?

A saw?

A carving knife?

And all those different body parts . . . . Horrible details became clear. The head with its blond hair, its beard, a hand, its fingers

cramped in fists, the feet, their toes, their toenails. She had separated one part from another. She had stuffed them into plastic bags
and, all alone, she had brought them down to the raft.

A wave of intense nausea rolled over him. He found himself on
the bathroom floor, vomiting into the shower drain.

Afterwards, the exhaustion. He stayed lying on the bathroom
floor. He noticed dust, pubic hair. He was quiet now, the taste of
vomit etched deep into his mouth.

What if other people began to suspect something? What if
someone had seen Sabina down by the raft? How could she be certain that no one saw her there?

Against his will, he knew what he must do. He would have to
return to Kvarnberga. He would tell Ingelize that he would accept
her offer of a job. At least for a trial period. He would have to be in
control of the situation. He couldn't do that from Södertälje. He
would have to return to the scene.

25

A CAR TURNED INTO THE FARMYARD. The crunch of gravel under the tires, the car was driving slowly as if the driver was unsure where to park.

"Who's coming?" Carl Sigvard asked Sabina. Sabina had been doing the laundry, running up and down the stairs all morning. There was something wrong with the machine; it stopped at every rinse cycle.

"I don't know," Sabina answered and pulled aside the curtain to look out the window. In the dim morning light, Carl Sigvard noticed that she was starting to look old. The skin on her face was drooping, and there were grey streaks in her hair; it was no longer a solid dark brown. Her eyes seemed smaller, as if they'd shrunk into their sockets.

"What's out there?" he asked.

"It's a police car."

"A police car! Why would they come out here?"

"Two police officers are getting out. They may want to come inside."

Frett had been sleeping by the heating element. He woke up, hearing the sound of the motor, and ran to the door. He stood there with his tail half-raised, not wagging. The ruff along his back stood straight up. He put his head to one side and let out a low growl.

"There's no danger, Frett," Sabina said.

When the knock came at the door, Frett began to bark wildly, insanely. He jumped against the door. Sabina had to push him aside with her foot when she opened it.

"Hello," a man's voice. "We're from the police station in Kisa. May we come inside for a minute?"

"What's this all about?"

"A missing person. We're knocking on doors all through the area. You're next in line."

"Come on in, then." Sabina bent down and shushed Frett. When they walked into the kitchen, Carl Sigvard saw that one of the officers was a woman. Both were in full uniform. They politely took off their shoes.

"Such a little puppy and already he's starting to guard the house," laughed the female officer. "That's nice. He'll keep the thieves away."

Frett had calmed down. He sniffed the officers and then their shoes. The woman scratched him on the head. Carl Sigvard could tell that she was used to dogs.

"What's his name?" she asked, looking up and smiling at Carl Sigvard.

"Frett."

"He's not that old, is he? A few months?"

"Something like that."

The male officer said, "I'm Jan Collin, and my colleague is Nina Axelsson."

"Please sit down," offered Carl Sigvard.

The two police officers moved to the kitchen bench. They unbuttoned their jackets. Carl Sigvard pulled the table closer to himself so they would have room to slide through.

"Can we offer you anything?" he asked.

"No thanks," said Nina Axelsson. "We had lunch at the guest house down the road."

"So they're still open this late in the season?"

"Yes, indeed. We had sandwiches and they were really good."

Sabina started down the basement stairs. "Excuse me, I'll be right back. I just have to check on the washing machine. It's got something wrong with it."

"If it's not one thing, it's another," Carl Sigvard said.

Jan Collin smiled slightly. A buzzing noise was heard from the radio on his belt.

"Nice place," he said.

"Can't complain."

"Lived here long?"

"Yep."

"How long?"

"My whole life. I was born here. I took over from my dad in the fifties. He'd taken over the farm from his father."

"Grow enough to live on?"

Carl Sigvard shrugged. "Well . . . ."

"How many in the household?"

"With or without the animals?"

"Not the animals."

"There's me. My name is Carl Sigvard Elmkvist, by the way. Then there's my partner, Sabina Johansson, and her son, Adam."

"Maybe we should go ahead and tell you why we're here," said Nina Axelsson. She had grey-green eyes and her face was a healthy red. She appeared to spend a great deal of time outdoors.

"Yes, by all means," Carl Sigvard said. "A missing person, I believe?"

"Hardy Lindström. His mother has reported him missing."

"Damn. She came around asking about him. And he never did show up?"

"No, he didn't."

Sabina returned from the basement, clumsy, huffing and puffing from the stairs.

"How's it going down there?" Carl Sigvard asked.

"That machine keeps quitting on me. We'll have to call someone to fix it, but repairs are so expensive."

"Well, sweetheart, that machine has lasted thirty years when most of them only last six or seven. It's one of a kind. We should donate it to a museum."

"Well, it chose a rotten time to quit. It's taking me forever to get the laundry done."

Sabina sat down on the edge of a chair, looked at the clock. Frett came over to her, wanted to jump on her lap. She bent down to rub his ears.

"The police have come here because of Hardy," he told her.

"So what's Hardy done now?"

"He's missing."

"Oh, that."

"Do the two of you know Hardy Lindström?" asked Jan Collin. He'd pulled out his notebook and a ballpoint pen.

"He often fills in when we're swamped with work here. And we sure could use him right now," Sabina stopped short.

"You see," Carl Sigvard explained to the officers, "I've had an accident. I haven't been able to work for quite some time, which is rough on a farming household."

The policewoman looked at him with sympathy. She had a pistol in her holster; Carl Sigvard also noticed handcuffs.

"What happened?" she asked.

"I fell from the hay loft. But see, I'm doing much better these days."

"When did this happen?"

"At the end of August, right in the middle of our busiest season."

"I understand. So you asked Hardy to help out."

"Yes."

"When did you see him last? Can you remember?"

Carl Sigvard thought for a moment.

"I haven't seen him since summer. But he's been here. He helped bring the cattle back from summer pasture out on Shame Island. What day was that, Sabina?"

Sabina got up and looked at the calendar over the kitchen bench. Flipped a few pages, said:

"Must have been the twenty-fifth."

"Of September?"

"Yes, September."

"What did you do on that day?"

"There was me, and my son Adam, and Tobias—that's Carl Sigvard's son. He lives in Södertälje. He isn't here right now, but he came down to help out—so we went out to the island, Shame Island; you must know it. That's where our animals have their summer pasture. And so Hardy was with us that day to help out."

"I see. Did you notice anything different about him that day?"

She was thoughtful. "No, nothing that I recall."

"Has he ever helped you out with this kind of job before?"

"In the spring, when we took them to the island."

"When you saw him last on the twenty-fifth, did he say anything specific?"

"Such as?"

"Well, see you tomorrow, or something of the sort? Did he agree to come back and help out some more?"

"No, nothing in particular. But he wanted his money that day, and I wasn't able to get to the bank, so I asked him to come back the next day."

"How did he react then?"

"He was irritated. I got the impression he really needed the money. But it was too late in the afternoon for me to get it, and there was nothing I could do about that. There was so much to do that day, I couldn't get to the bank."

Sabina drew her fingers through her short hair.

"Did he return the following day?" the policeman asked.

"Yes, he did."

"That was Wednesday the 26th, was it not?"

"Yes, it probably was. I don't remember it all that well."

"The twenty-sixth was the same day that he went missing."

"I see."

"How did he get here?"

"He has his old Vespa. He drives that thing no matter what the weather."

"Can you remember what his mood had been that day?"

Sabina reflected. She blew air from her lips, tapped her finger on her mouth.

"Hmm . . . he was, well, not in the best of moods, to be honest. Because I didn't have the money the day before. He really wanted it."

"How large was the sum in question?"

"Two thousand crowns. And he'd helped us earlier, too, so he had a lot coming to him."

"I see."

There was the sound of another car's motor.

"That's the mail truck," said Carl Sigvard.

"Are we in the way?" Jan Collin stood up to look out the window. Frett had already reached the door and was barking happily.

"Shh, quiet now, Frett, it's just the mail!" Sabina commanded. "No, don't worry, he has enough room to turn his truck around."

Nina, the policewoman, also stood up. She was able to move as quiet as a cat, thought Carl Sigvard. How would it feel to be arrested by a policewoman? How would it be to have a woman bring you to the ground and cuff you?

"Do you remember what Hardy Lindström was wearing that day?" Nina asked, turning toward Sabina.

Sabina sat back down, put her chin in her hand.

"Just the usual. The stuff he always wears. A brown leather jacket. Boots. The kind you stuff your pants legs in. Sometimes he wears this hat, it almost looks like a cowboy hat. That kind, you know?"

Jan Collin kept taking notes.

"Do you really have enough men to search for a guy like Hardy who hasn't even been gone all that long?" asked Carl Sigvard. "I've heard there's not enough people on the force, especially here in Östergötland province. It's not a popular occupation these days, I understand. Especially after that event in Malexander."

"We're looking for him for other reasons, which I can't go into."

"I understand."

"May I ask another question?" asked Jan Collin. "The other two people who were here that day, where are they now?"

"My boy Tobias has gone back to Södertälje. He's a writer. Maybe you heard of him. He's written a mystery called *Night.*"

"Sorry, haven't heard of him."

"It's about a policeman. But in Stockholm, of course."

"Not much time to read, I'm afraid."

"Not much time for that here, either," agreed Carl Sigvard.

"The other guy. Adam was his name?"

"Yes, Adam," said Sabina. "He's my son. Right now he's in his room."

"May we talk to him?"

Sabina cleared her throat.

"You must understand . . . . He's not like other people."

"He's not?" The policewoman looked at her, questioningly.

"He has mental issues."

"What does that mean?"

"It's hard to explain."

"Is he developmentally disabled?"

"Yes, you could say that."

"But he can help out on the farm?"

"Yes, sometimes."

"I've heard that he makes appearances as an entertainer sometimes. He's a good singer."

"Who told you that?"

"Hardy Lindström's mother."

"That's true, he's given some performances."

"Hardy was the one who convinced him to appear on stage, is that right?"

Sabina nodded.

"I would like to speak with Adam."

"I'm sorry. It's difficult right now."

Nina Axelsson squatted down next to Frett, who rolled on his back and wagged his tail. She petted his soft, exposed stomach. "You're a good one, aren't you, pup-pup! You'd make a good police dog, wouldn't you? We do need good police dogs!"

Nina looked up at Sabina.

"Still, I must speak with your son."

26

SABINA HAD STARTED TO MAKE A HABIT of accompanying Carl Sigvard to the outhouse. She would leave him alone there and return after a little while, when she guessed he would be done. She was turning into a real mother hen, scared to death that he would slip and fall while using his crutches. Instead of his sacks of lime, she'd brought in a bucket of some kind of new-fangled chemical. At least now there was more room in the outhouse.

"We're not living in the nineteenth century anymore," she said, looking at him teasingly. "Lime is old-fashioned. We're not talking about mass graves from World War One in here."

"Listen up, woman, I'm not that old!"

He enjoyed her moments of feistiness, since she was often in a bad mood these days, worn out, exhausted, he knew, from the farm work and from taking care of him and Adam.

When they got back to the house, she told him she was going to out in the evening.

"I'm going to head over to the Vesterberg house for a while and see if Tobias has everything he needs."

"I can't understand why the boy hasn't called!"

"He probably wanted to surprise us, that's all."

"If you ask me, I think it's very strange. Rent a house for real money when we have lots of room here at home!"

Sabina set a coffee mug in front of him.

"You must make an effort to understand him, Carl Sigvard. He's a writer. He's not like the rest of us. He has to have some peace and quiet. Don't you need your peace and quiet at times?"

She laughed again, that teasing laugh.

Of course he needed his peace and quiet at times. Just the thought of her standing out there near the outhouse and waiting for him was inhibiting and made it impossible to do his business, which he hadn't accomplished in two days now.

Sabina slung her jacket over her shoulders and was ready to leave the house.

"Give him my best anyway," he growled. "Tell him that his own home is always open to him!"

Before Sabina left, she turned on the TV for him. Carl Sigvard found the noise irritating, and found the remote to turn it off again. He thumbed through the newspaper, but didn't have the energy to read more than the headlines. Something was eating at him, but he couldn't put his finger on it. Maybe it had to do with Sabina's strange mood and her feisty humor, as if she were hiding something from him. He wanted to make love to her, be close, find their rhythm, both his and hers. Still, he was not yet up to that kind of exercise. The pain in his body still kept him from it.

Sabina was also very tired these evenings. She slept on her stomach. Her breathing was deep and long, but he knew that she wasn't always asleep. She would clear her throat when she thought he wouldn't notice, and then he would realize that she was awake but did not want him to know.

Nothing was the way it should be. Not just his useless body. His life. Her life. Their routines. This was all his fault and he knew it. Even Adam had changed after the accident. He kept to his room and seldom came out. This tortured Sabina, even though she did everything to hide her feelings from him.

Sitting up and thinking made his intestines shift. He could use the inside toilet, as no one would bother him, but he did not want to. He wanted to rule his life again and be the master of his own routines.

Of course it was dark outside, but he knew every inch of the path to the outhouse and his eyes would get used to the darkness as soon as he left the house.

It took a little effort to walk to the mud room. Sabina had wrapped the handles of the crutches in foam strips so his palms would not hurt too much and get blisters from supporting his entire weight. He leaned them against the doorjamb and put on his jacket. He left the lights on in the house. The weather was cold, but the snow was gone. The stars in the heavens twinkled down upon him while he stood still to collect his strength.

In spite of the darkness, things went better than he'd even imagined they would. He was able to balance on his crutches and pull himself forward along the frozen path. Sabina had never given him a hard time about his need to use the outhouse in peace and quiet, but Svava used to find it intolerable.

Svava. These same stars were shining above her, too, wherever she was. Maybe she was asleep? Maybe she was making violent love to an Icelandic Viking? He realized that thoughts of her no longer bothered him. What she'd done to him was insulting and hurtful and he'd never been so hurt before, but that was all over now. No such thing could happen to him now.

It was easier to totter along without Sabina. None of her nervous glances. *Don't put your crutch there! Watch out for that rock!* He could rely on himself again. He reached the outhouse, and he had to stop and catch his breath for a moment.

He would recover. He would be totally recovered.

When he left the outhouse, he saw movement by the barn; someone was moving there hugging the wall. Was someone coming to hurt his animals? Could this be Hardy Lindström, since the figure seemed to have a tall, male shape? He heard the sound of the barn door opening. The dogs were quiet, but of course they would recognize Hardy, so they wouldn't raise an alarm.

What was Hardy doing in their barn? Was he hiding from the police?

Wrath started to rise in his body. That young, strong Hardy Lindström with his shady glances, his slick ideas, his idiotic schemes such as dressing up poor Adam in those god-awful glittering clothes, turning that poor child into an exhibit. What surprised Carl Sigvard was that Sabina didn't seem to notice it and so blindly would defend Hardy. If someone would try and teach something to Adam, it should be something sensible! Not dress him up and bring him to market like the Bearded Lady or the Elephant Man! Come and see what the Cretan can do! Adam needed to be treated with respect and no one should demand things from him that were so meaningless. Instead, people should put their energy into training Adam to do something useful so that he could have a proper life. Maybe even be able to move out and have his own apartment. Then he and Sabina could live a normal life.

Carl Sigvard placed his crutches on stable ground as softly as he could. He hopped as quietly and swiftly as possible. He'd surprise that Hardy and turn him over to the police. They certainly would not be looking for him so hard if he hadn't done something really bad. Hardy could be up to no good in the barn and the animals were in there unprotected. It was time that Carl Sigvard returned to his position as the man of the house. His rising anger gave him extra strength.

The barn door was ajar. A bit of air, warm from the animals, came to him. He took the point of his crutch and used it to push the door open. He heard noise, a yowl, then an awful roar which made him stop and hold his breath. Then he heard thuds, as if two people were fighting with fists and skulls, and then the clang of metal. Fear touched his anger, but his anger was stronger and forced him into the hallway, where he clicked on the light switch.

The noises stopped immediately. Adam was standing there. Alone. One hand, holding a pitch fork, was raised ready to attack. Adam's face was red and his nose was running. His chest was heaving, and he panted with his mouth gaping open.

"Adam!" Carl Sigvard yelled.

The boy didn't seem to hear him. He hefted the pitchfork as if ready to lunge at an unseen, attacking enemy.

"Adam!" he yelled again. "What in the hell do you think you're doing?"

A clang on the floor. Adam had dropped the pitchfork and it landed in the hallway. The animals, who had been silent, began to squeal and howl. Adam stood there, still panting with a rasping noise, while his shoulders heaved. Adam's whole body seemed wrong; he was much thinner than before.

Carl Sigvard's grip on his crutches loosened. He realized he was freezing.

"Adam," he said. "Let's go inside and wait for Sabina. Your mamma will soon be home again."

When Adam heard his mother's name, he seemed to relax. His shoulders settled down, his front teeth met his lips. A heavy, mournful sound came from his throat.

Carl Sigvard took a deep breath.

"Are you alone out here?" he asked.

Adam's stare was empty.

"Who were you fighting with, boy?"

No answer.

"Pick up the pitchfork and put it back where it belongs."

To his surprise, Adam obeyed him.

"Let's go inside, now," Carl Sigvard said, keeping his voice steady. "Let's go in and wait for Mamma."

27

ALL THOSE YEARS, HOW HER MOTHER WOULD STAND BY THE CLEAN-ING CUPBOARD and pull out the vacuum cleaner to assemble its parts. Then the sound of the vacuum cleaner's motor, a sound which Marit had found grating since her earliest childhood.

How her mother seemed to step inside the noise and hide behind it. This aggressive hum began every Saturday morning until it woke Marit from her pleasant sleep. Her door had to be ajar so mother could use the brush attachment on the wall-to-wall carpet right outside her room—aggressive sweeping, since there might be a stain just outside the room of a teenager. Maybe a drop of milk which had been spilled and hardened to an invisible crumb.

Marit and her father, with sleep-filled eyes, would stumble out to the kitchen. They would stand by the counter, fumbling with tea leaves and water. Then it would be the kitchen's turn. The vacuum cleaner would roll over the threshold with a bump on its hard stomach. Her mother's mouth would be hard and thin and have no color; she didn't even look at them, but drove them out of her way as the brush nipped their bare ankles. The vacuum cleaner was a weapon against the defenseless. How could Marit and her father fight it?

As soon as possible, Marit's father would disappear into the garage. He would occupy himself with his car. There was always something to do under the hood, even if her father was really not all that mechanical. Marit would arrange her school books on her desk but did not dare shut her door; that would be like setting off a hand grenade.

Later on, during the afternoon, as the washing machine was thumping full bore, her mother would prepare dinner. During the entire long day, her mother would not sit down once until they all sat down to eat, but even then she wouldn't stay seated for long. She'd leap to her feet in order to start doing the dishes.

"Let me do them for once!" her father would plead, too late, because once she'd started, she did not stop until they were done. Afterwards she would fall into bed with her feet on a pillow. Her feet were sore and burning, and the cracks in them were her stigmata.

"Mamma, please, you don't have to do that!" Marit was all grown up now, but her voice sounded like a little girl pleading. Her mother was an old woman with a bent back, but she still attacked the floor with the vacuum cleaner so that not a single crumb would be left in the corners or under the table.

The two women were in their old, frozen places.

Marit gave up and went into the bathroom, locking the door behind her, making sure it was locked. The roar of the vacuum still reached her, but much weakened.

She looked at herself in the mirror and whispered, "Tobias!"

She thought about the woman who'd called him on his cell phone. Gave no name, was totally formal, yet not so formal she gave the impression she didn't know him. "I'm trying to reach Tobias. Is he there?"

The woman's voice was a slap in the face.

"May I ask who's calling?" she'd replied, but the woman did not answer. She just hung up.

Tobias hadn't contacted her since he left. Maybe it was true that cell phone connections from the country were bad.

Was he with her now? The woman who called him? Marit cursed herself for not tracking the call. Still, it was Tobias' telephone and she had no right to snoop in his private life. Or did she? Wasn't she a part of his private life?

He was not being honest with her. He was hiding something. He seemed totally distracted, and, although he blamed it on his book, she knew that it was something else. What was really going on? Had she destroyed their relationship by trying to force him to admit who the woman was? Had she been too demanding?

Her mother had finished vacuuming, the machine was turned off. Marit opened the door and walked out. She felt her heart beating.

Her mother sat at the kitchen table, her legs wide apart, her brown socks falling down.

"I decided to do your vacuuming for you," she said, as if Marit hadn't noticed.

"Thanks, but you really didn't have to do it," she said again. Marit forced a laugh so that she could take the sting out of the implied criticism.

"No, but I thought I'd do it just the same."

"Do you think my place looks that shitty?"

"Such language from an educated woman, a librarian to boot! I'm disappointed in you."

"Well, then, I meant to say dirty."

Marit poured a glass of orange juice for each of them, and put the vacuum cleaner away.

"Mine is better," her mother said. "Even though it's older, it has much better suction."

"I'm sure it's a different machine than the one you had when I lived at home!" Again the forced laugh like a shield. Her mother drank some juice.

"Of course not. Ours is ten years old. Your dad and I went together to buy it at a warehouse store in Bromma. Have you ever been to Bromma?"

"No, I haven't."

"Well, I'm sure you have no business in that part of town."

Marit noticed that the clouds were hanging low this morning, threatening to snow.

"So Tobias hasn't called you yet?"

Marit was expecting that question. "No."

"Isn't it a bit strange?"

"How so? You can't use a cell phone in Kvarnberga. The connections are bad."

"That may be, but there are still normal telephones in Kvarn-berga, aren't there?"

"Maybe he hasn't had the chance."

"Marit, I don't want to get mixed up in your life and your choices, but I do have eyes . . . ."

"What are you talking about?"

"My dear child, please don't take this the wrong way. I just want . . . you to be happy."

She looked at her mother's flecked, knotted hand, wanted to cry as she looked at it, wanted to cry because they had never been able to reach each other.

"Are *you* happy?" Marit asked quietly.

Her mother jumped as if she'd never heard such a question before. She drummed the table with her fingers.

"Happy? I am old. I've lived my life. But you, you have lots of time left. Many years. I just wish that you had a man who treated you with respect."

This was too much to take. Marit felt she had to get out. She ran into the hallway and buried her face in her coat. Her shouted words were muffled.

"Respect! He respects me in his own way! You can't see it; you won't see it! It may not be something you see just with your eyes!"

Her mother's voice came from the kitchen. She was already standing at the sink and running the hot water.

"My girl, you can only speak from what your life tells you."

At that moment Marit made a decision.

28

A SOUND WAS HUMMING THROUGH HIS MIND WHEN TOBIAS WOKE UP. It was almost inaudible, but stubbornly insidious. He heard it inside himself the moment he opened his eyes. He was far from being rested; he drew up his knees inside the sleeping bag, and the events of the previous evening returned. His balls ached. He held them for a moment. He was freezing.

It was quarter to six in the morning. He lay there, trying to fall back to sleep, but the tune in his head wouldn't let him. It made him nervous. The darkness outside the windows was thick and threatening. In spite of the chill in the room, he decided to get up and take a cold, military-style shower. He stripped off his underwear and looked at his body. He momentarily straightened his back, but could not keep it straight. His toenails needed to be clipped; they were long, broken, and had torn holes in his socks. He shivered and got into the shower. It took a few minutes before the water was warm enough to relax in.

Then he remembered he still did not have a towel. As luck would have it, a worn-out guest towel was hanging on a hook. It would have to do.

He also realized that he hadn't brought the right clothes, not if he were shoveling manure in Ingelize's stable.

Things had gone too fast. Tobias pulled on his shirt and his black jeans. They'd been washed so often that they now looked a shabby gray. Maybe he could dye them black again? His hair hung much too far down in front of his eyes. He should have had it cut long ago. He found scissors in one of the kitchen drawers and although they weren't sharp, he managed to clip a few centimeters off. The cut was uneven, but that didn't matter. He brushed the tufts of hair into the toilet and flushed.

While the water for coffee was coming to a boil, he started to look for a coffee filter. Finally he found a yellowed heap of filters under a tray. The morning news was on TV. It had been over a month since the hijacked planes had flown into the World Trade Center, but the news still focused on the catastrophe.

He sliced some bread and made salami sandwiches. The coffee had a bad aftertaste. He ought to thin it out with more hot water, but he didn't move from the table. He sat and chewed and listened to the news without hearing what was said.

Sabina, he thought with a suffering moan.

Tobias picked up his cell phone. No one had called. There were enough bars to make a call, but who should he contact? He tapped the number for Görel and Klara. He had to hear the voices of people he was close to. Görel answered. He had the impulse to hang up, but he didn't. Then it was too late.

"Tobias, is that you?" she was surprised. "Where are you?"

"In Kvarnberga. Imagine, you're up so early!"

She laughed quietly.

Tobias continued. "Is everything all right with you?"

"Everything's going very well, thank you."

"Even with . . . Rikard?" He had trouble spitting out the psychiatrist's name.

Görel laughed again. "He's good for me. Very good."

"That makes me extremely happy."

"Mmm. How is everything with you?"

"What about?"

"How's your librarian?"

Tobias had no desire to talk about his private life with his ex-wife. Especially at this hour of the morning.

"Is Klara home?" he asked.

"Of course, but she's asleep. She has a late start this morning."

"Please give her my best."

"What *is* up, Tobias? Is something wrong?"

"Oh no, not really."

"And how is Sitting Bull?"

"Dad? He's better, I believe."

"Say hi to him from me. And take good care of yourself. Bye now."

Tobias walked around outside the house and smoked his fifth cigarette. He saw a bird with red feathers in one of the bushes. Robin Redbreast, who received his color when he pulled a thorn from Jesus' brow.

The garden was well taken care of and bedded down for the winter. There was a shed behind the house. He opened the door, went inside, and found that all the summer things were stored there: The garden furniture. Large clay flower pots. The lawnmower. A striped umbrella, closed. Two ladies' bicycles. With a bit of effort he untangled one. The tires were low, but there was a bicycle pump in the basket. Tobias squatted down and began to pump.

His fingers froze while he was riding. And that tune, always in the back of his brain, weak but always there. The seat was too low and he kept banging his knees. He'd have to borrow some kind of tool to raise it. He'd ask Ingelize.

Ingelize was coming out of the stable as he turned into her driveway. She waved at him.

"Good morning! Nice that you're early! Welcome!"

Tobias got off the bicycle. "Thanks."

"Did you sleep well last night?"

"Yes, indeed."

"Have you had your breakfast already?"

"Yep."

"So have I. I was just going to make a cup of mimosa tea. You can have a cup, too, if you want."

"I didn't bring the right kind of clothes with me."

Ingelize measured him with eyes whose lids were blue with make-up.

"You can certainly borrow Jens'. He has everything you'll need, even a security vest for jumping, although he's never once sat on the back of a horse. He did intend to ride with me, you know, but he's never had the time. I think that the two of you are about the same size."

"That'll work."

They went inside to a warm and cozy kitchen. A cat came up to them, stretched, meowed. Ingelize talked to it as she made it a bowl of milk.

"Her name is Vanja. She was just sitting outside one day, and has been here ever since. No owner has ever claimed her. She's been here for a year now."

"This area is crawling with cats."

"It's crawling with mice, too, so these kitties are needed. By the way, I'm thinking of getting a dog."

"Why would you want a dog?"

She was silent for a moment. "It's kind of silly, actually. I've never been scared of the dark before, but lately I've developed such a . . . fear. And now, in the autumn, when it's so dark, I decided I really needed a guard dog."

"Did something happen?"

"I don't really know for sure. But I lock the door at night, too. I never used to. It's my old age, I guess."

She put a thermos on the table and a plate with a sugar cake. He took up a piece of cake; it was still warm, and it crumbled.

Ingelize sighed. "And the paddock. It just stands there half-finished."

"The one Hardy Lindström was supposed to build?"

"That's the one."

The tune inside his ears increased in strength.

"He'll be back soon," he heard his own voice say.

"Do you really believe that?"

"Sure. Just be patient. Besides, it'll soon be winter. Nobody can work on a paddock in the wintertime."

"No, you're right there."

The wall clock over the kitchen sink struck the half hour. It was seven-thirty. From far away, the sound of a diesel motor could be heard. Probably the school bus. The cat jumped up onto the sofa and turned its green eyes on Tobias. Ingelize stroked its mottled coat.

"Were Sabina and Sigge happy to see you?" Ingelize asked.

Tobias nodded.

"Do you think you can write out here? Will inspiration come to you?"

"We'll see. At least my laptop is here."

"I certainly hope you'll be able to write! Your books are so good!"

"Thanks."

"By the way, there's one thing we haven't talked about. Your pay."

"No, we haven't discussed that."

"Well, I thought . . . maybe you could work half-time? I'm not the wealthiest woman on the planet, as you know."

"You're not?" Tobias attempted a joke.

"No, seriously. But what if I give you seven thousand crowns a month? And, of course, you'd be able to ride as much as you want. You certainly couldn't have that in Södertälje."

"It's fine by me."

"Great! I'm so happy about this! Shall we sign the contract now? Since we're in total agreement?"

"No, well, let that wait. Let's see if this works out first."

Ingelize got up and went into her living room, returning with three books. His books.

"And while we're at it, I still have these. If you would be so kind, please scribble something in them?"

Tobias remembered Ingelize had told him she was on the way to get these books that Wednesday when she'd gone into the barn and seen Sabina washing away the blood.

The sound whirling in his brain amplified to a shriek. Mechanically he lifted the pen, opened the covers and wrote.

Ingelize took back the books and read:

To Ingelize. For old friendship's sake. Tobias Elmkvist.

"That's strange," she said, wrinkling her nose. "All the men I know have the same handwriting."

"Really?"

"Yes, small and spiky, if you don't mind my saying so."

"Maybe we're not so small and spiky in other places," he joked.

She giggled, holding the pen. On the kitchen table there was a memo pad filled with doodles, words, and numbers, written any which way wherever there was room. Obviously written while she was talking on the phone. She'd drawn some flowers and abstract patterns, too. She flipped to a new sheet and wrote her name: Ingelize Moberg. She had what people call a driven style of handwriting: large, slanted, and round.

"I wonder what a graphologist would say about yours?" he said.

"A strong person, willing to take action. Good character. Gifted." She laughed.

She was interrupted by the telephone. The noise beat against his temples. She turned her back as she picked up the receiver.

"Yes. Yes, that's me. I see. I heard about that. Sure. That'll be fine. Certainly. This afternoon, then. Are you able to find my place?"

After she hung up, she went upstairs and came back with Jens' riding clothes.

"Try these on," she said.

Tobias went into the guest bathroom. It seemed to have been recently renovated. The walls and floor had tiles set in a black-and-white pattern, and a black lace curtain covered half the window. It reminded him of Halloween. The overwhelming perfume from the soap irritated his sinuses and made him sneeze a few times. He took off his clothes and tried on the riding pants which were green with leather protection down the inside of the legs. They had obviously never been worn before. The accompanying plaid shirt had sleeves which were too short to match the legs of the pants which were also too short.

"Do they fit?" Ingelize called from the hallway.

"Fine."

"I have a sweater here, too. And rag socks and boots. What size boot do you wear?"

"Forty-four."

"Well, we'll find some boots out in the stable. Like the other day. Jens has amazingly tiny feet. As a matter of fact, his feet were the only thing that frightened me when I first met him."

Tobias opened the door and came out.

"Well, look at you! That'll work. You can keep the sleeves unbuttoned and then wear the sweater over it, and you can pull the socks over the pants all the way to your knees."

"Frightened you?" Tobias asked about her earlier comment.

She shrugged her shoulders.

"As a matter of fact, they were a real turn-off," she confessed. "But thank God he had ... um ... other qualities."

Her small office was in a room next to the stable. Ingelize kept her booking record there. On the walls there were posters of Icelandic ponies, and in one corner there was an old portable typewriter.

Tobias depressed the keys.

"You've got to be kidding me. Do you really use this old thing?"

"Well, sometimes. It's handy for typing out receipts."

"This has to be at least one hundred years old!"

"No, it was made in the sixties. It works really well, though soon it will probably be impossible to find color ribbon for it."

"You'll have to computerize."

"I already have, actually, and I even have a website. I'm not that backwards."

She flipped through her booking record.

"Nothing going on today," she said. "That's good, because I'm having unexpected visitors this afternoon."

"Who?"

"The police."

The sound in his ears, like a metallic thread tightened to its limit.

"Yes, I heard they're going door to door," he heard his own voice say. "Sabina said that they'd been to their place the other day."

"They came here when I was in Stockholm."

"I can't believe they'd call this early in the morning! They have their nerve!"

Ingelize flipped through her book. Her fingernails were shining red. She changed the subject.

"Tomorrow, however, things get busy," she said, and she raised her eyes to look at him. "Tomorrow at eight in the morning seven people are coming from a computer company. They want to kick off their autumn events with a riding tour."

"Have any of them ever ridden before?" Tobias' voice, disconnected.

She took up her pen and wrote something in the book.

"Not enough to do the tour on their own."

"So what do we have to do?"

"First, we help them choose their horses; they go with us to the pasture and choose. People usually think that's a lot of fun. And then they start to get to know their horse. Then we show them how to clean their horses' hooves. We have to saddle up ourselves. They certainly wouldn't know how. And then we help them mount, and we adjust their stirrups and make sure they're ready to go."

"That's a lot of work," he said.

"Yes, indeed. That's why I do appreciate having someone help out. And then I let them take a few turns inside the stable so that they get used to riding. Many of them are nervous or even fearful. The guys don't like to mention that, but you can tell from their body language. They sit like this."

She hunched her shoulders and nervously clutched at a pair of imaginary reins, throwing mistrustful glances right and left.

Tobias laughed.

"Aren't there any women who are afraid?"

"Sure. The difference is the women are not afraid to say so."

"I see."

"Then we ride outside," she continued. "But we start carefully. A trot, or even a canter, is usually fine for everyone, but not everyone wants to gallop. We take those who don't want to go so fast up the hill first. You should never force anyone, or things can go really bad."

Ingelize opened a cupboard and took out some banana-shaped saddle bags.

"We usually ride up the mountainside, you know, where we rode the other day. It's so wonderful up there. The view usually impresses the guests. Then we have a picnic. I usually have some sandwiches ready beforehand, and I bring hot water in a thermos, coffee powder, and tea bags. I usually take these throwaway cups back home and wash them out to reuse. I feel you must watch your money, hee, hee, but you don't have to tell anyone about that, it can appear too stingy."

29

AFTERWARDS TOBIAS THOUGHT INGELIZE SHOULD HAVE REALIZED WHAT WOULD HAPPEN. She should have seen it in him and she should have heard what he heard, that ringing, shrieking sound, constantly increasing in strength, becoming more difficult to withstand. She should have read it in his face; she should have defended herself. She should not have lured him to come with her the whole way.

"Let's go for a trial ride, so that you know the way."

She was looking him right in the eye. She was short, tiny even, and her boots hugged her calves.

"I know my way," he said. *I grew up here, you know.*

He did not say the last aloud as she'd already left for the stable. A lot of horses stood in their stalls, impatiently shaking their heads.

"You can ride Elfur today. He's a real firecracker, so you'll have your work cut out, but I think you'll grow to like him."

Ingelize pointed toward a stall half-door where he saw a black, finely formed horse looking out.

"One piece of advice. Hold the reins low, as he has a really tender mouth. And never, ever use the spurs."

What was she up to? Was she trying to test him somehow? Was she trying to see if he was good enough to help her out? Whether he would be worth seven thousand crowns a month?

"Elfur doesn't like to be with the other horses," she called from the other end of the stable. "But he has to or he won't be of any use."

Elfur shied as Tobias opened the stall door. He backed right into the wall with a loud thump.

"There, there." Tobias soothed the animal and managed to place his arm around the horse's neck and slowly worked the bridle onto his head. Then he led the horse out and tied the reins to a post.

Ingelize was getting her usual white horse ready.

"This is Snær. You've met him before." She babbled. "He's my private horse. He's just wonderful. He's smart and sure."

Tobias put on the saddle in stages. First he checked the right side, then the left. He checked the girth. Only then did he realize he hadn't brushed Elfur down or cleaned his hooves as he should have.

The sound sizzled in his brain.

Tobias went to get a hoof pick and decided to try on a helmet at the same time. The minute he fastened the chin-strap, the sound stopped, only to return a second later, clearer, higher, stronger.

He found a jacket as well. Its cloth had stiffened as if it had hung on the hook so long the wrinkles had turned to stone. There was a pair of riding gloves in the pocket.

Tobias finished working on Elfur and untied him. He swung up. Immediately, the horse began to buck a little, so Tobias let his full weight sink into the saddle. The animal's body vibrated between his legs. The image of his mother, Svava, came to him and he almost felt as if she were sitting behind him, her stomach against his back. Carefully he let the horse skitter toward the ring. Elfur was hard to hold. Every time Tobias moved his hands, the horse danced away.

"How's it going?" called Ingelize. She was tying on a saddle bag. Tobias didn't answer, but touched his heels lightly to the horse's sides. The horse snorted and attempted to rear. Reflexively, Tobias leaned forward so that the horse came back down. Tobias talked softly to it, "*hou, hou,*" the old Icelandic word of comfort which he remembered from his childhood.

"He's a powerful one, isn't he?" Ingelize called. She was in the saddle now, and she rode toward them. Elfur reared, flattening his ears.

"Let him know he can't act like that!" commanded Ingelize. "Sometimes I think that horse is crazy, but I know you can handle him. Just show him who's the boss!"

Ingelize let Tobias take the lead as they rode out of the stable. He sat mechanically in his saddle and listened to the sound in his head. The horse followed his lead and broke into a trot. They rode past the fields and across the clearcut, where they had to be careful as the ground was covered with branches and twigs and there could be hidden holes. Then they rode onto the sandy forest path and broke into a crazy gallop. Ingelize kept close behind Elfur's hooves, chasing him so that the horses' bodies were close to crashing.

It was a cold, still day. No color in a sky as transparent as a drifting fog. A flock of jackdaws lifted from the treetops, screeching as they circled above. Tobias turned to look at Ingelize, and she was so close behind him she had tears in her eyes from the wind. *Shouldn't she have felt an inkling of his fear by now?*

She should have realized something was wrong as they approached the cliff over Mörkviken. She should have known and stopped the chase. She could have halted her horse and been content to point at the lookout and say, "We usually take a break there, but not today. Now we'll ride back and go tomorrow with the group."

She could have said something like that.

But she didn't.

Instead she stayed right behind him. She did not slow down one bit—so there was no chance to stop what was going to happen.

They tied the horses a little apart from each other. Ingelize undid one of the saddlebags and walked near a stump, where she spread out a picnic blanket and set out the thermos and a few beat-up throwaway cups. She didn't say anything. Later he realized that that was strange, since she usually babbled on and on.

Tobias didn't say anything either. He took the can of powdered coffee and spooned three tablespoons into each cup, pouring hot water afterwards.

Ingelize was squatting.

"You have to be especially careful that no one goes too close to the edge," she said, after she finished drinking her coffee. "The ground is very unstable. Every year more and more of it is undermined."

He nodded and did not take his eyes from hers.

He watched her stand and walk a step or two.

The grass beneath her feet was dry and yellowed.

He got up, too.

"Here, but no farther," she said. She turned her back to him.

He was right behind her. He'd taken off his gloves. His hands were naked.

He could feel her spine through the cloth of her red jacket.

She was absolutely silent as she fell.

30

TOBIAS UNLATCHED HIS HELMET AND HELD HIS BREATH. The sound in his brain had stopped. He found himself on the edge of the cliff over Mörkviken, wearing Jens' riding clothes that were too small and realizing that the sound had stopped and he was all alone at the top of the mountain. The horses were there, of course, and they snorted, stamped, and pulled at their reins. The thought came to Tobias that he would have to get the horses home somehow, but it would not be easy, since they did not tolerate each other. Slowly he closed the thermos and put everything away in the saddle bag.

The sound in his head had gone, but was replaced by an intense headache. It started from a single point in the middle of his forehead and expanded outward. Every time he moved his head he saw spots.

"Ingelize," he said. His voice was hollow. "Ingelize!"

Tobias got onto his stomach and crawled toward the edge. He could see Shame Island in the distance, and he kept looking toward the horizon for a long time before he dared to look down. The pain drummed the inside of his head.

At first he did not see her body, just the signs of her fall. She'd pulled gravel and branches out with her, and even a small birch tree had been broken in half during her way down. He edged closer and called out her name.

He could see something red near the rocks by the water. Her jacket. He discovered suddenly that he was crying. He wormed his way backward like an eel until he could sit up, and then he wiped away tears with his sleeve. He blew his nose with his fingers, and then wiped his fingers on the grass. He had to be sure. He crawled back to the edge. Yes, he could see her clearly now. She lay twisted between two jagged rocks. She was on her back, and her head hung crookedly from her neck. She didn't move.

Tobias had not brought his cell phone; he'd left it in Ingelize's house.

He had to hurry. He tied the saddle bag to the white horse's saddle, made sure the girth was properly tight, and unfastened the reins from the bridle, so that the horse was free.

"Go home!" he said.

The horse turned its head toward him then bent it to bite at some grass. Tobias decided to simply let it alone. He wrapped the loose reins around his waist and walked over to Elfur.

Elfur was pawing his hoof on the moss; the shoe clanged whenever it hit the stone underneath. The horse snorted and pranced, making the saddle squeak as it moved. Tobias drew up the girth another notch. Elfur bared his yellow teeth and snapped so that Tobias hit him on the side with his fist and yelled.

He swung up, but before he was fully settled in the saddle, Elfur leaped away. Tobias was startled for a moment, alarmed he might be thrown off, but then he gathered in the reins and controlled himself. The trail back was steep, and Tobias pulled down his horse. From the corner of his eye, he saw Ingelize's white horse following them at a distance.

Tobias got back to the stable without seeing anyone else. He dismounted and led the lathered and panting Elfur into a stall. Snær wandered in behind them but stopped on the lawn and began to graze.

"Hello." A girl's voice.

Tobias jumped. He thought he was alone.

The girl walked over to him. She was only a year or two older than Klara. She had blonde, wavy hair which hung over her collar.

"There's been an accident!" he said quickly. "Do you have a cell phone that works out here?"

The girl bit her lower lip.

"Do you have one?" he roared.

"No."

"Damn it all! We have to call for help! Ingelize has fallen off Mörkviken's cliff."

"No!" the girl shouted. Her mouth was wide open and Tobias could see she had braces with pieces of food stuck in the wires.

"Run up to the house and call Emergency!" he yelled. "Tell them to hurry, goddamn it!"

She still hesitated as if she wanted him to make the call. He raised his hand in a crazy gesture, and she ran.

He had one thought in his mind. He had to deal with the contract! If they had signed that damn contract, he would have a reason for being out here. It would prove to everyone that the reason he'd returned to Kvarnberga was to help Ingelize and write his book.

There was no other reason for him to return!

Tobias hurried into the office, pulled out a piece of paper, and inserted it into the typewriter. Then he froze.

He leaned to look out the window toward the house. His fingers moved over the typewriter keys.

Contract, he typed. From then on it was easy.

Today I, Ingelize Moberg, have employed Tobias Elmkvist to assist half-time in my riding stable at the rate of seven thousand crowns per month.

Östra Kvarnberga, the 10th of October.

Ingelize Moberg.

He found her signature in the booking record. He pulled the paper out of the typewriter and placed it over the signature, picked up a ball-point pen and traced it. He did not think, he did not hesitate, and he was satisfied with the result. Quickly he folded the paper in half and stuffed it into the pocket of Jens' plaid shirt.

Just as he finished, the door flew open and the girl ran across the threshold. Her blonde hair had gotten tangled, and she looked about to throw up. He hadn't heard her coming.

"It's locked," she wailed. "She never used to lock her doors, but this time it's locked!"

He thumped his palm on the table.

"Damn it all! She did tell me that!"

"What are we going to do?" The girl had started to cry and Tobias wanted to slap her.

"My cell phone's in the house too. I had to charge it. And now we can't get at any telephone. Where do you live?"

"Next to the grocery store."

"Bike home as quick as you can and find a telephone. But hurry, for Christ's sake. She needs help as soon as possible! She's fallen off the mountain and she's lying on the beach between the rocks!"

The girl ran toward her bike, leaning forward. Tobias watched how she jumped on the bike so fast that she wobbled. He saw her pick up speed and pedal away.

He felt that his mouth was full of glue.

31

"ARE YOU CERTAIN YOU'RE UP TO IT, CARL SIGVARD?"

Sabina settled a pillow into the back of the chair and helped him take a seat in front of the desk. Carl Sigvard had decided that the least he could do was go over the books. There was no need to burden Sabina with that.

He soon realized that he couldn't sit for a long time and often had to take a break.

"Where are the envelopes?" he asked worriedly. "Do we have any left?"

"Sure, let me get them."

The pile of bills was huge. He waded through them, and noticed that many of them were past due. That irritated him, as he had always paid his bills on time.

Sabina came up behind him, bent over him and kissed the back of his neck.

"Are you all right sitting here?" she asked, as she put envelopes on the table.

"I'm fine, thanks."

"I wonder how long we'll have bills on paper. Everything is supposed to be done by computer these days."

"Maybe I should take a class in my old age," he joked.

Sabina smiled. "You're not that old, my sweet man."

"Well, but most people my age never even start using computers."

"Don't say that."

"It's different for Tobias and his generation. He even writes books on them."

"I think most writers do these days."

Carl Sigvard sorted the envelopes next to the bills.

"Well, maybe we should ask his opinion," he said, "if it makes any sense for an old goat like me to buy a brand-new computer."

"I saw an ad in the paper," she said. "They can put a whole package together for only twenty thousand crowns. Plus tax, of course."

"A whole package, indeed," he snorted. "You have to be able to use the damn thing, so it doesn't just sit around and collect dust."

"Let's talk to Tobias, then. We can invite him to dinner this week."

"Yes, that sounds good."

Carl Sigvard was still sitting and signing the checks when a car drove into the yard. A Toyota, he realized, as he leaned forward to look out the window. A strange woman climbed out. She had a small backpack in her hand, and she stopped to look around as if she was unsure what she should do.

In the kitchen, Frett began to bark.

"Sabina!" Carl Sigvard yelled. "We have a visitor!"

Carl Sigvard heard Sabina open the door and how Frett ran out into the yard, barking wildly. Then he heard the sound of two women's voices in a polite exchange.

Carl Sigvard reached for his crutches and was able to push back the office chair to get to his feet. It was a quarter to eleven in the morning. He managed to get half way to the kitchen when the woman came in with Sabina. The visitor took off her shoes at the door.

"You don't need to do that," Sabina said politely.

The woman smiled nervously. Wearing just her socks, she walked over to Carl Sigvard and placed her hand over his hand on his crutch.

"Let me introduce myself. I'm Marit Stenhägg," she said. "Tobias and I are in a relationship. And you must be . . . his dad."

Once they were settled at the kitchen table with their cups of coffee, Marit told them that she'd started driving very early that morning.

"I just felt the urge to see how things are here in Kvarnberga. Tobias has told me a great deal about all of you. But he doesn't know I've come. It's supposed to be a surprise."

"So was he right?" asked Carl Sigvard.

"About what?"

"About how things are around here?"

"Maybe not in all the details," she said quietly.

She had a thin, tiny doll face with a pointed chin. Her palms were damp, as Carl Sigvard had noticed when she touched his hand. The poor thing looked extremely delicate.

Carefully he said, "Tobias is not staying with us this time."

Marit swallowed and looked down.

"At least it's good to see that his father is doing much better," she said.

"That's right! I'll be completely back to normal in no time!"

"There, there, take it slowly and don't rush," Sabina said as she offered them a plate of her home-baked cinnamon buns. Marit took a bite then set it down.

"Somehow I got the feeling that something had gone wrong," she whispered. "Something about his father that made him rush down here."

"Something happened to me?" Carl Sigvard and Sabina looked at each other over the table. "As far as I know, he was supposed to come down here to work on his book. He's rented a house. You must have driven past it on your way here. It's a two-story, white-washed stone house."

"Rented a house?" the woman repeated.

"And then he was going to work for Ingelize. He was going to help out with the horses. Ingelize Moberg. She's a woman who owns a stable and runs a tour group operation. With Icelandic ponies."

The woman put her head down. She picked at a hangnail, and Carl Sigvard wanted to tell her to stop pulling it since those things hurt like hell until they healed up. Carl Sigvard felt anger rising. His damned selfish son, did that boy have a single ounce of sense in his body? Such a sweet, dear girl!

"You'll have to talk to him," Carl Sigvard said. "There must have been some kind of misunderstanding. He's got a lot on his mind, that boy, and sometimes he lives inside his own world. That's the way writers are. They're not like the rest of us normal people."

The telephone rang. Sabina went to answer it. Carl Sigvard heard that she wasn't saying much, just a few words of acknowledgement as she stood with her head turned away from them. When she replaced the receiver, Carl Sigvard knew right away it was bad news.

"What happened, Sabina?" he asked, as a pricking sense of worry shivered through his entire body all the way to his palms.

Sabina sank into a chair and placed her head in her hands. Carl Sigvard took her shoulder and shook it.

"Tell me, Sabina! What has happened?"

Then Sabina lifted her head and looked at the ceiling. Her voice was thick and broken as she began to speak.

"It's . . . horrible. Maria Vesterberg called. It's Ingelize . . . she fell from the cliff . . . she's dead."

32

TOBIAS DID NOT KNOW WHO HAD UNLOCKED THE DOOR, but he was finally able to go inside. He started searching for his own clothes. He changed. A great number of people were gathering in the yard. Two police cars. Some neighbors. He didn't know them. They must be new to the village.

After the girl had biked away, he had taken care of the horses. He unsaddled them, curried their coats, gave them some water. Then he left them in their stalls. The girl would have to take over later. She would know best what they needed.

Tobias sat on the front stairs and the cat came up to him. It kneaded its paws on him and began to purr. He began to cry again, loud and wailing, so loud in fact that the sound scared him. The cat stayed close to him for a while and watched him. Then it slid away behind the corner of the house. Tobias smoked a few cigarettes and undid the buttons on the riding pants; they were too tight and made him feel nauseous.

While he sat there, another girl biked into the yard. She was older than the first girl. He could tell right away that she knew what had happened.

"What's your name?" he asked in a voice scratchy from all his crying. He saw the girl's eyes were red.

"Emma."

"Do you often help with the horses?"

She nodded.

"You must be strong now, Emma. You're going to have to keep on helping with them until we know what will happen."

"Yes . . . ." She wiped away snot.

"We took Elfur and Snaer riding this morning. I've put them in their stalls now, curried them, given them some water, but I don't know what to feed them. Ingelize . . . didn't have time . . . to tell me what they need."

He couldn't talk any longer. He leaned his forehead against the wall and, although his eyes stayed dry, he choked up. Emma stood crying, too.

"She was so nice . . . she was so nice. This is so wrong." Emma said.

"Yes."

"What are they doing with her now?"

"I imagine they're taking care of her. They'll wash her, make her look nice."

"But she's dead!" Emma howled.

He stood up to hug her and try to comfort her.

That's when the first police car drove into the yard.

They sat in Ingelize's living room. There were two police officers, a man and a woman. He had to tell them what had happened.

"We were supposed to come here this afternoon to interview her," said the male police officer, who had introduced himself as Jan Collin.

Tobias nodded. "I know. She told me."

A great calm spread over him. Also a great sense of exhaustion.

"We were going to ask her about a missing person."

"I heard that, too. Hardy Lindström."

"We wanted to talk to you, too, at some point. You met Hardy on the day he disappeared. You were all out together on a raft, I understand. But we'll deal with all that later. It's too much on a day like today."

"Thanks," he said.

"Let's try and reconstruct what happened, shall we? The two of you were out riding, Ingelize and you, am I right?"

"That's correct."

"How come?" The police woman gave him a sympathetic look as she asked the question.

"I was just about to start working for Ingelize. She needs . . . she needed someone to help out. This was my first day on the job." Tobias fell silent and began to massage the skin over his temples.

"Do you have a headache?" the police woman asked.

"Yes . . . horrible."

"Have you taken anything for it?"

"No, I don't have anything with me."

"I'll go look in her bathroom cupboard." The police woman stood up and Tobias noticed more muscles in her rear end than he would have expected.

"Do you often have headaches?" Collin asked.

"Only when I'm stressed."

"Well, yes, this is certainly a stressful day."

They sat quietly waiting for the woman to return. She was quick. She held out two pills and a glass of water.

"Thanks." Tobias searched in his shirt pocket for the contract. Luckily he'd remembered to switch it into his own shirt.

"Here's the paper," he said.

Collin took it and read it, nodding.

"Well, that job's over," he said with a touch of sorrow.

"Yes," Tobias said.

He drank the rest of his water. "Have you managed to reach her husband?"

"We won't do it ourselves. Some colleagues of ours in Stockholm will get in touch. He's in Parliament."

"I know."

"So why did you decide to go up the mountain?"

"It was her idea. She often brings tour groups up there. She wanted to show me the route, so we were doing a test ride." Tobias interrupted himself. "Oh, fuck! There's a group coming tomorrow morning! They're supposed to take that tour! We'll have to call them and cancel."

"Don't worry, we'll take care of it. Do you know who they were?"

"She has a booking record in her office by the stable. She always keeps track in it."

Collin had gotten up and begun to wander through the room. He stopped when he saw the books on the dining room table. He picked one up. It was Tobias' short story collection.

"You're the one who wrote these books?"

"Yes, I am."

"Hmm. *The Fountains of Family*. Please excuse my ignorance, but what is that supposed to mean?"

"It's kind of hard to explain."

"Did you give these books to Ingelize?"

"No, she bought them herself. She asked me to sign them so I did. This morning, in fact, the same day she . . . ."

"So you're a writer?" the police woman asked.

"Yes."

"Are things going well?"

"Not really."

"Your father mentioned you'd written a mystery."

"Yes. It's called *Night*. It's out in paperback now."

"We'll have to read that one, won't we, Janne?"

Collin nodded.

"Are you writing anything now?"

"That was the whole point of me coming to Kvarnberga. I was going to write. I rented a house from Maria Vesterberg. I was going to help out with the horses half-time and write half-time."

"I see." Collin sat back down and uncapped his pen.

"So, can you tell me what happened up on the mountain?"

"I need a cigarette."

"Maybe you shouldn't smoke in here," the woman said.

"It doesn't matter now," her colleague replied.

There were no ashtrays, so Tobias got a saucer. A normal saucer for a tea cup. The last time it had been washed, Ingelize must have been the one who held the dish brush. It hurt him to think of that. He dragged smoke deep into his lungs, as deep as he possibly could. He blew it out in puffs.

"So, up on the mountain . . . ," Collin began again.

"We took a break up there. She often does it with the groups. It's an unbelievable view. She told me that people enjoyed the view. She'd brought some coffee so we drank a cup. And we talked . . .

about her business, yes, well, things that I was supposed to do. Or that I was supposed to do but won't."

"Were you sitting down while you drank your coffee?"

"Sitting down? No, we weren't."

"I was just wondering since the ground is damp this time of year."

"We were squatting next to a tree stump."

"What about the horses?"

"We'd tied them to some trees."

"And then?"

"And then I asked if it wasn't risky coming up here. She had said that the ground was being undermined by erosion and the like, and I thought it would be too risky for groups and such. But she said she always kept her eye on the people, and then she got up and she walked close to the edge and, like . . . she stood there and was pointing and I thought . . . Good God, don't stand near the edge like that, but it was like . . . like she wanted to tease me about it . . . what can I say . . . I don't know . . . and then, suddenly . . . ."

He stared at them and his eyes were burning.

Collin gave an encouraging nod.

"There was no way I could stop it," Tobias finished.

"I understand."

Tobias stubbed out one cigarette and lit another.

"Was there any, how should I put it, attraction between the two of you?" Collin asked.

"Attraction?"

"Was she interested in you, as a man, that is?"

"I wouldn't know."

"What about you?"

"What the hell? I have a steady partner."

"Don't get angry. I just need you to tell me what happened."

"She's not my type. And she's married."

"Yes, true enough, but even married people can feel tempted at times."

"What are you trying to get at?" Tobias was furious. "Do you really believe that I would have run after her and tried to fuck her and drove her over the edge? Is that what you're implying?"

"I am not trying to imply anything. My job is to find out the truth."

"All right," the police woman said, trying to calm the situation. "She walked too close to the edge and she fell over."

"That's right."

"How did you react?"

"My first thought was to call for help, of course. But then I realized I'd left my cell phone at the house. You carry the damn things with you everywhere, but when you really need them . . . . Well, I didn't have mine and I'm not sure I would have been able to get a connection up there."

"True."

"What was I supposed to do? She was lying there. I could see her, but I had no way to get to her, and how would I have been able to help her if I did? It's fucking steep all the way down. And I understood right away that if she wasn't already dead, she would be seriously injured. I did not see her move. So I took one of the horses and rode back here as fast as I could to get help."

"A neighbor was the one who called us."

"Yes, there was a young girl here in the stable when I got here and I sent her to make the call, since she would find a phone more quickly. I mean, she knows her way around here."

"I think we have enough information, now," Collin said. "You need to recover, Elmkvist. How long do you intend to stay in the village?"

"Well, now I have no idea."

"You'll still be here tomorrow, though?"

"Yes, yes, absolutely."

"Good. Then we'll meet again tomorrow. Please give us your cell phone number."

Tobias gave them the number.

The woman said, "It's not certain we can reach you on a cell phone since we have such bad connections in this area. We'll need to exchange a few words with your father and Sabina Johansson tomorrow as well, so can we say that we'll meet you there around eleven o'clock in the morning?"

Tobias nodded. He could not think of a single reason to say no.

33

MARIT'S TOYOTA WAS PARKED IN FRONT OF THE VESTERBERG HOUSE. Tobias recognized it immediately. Marit was sitting in the car and she looked like she was freezing. He leaned the bicycle against the stairs and walked over to her car.

"Hi. You came."

"Yes," she said curtly.

"Sweetheart." Tobias thought that she might start to cry, but her eyes were cold and blue.

"Why did you lie to me?"

"Lie to you?"

"Why did you tell me that your father had gotten worse?"

"Sorry. That was stupid of me."

"I don't know why you felt you had to lie. I've just been to your father's place. I met him and Sabina. What you told me was not true. Your father was not worse at all."

Tobias grabbed the handle to open the car door. It was locked.

"You lied to me, Tobias!"

"Sorry. I had to be by myself to write," he said. "I thought you would be sad. I thought you'd think I was selfish if I told you the truth."

"Why would you imagine that?"

"That's what I thought, that's all. I see now that it was stupid of me."

"Yes, it was very, very stupid of you."

"Marit, I've been through some terrible things today . . . ."

Marit seemed to shrink. "I heard. Sorry."

"Come on out of the car. Let's go inside the house."

For a moment, he thought she would refuse. Then she opened the car door and climbed out.

Marit had brought three bottles of wine, and they drank all three that evening. They sat next to each other, close together, skin to skin.

"I sent my mother packing," she said drunkenly. "I couldn't stand having her around. The only one I wanted was you."

He took her delicate face between his hands and kissed her.

"We'll go to Thailand," he said. "As soon as we get back, we'll call a travel agent and go."

"Yes, Tobias, we'll go to Thailand!"

They went to bed. Side by side. He remembered the spider but was too drunk to see if it was on the ceiling. He thought about asking her to look but realized that might not be a good idea; besides, they were much too drunk to do anything about it.

When he closed his eyes, he saw how Ingelize flew through the air. Her arms were wide and her red jacket fluttered like wings. He saw the picture in his mind when he went to sleep, and he saw it again when he woke up.

The picture did not bother him one bit. It was over.

34

SHE'D COME BACK. NINA POLICE. Police Nina was in their house. Nina Police.

Adam had thought a great deal about Police Nina. He remembered her voice and her words. She had come to his room and talked to him. She talked for a long time.

She knew all of Elvis' songs. Just like he did.

"I am going to sing for Police Nina," he told Mother. He had gone downstairs to breakfast. Mother had made oatmeal for him. Mother poured flowing honey right into the middle. He watched the golden string sink into the sea of gray. It looked like snot.

Mother ruffled his hair.

"What are you talking about, Police Nina?"

"Yes. Nina Police."

"You have to eat, Adam, my boy. Now that you've gotten out of bed, you need to take a shower, too. Don't forget to shave."

He did not know that today was the day Police Nina was coming. It was just that he thought of her. He could see her in his mind. She had sat next to his bed and talked to him. She loved all of Elvis' songs and she knew them by heart.

For Nina Police he would eat his oatmeal. The first two spoonfuls went down well.

Then he remembered. He had to turn his whole body away from the table so he would not vomit.

"Mamma," he said once his stomach had calmed down.

Mother was not listening.

"Go and take a shower now. People are coming today. They are coming at eleven o'clock."

Mother did not say who was coming, but somehow he knew. So he did what she asked. He went into the shower and scrubbed clean with soap and shampoo.

You need to be clean when you perform, Hardy had said. "You need to be nice and clean, Adam, or you'll give off the wrong signals. The girls don't like it if you smell like a gorilla. And look at this photo! This is what Elvis looks like!"

Hardy held out a record. Elvis with his guitar. Elvis' cheeks were rosy and clean.

"Doesn't Elvis look good? He keeps clean! You have to keep clean, too!"

Hardy was his manager.

"You're going to be a Big Star, Adam. But you have to do everything I say."

He stood in the shower. He felt weak. He had no energy. He did not recognize his own body. His stomach was much smaller. That is what happened if you don't eat enough food. He looked at his penis. He looked at his feet. He thought of the shoes that Hardy had given him. The shoes were too small and hurt his feet. He couldn't wear them.

He shaved without looking in the mirror.

The red pants with the silver spangles were too large. They made him throw them on the floor. He stomped on them, stomped them into the rug, into the floorboards. He saw his belt hanging over a chair. His anger rolled away. He lifted the pants and drew the belt through the loops. If he pulled the belt tightly, the belt would hold his pants up.

He studied his reflection in the mirror. The silver shone like fish scales.

He heard the car pull in. He recognized the sound. It was the same car Nina Police drove in last time. The police car. Her name was Nina and she was a police officer. She could drive the police car she came in.

His legs began to itch. He lifted his pants leg and scratched as hard as he could. Small, dry skin flakes fell onto the floor. He looked around the room. What if Nina Police came inside? He must make the bed.

I am going to sing, Adam thought, but he could not remember a single melody. Hardy was the one who got him going. Hardy would sing the first two words and that would get him started. Then he could sing.

Hardy was his manager.

He shook, went to his wardrobe. His hair was still wet from the shower.

"It doesn't matter what you look like, Adam, as long as you're fresh and clean. Try a little hair gel, too. Then your hair will be shiny. You don't have hair gel? Your mother doesn't have any either? Don't worry, I'll get you some."

He did not have any hair gel. But his hair was washed and clean.

He opened his wardrobe door and climbed inside. All his clothes were hanging up inside. His Elvis clothes. His Adam clothes. Jeans and the nice good black pants. The jacket and the shirts. There were boxes, too. All his things were there. The things he liked the best.

The new dog was barking downstairs. And voices. He recognized the voices. The smell of coffee reached him. The smell made him weak. He could not stand smells any more. He couldn't stand food any more.

Big Star, he repeated. Big Star. Like a sing-song.

He had put it as far back in the wardrobe as possible. It was behind the box with his stuffed animals. He used to have the stuffed animals in his bed when he was little. Sometimes he still took them out and felt their fur. They liked the box. They slept when he didn't need them.

There it was, all the way in the back. Hardy Lindström's hat. He had not been able to look at it after the thing. This was the first time. His ears rang as he pulled Hardy's hat into the light. He stood in front of the window. He saw the sun on the barn roof. He looked at the brown stains on Hardy's hat.

Police Nina. He told Police Nina he was going to sing for her. He did not remember any melody. He did not remember any words. He stood at the window and looked at the yellow leaves on the birch trees.

He lifted the hat and put it on his own head.

Hardy's hat was too little.

He knew that. He had seen Hardy's head. Hardy's head had been on the floor. He had seen Hardy's head in red blood on the floor. It was all by itself and it looked very small.

Mother had washed away the blood later. She washed the walls and the floor and even the desk.

He was hiding. He did not dare show himself.

A new car drove into the yard. It was the Toyota. It was the same car as yesterday. He saw it come while he was huddled on the top stairs. There was a tiny window at the top of the stairs. He saw a woman. She had a backpack. He did not know who she was. He did not want to know.

Today the Toyota was back. The puppy barked. He thought about the Eye. He remembered Hardy's eyes. He thought about how the blood glittered on Hardy's beard.

He felt ice cold. His fingertips were dry.

It was time for him to go downstairs now. He had Hardy's hat on and if he walked slowly and held tight to the handrail, Hardy's hat would stay on. Hardy's hat would be on his head when he walked into the big room.

They were all there. He heard them. He heard their voices.

And she was there. Nina Police. He wanted to sing for her, as he promised.

But he did not remember the words. He did not remember the melodies.

She had been looking for Hardy. Hardy was gone.

He remembered that.

He would tell her.

He would tell her and she would talk to him and she would listen.

BOOKS FROM PLEASURE BOAT STUDIO: A LITERARY PRESS

(Note: Caravel Books is a new imprint of Pleasure Boat Studio: A Literary Press. Caravel Books is the imprint for mysteries only. Aequitas Books is another imprint which includes non-fiction with philosophical and sociological themes. Empty Bowl Press is a Division of Pleasure Boat Studio.)

God Is a Tree, and Other Middle-Age Prayers ~ Esther Cohen ~ $10

Home & Away: The Old Town Poems ~ Kevin Miller ~ $15

Old Tale Road ~ Andrew Schelling ~ an empty bowl book ~ $15

The Shadow in the Water ~ Inger Frimansson, trans. fm. Swedish by Laura Wideburg ~ a caravel mystery ~ $18

Working the Woods, Working the Sea ~ eds. Finn Wilcox and Jerry Gorsline ~ an empty bowl book ~ $22

Listening to the Rhino ~ Dr. Janet Dallett ~ an aequitas book ~ $16

The Woman Who Wrote King Lear, and Other Stories ~ Louis Phillips ~ $16

Weinstock Among the Dying ~ Michael Blumenthal ~ $18

The War Journal of Lila Ann Smith ~ Irving Warner ~ $18

Dream of the Dragon Pool: A Daoist Quest ~ Albert A. Dalia ~ $18

Good Night, My Darling ~ Inger Frimansson, Trans by Laura Wideburg ~ $18 ~ a caravel mystery

Falling Awake: An American Woman Gets a Grip on the Whole Changing World — One Essay at a Time ~ Mary Lou Sanelli ~ $15 ~ an aequitas book

Way Out There: Lyrical Essays ~ Michael Daley ~ $16 ~ an aequitas book

The Case of Emily V. ~ Keith Oatley ~ $18 ~ a caravel mystery

Monique ~ Luisa Coelho, Trans fm Portuguese by Maria do Carmo de Vasconcelos and Dolores DeLuise ~ $14

The Blossoms Are Ghosts at the Wedding ~ Tom Jay ~ $15 ~ an empty bowl book

Against Romance ~ Michael Blumenthal ~ poetry ~ $14

Speak to the Mountain: The Tommie Waites Story ~ Dr. Bessie Blake ~ $18 / $26 ~ an aequitas book

Artrage ~ Everett Aison ~ $15

Days We Would Rather Know ~ Michael Blumenthal ~ $14

Puget Sound: 15 Stories ~ C. C. Long ~ $14

Homicide My Own ~ Anne Argula ~ $16

Craving Water ~ Mary Lou Sanelli ~ $15

When the Tiger Weeps ~ Mike O'Connor ~ $15

Wagner, Descending: The Wrath of the Salmon Queen ~ Irving Warner ~ $16

Concentricity ~ Sheila E. Murphy ~ $13.95

Schilling, from a study in lost time ~ Terrell Guillory ~ $16.95

Rumours: A Memoir of a British POW in WWII ~ Chas Mayhead ~ $16

The Immigrant's Table ~ Mary Lou Sanelli ~ $13.95

The Enduring Vision of Norman Mailer ~ Dr. Barry H. Leeds ~ $18

Women in the Garden ~ Mary Lou Sanelli ~ $13.95

Pronoun Music ~ Richard Cohen ~ $16

If You Were With Me Everything Would Be All Right ~ Ken Harvey ~ $16

The 8th Day of the Week ~ Al Kessler ~ $16

Another Life, and Other Stories ~ Edwin Weihe ~ $16

Saying the Necessary ~ Edward Harkness ~ $14

Nature Lovers ~ Charles Potts ~ $10

In Memory of Hawks, & Other Stories from Alaska ~ Irving Warner ~ $15

The Politics of My Heart ~ William Slaughter ~ $12.95

The Rape Poems ~ Frances Driscoll ~ $12.95

When History Enters the House: Essays from Central Europe ~ Michael Blumenthal ~ $15

Setting Out: The Education of Lili ~ Tung Nien ~ Trans fm Chinese by Mike O'Connor ~ $15

Unnecessary Talking: The Montesano Stories ~ Mike O'Connor ~ $16

OUR CHAPBOOK SERIES:

No. 1: The Handful of Seeds: Three and a Half Essays ~ Andrew Schelling ~ $7

No. 2: Original Sin ~ Michael Daley ~ $8

No. 3: Too Small to Hold You ~ Kate Reavey ~ $8

No. 4: The Light on Our Faces: A Therapy Dialogue ~ Lee Miriam WhitmanRaymond ~ $8

No. 5: Eye ~ William Bridges ~ $8

No. 6: Selected New Poems of Rainer Maria Rilke ~ Trans fm German by Alice Derry ~ $10

No. 7: Through High Still Air: A Season at Sourdough Mountain ~ Tim McNulty ~ $9

No. 8: Sight Progress ~ Zhang Er, Trans fm Chinese by Rachel Levitsky ~ $9

No. 9: The Perfect Hour ~ Blas Falconer ~ $9

No. 10: Fervor ~ Zaedryn Meade ~ $10

FROM OTHER PUBLISHERS (in limited editions):

Desire ~ Jody Aliesan ~ $14 (an Empty Bowl book)

Deams of the Hand ~ Susan Goldwitz ~ $14 (an Empty Bowl book)

Lineage ~ Mary Lou Sanelli ~ $14 (an Empty Bowl book)

The Basin: Poems from a Chinese Province ~ Mike O'Connor ~ $10 (an Empty Bowl book)

The Straits ~ Michael Daley ~ $10 (an Empty Bowl book)

In Our Hearts and Minds: The Northwest and Central America ~ Ed. Michael Daley ~ $12 (an Empty Bowl book)

The Rainshadow ~ Mike O'Connor ~ $16 (an Empty Bowl book)

Untold Stories ~ William Slaughter ~ $10 (an Empty Bowl book)

In Blue Mountain Dusk ~ Tim McNulty ~ $12.95 (a Broken Moon book)

China Basin ~ Clemens Starck ~ $13.95 (a Story Line Press book)

Journeyman's Wages ~ Clemens Starck ~ $10.95 (a Story Line Press book)

ORDERS: PLEASURE BOAT STUDIO
books are available by order from your bookstore, directly from PBS, or through the following:

SPD (Small Press Distribution)
Tel. 800.869.7553, Fax 5105240852
Partners/West Tel. 425.227.8486,
Fax 425.204.2448
Baker & Taylor 800.775.1100,
Fax 800.775.7480
Ingram Tel 615.793.5000, Fax 615.287.5429
Amazon.com or Barnesandnoble.com

HOW WE GOT OUR NAME

…from "Pleasure Boat Studio," an essay written by Ouyang Xiu, Song Dynasty poet, essayist, and scholar, on the twelfth day of the twelfth month in the *renwu* year (January 25, 1043):

> "I have heard of men of antiquity who fled from the world to distant rivers and lakes and refused to their dying day to return. They must have found some source of pleasure there. If one is not anxious for profit, even at the risk of danger, or is not convicted of a crime and forced to embark; rather, if one has a favorable breeze and gentle seas and is able to rest comfortably on a pillow and mat, sailing several hundred miles in a single day, then is boat travel not enjoyable? Of course, I have no time for such diversions. But since 'pleasure boat' is the designation of boats used for such pastimes, I have now adopted it as the name of my studio. Is there anything wrong with that?"

Translated by Ronald Egan

Look for these two new mysteries coming SOON
from Caravel Books:

Russell Hill's The Lord God Bird
"Russell Hill has one of the strongest voices I've read in years,
his prose lyrical, haunted and evocative, his settings palpable
and his characters unforgettable. The Lord God Bird will stick
in your mind long after you've turned the last page."
—Charles Ardai, Publisher, Hardcase Crime
and Edgar Allan Poe winner

and

Michael Burke's Swan Dive
First-time novelist Michael Burke has created a sexy and fast-
paced jaunt which focuses on a down-and-out detective with a
roaming eye who gets involved with a complex business deal,
a deal which results in embezzlement, swindling, and murder.
Along the way, the detective (named Heron, nicknamed "Blue")
discovers a great deal about himself while trying to understand
the subterfuge. For a smart-guy detective, he is surprisingly
naïve and innocent.